Taming *the* Savage Duke

BARBARA RUSSELL

OLIVERHEBERBOOKS

Cover art by Dar Albert at Wicked Smart Designs

Published by Oliver-Heber Books

0 9 8 7 6 5 4 3 2 1

one

London, 1880

FOR MADDIE, FINDING a husband during the next London Season was as probable as the members of the Lord Byron's Society remaining celibate. She couldn't endure another dull series of balls and dreadful conversations about the weather.

Not that she didn't take the pursuit of finding a suitable husband seriously but...actually, she didn't. Not anymore. Because she'd just received *the* letter that was going to change the course of her life forever. Who needed to secure her future with a marriage when she had the chance to receive a fellowship to attend the Royal Women's Art Academy and become the painter she'd always wanted to be?

A husband could wait. Her biggest dream couldn't.

Maddie clenched the letter against her chest, twirling around her room as she imagined her paintings being displayed at the National Gallery and admired by the most prominent art critics. She fell over the four-poster bed in her enthusiasm thanks to her skirts wrapping around her legs. Her chest heaved as if after a long horse-riding session in the park.

With happy tears brimming in her eyes, she read the magical

letter again. Mrs. Bridget Blanchet, the most acclaimed female artist in the world, would soon be in London for an exhibition of her work and wanted to meet Maddie! All those months spent corresponding with Bridget had brought fruit. She would never complain again about painful writer's calluses or long waits for a reply.

A knot of anxiety tightening in her belly doused her enthusiasm. Maybe it was too soon to celebrate. If Bridget found Maddie's work impressive, she would help Maddie receive a full fellowship for the academy. Six thousand pounds per year. The sum would cover everything from the lessons and the material for painting to the accommodation.

Painting. All day. Every day. Surrounded by other artists.

The room tilted as Maddie contemplated the enormity of the sum and how her life might change. She could focus on painting, learn about the latest techniques, be in contact with other artists, and plan for her future as an independent professional. A future of canvases to be filled with colours and emotions. Speaking of which. She put the letter on the vanity, shoving aside her jars of rouge and face powder mingled with bottles of turpentine, and wiped the drops of burnt sienna from her fingers with a cloth, lest she stain her precious letter.

As she cleaned her hands from the stubborn dark-red pigment, an unbidden sob tore out of her. Not many unknown artists could claim to have attracted the attention of a famous painter like Mrs. Blanchet. But Maddie had. She wasn't sure how it'd happened. Well, she'd sent many letters to Mrs. Blanchet to Paris, writing how inspiring her work was after having seen an exhibition of her portraits. But she hadn't believed Mrs. Blanchet would have replied.

But Mrs. Blanchet hadn't simply replied. She'd started a regular correspondence with Maddie, asking for samples of her sketches, encouraging her, and giving her suggestions for the sfumato—it was difficult to paint in soft tones by blurring the edges without making the painting looking as if created by a drunken artist—and the colour mixing. And now Maddie would meet her. She wasn't deluded. Mrs. Blanchet was going to judge her work, and if she wasn't impressed, Maddie would need to swallow her pride and reconsider her plans for the Season.

Oh, Lord. Her stomach churned at the thought. Not only because she would renounce her dream, or at the very least postpone it, but because her mother would never stop telling her, 'I told you so.'

No proper lady should ever earn her living from painting scandalous portraits—Mother's words. Not hers.

But if Maddie succeeded...Her legs grew weak, and she plopped down onto the stuffed stool in front of the mirror, inhaling the scent of her lavender perfume and that of her colours and oils. Tears blotched her emerald skirt. She, Madeline Josephine Debenham, was going to study at the prestigious academy—perhaps she should rein in her imagination and focus on producing a painting so stunning that Mrs. Blanchet could do nothing but be impressed.

Wiping her tears, Maddie folded the letter and put it in her pocket. Dreams and plans were two different things. She preferred the latter.

There was also another problem to deal with, and it'd be better if she dealt with it now. After all, creativity required courage, and courage required...she didn't know what. Desperation, perhaps? Or maybe simply a tad of madness. She had a lot of desperation and certainly more than a tad of madness.

So she stood up and patted her chignon. Determination, that was what courage required, and she was determined to talk to her mother. Yes, sir, she was. Of course she was. Right now. Immediately. Perhaps after a fortifying cup of tea. No, now.

Still, it took her two attempts to open the door and step into the hallway. The smell of freshly baked scones wafting from the kitchen downstairs was refreshing compared to that of paint and turpentine oil in her bedroom. She didn't mind the smell though, and when she painted, she barely noticed it so focused she was...and she was stalling.

Right. Determination.

She lifted her chin and gathered her courage, marching towards her mother's parlour on wobbly legs.

"Mother?" She knocked and held her breath, half-wishing Mother had gone out for an early call.

"Come in." Her mother's voice carried a hint of annoyance. Or maybe Maddie was nervous on top of determined and desperate.

Pulse spiking, she inched the door open, and her resolve dithered at the sight of her mother's scowl. They shared the same raven hair, too-pale complexion, and green eyes, but Maddie wondered if she looked as menacing as her mother did when she frowned.

She cleared her throat. "Good morning, Mother. I'm here because I wish to talk to you."

"Obviously." Mother lowered her embroidery and waved Maddie in.

The long string of pearls around Mother's neck clinked when she shifted in the armchair. Those pearls would likely pay Maddie's fee at the academy if her mother wanted to.

"What did you wish to talk to me about?" Mother asked.

Keeping her gaze on the intricate pattern on the carpet, Maddie sat in front of her mother. The roaring fire in the hearth didn't seem to shed any ounce of warmth, and the sunlight filtering through the voile curtains dimmed as if scared. She tugged at the hem of her shirt and reminded herself six thousand pounds were a good argument.

"I've received a letter." Goodness, what a clumsy start. "See, you don't know, but I've been writing to Mrs. Bridget Blanchet regularly. She's the artist who painted *The Witches' Night*." And many other scandalous paintings Maddie wasn't going to mention like *The Naked Goddess*. "Mrs. Blanchet lives in Paris with her husband and..." She closed her fists not to show how much her hands trembled. "I thought that, if she met me and if she liked..." Tarnation. She wasn't making any sense at all. She chanced a glance up and regretted it, seeing her mother's icy expression. She'd catch a cold from it. "Six thousand pounds," she whispered so low she doubted her mother had heard her.

Mother's gaze was ablaze with green fire. Her lips were pursed into a severe expression Maddie hoped she hadn't inherited.

The silence was so thick Maddie could grow potatoes in it. Her tongue knotted. As much as she wanted to talk about the darn six thousand pounds, she could only stare at her mother. Drops of perspiration dampened her back, and her heartbeat drummed in her ears.

"Let me help you." Mother put the embroidery on the low table in front of her and sighed heavily. "If you think I wasn't aware of your little..." She flourished a hand dismissively. "Friendship with that woman, you're sorely mistaken. Nothing happens in my house without my knowledge. I'm aware of what that woman wrote to you and you to her, including all those inappropriate details on how to draw naked male bodies." Her voice rose.

A chill crawled down Maddie's spine. "Did you read my letters?"

Mother pinched the bridge of her nose. "You're as gullible as your father. I wonder if you and your sister took after me at all."

"You read my letters." Maddie's voice hardened. All that time, Mother had been reading Maddie's correspondence and knowing what she'd been planning. "But the envelopes were sealed when I received the letters."

Mother's gaze travelled skywards. "Oh, dear child."

Honestly, Maddie didn't know if she should be furious or impressed by her mother's Machiavellian skills. Right now, she leant towards furious. "Those letters were private."

Mother thumped a fist on the armrest. "Not as long as you live under my roof. I pay for your food, clothes, coal, and even for your books and painting supplies. I have the right to know what you're doing."

Maddie gnashed her teeth. "Why didn't you say anything then?"

"Because I wanted to see where this madness led you," Mother said. "I'm not against learning a craft. Playing the piano, writing poetry, and even painting, as disgustingly untidy as it is, are all skills that enhance a woman's value. But thinking of becoming a painter as a way to make a living? Painting naked bodies?" She placed a hand on her tightly buttoned bodice. "I want you to be respected and admired, not despised and ridiculed for being a promiscuous woman. Why do you think Mrs. Blanchet had to leave London? Because she couldn't cope with the gossip and the hatred. Her name appeared on the scandal sheet twice a week."

Did the scandal matter though now that Mrs. Blanchet had been vindicated?

"The fellowship would provide me with six thousand pounds." Maddie handed the letter to her mother, which was useless since she'd already read it.

"That's wonderful. But after that? After you attend this prestigious academy, what will happen to you?" Mother didn't seem to want Maddie's answer, so she didn't provide any. "Do you think you will earn enough money to sustain yourself? No one in London would rent you a room, invite you to a soirée, or simply want to be your friend as happened to your Mrs. Blanchet." Mother let out a polite scoff. "Absurd. Painting isn't a secure future for yourself. Art is a fickle affair. It brings you money one day and takes it from you the next. You'll starve, Maddie, become an outcast, die in solitude, and I will not allow it."

The future couldn't be so grim. Maddie inched closer to her mother. "But Mrs. Blanchet—"

"She's married to a rich man who allows her to indulge in the nonsensical belief that she's an artist."

"Mother!" Maddie placed a fluttering hand on her chest. How

could her mother talk in such fashion about one of the most appreciated artists of the moment? "Mrs. Blanchet's paintings are worth a fortune. Yes, her husband supports her, but he doesn't allow her to be an artist. She is one."

Mother's features tautened. "I've been generous to you so far, enduring all that wasted time to let you be a dauber, but enough of that."

"Dauber!"

"We're talking about your future." Mother spoke with the tone of someone who was losing their patience. "What will you do when you're old and poor and with only a handful of canvases no one wants to pay for? Alone, shunned, without a husband? Mrs. Blanchet was lucky after society had mocked her, but you? You showed no interest in the gentlemen I introduced you to, and the last Season was a complete disaster. I received more invitations to dance than you did. The only thing you can converse about is paintings. Do you realise how dull it is?"

"The gentlemen you introduced to me could only talk about themselves."

"Oh, shush." Mother rubbed the spot between her eyebrows.

Maddie swallowed past the lump swelling in her throat. It wasn't her fault if the gentlemen she'd met during the last Season hadn't appreciated her passion for painting. It was her fault if a couple of said gentlemen had stormed out of the ballroom because she'd offended them with her opinions on what *didn't* constitute a scandalous painting. Artists had painted naked bodies for centuries.

"This madness ends this instant." Mother picked up her embroidery. "No more talking about this silly academy."

Silly academy? Anger flared up in Maddie's chest. "I want to meet Mrs. Blanchet," she said in a low voice cracking with emotion. When her mother didn't reply, she spoke in a firmer voice, "I want to—"

"I heard you." Mother glared, pausing her embroidery again.

"As your mother, it's my duty to protect you from disappoint-ment, or, in some cases, stupidity. But do you want to make a fool out of yourself? By all means, show one of your paintings to that woman."

That hurt. Maybe Maddie wasn't as talented or prepared as Mrs. Blanchet, but she worked hard and, with the right training, she was sure her technique would improve.

"But if she doesn't like it, you're going to do whatever I say. Is that clear?" Mother asked.

Well, if Maddie couldn't receive the fellowship, her chances of entering the academy were nought. She gave a curt nod. After all, she wanted to impress Mrs. Blanchet.

Mother focused on her embroidery—the silhouette of an angel, ironically. "At your age, I was married and carrying my first child. Painting. Travelling. Adventures." She huffed. "Nonsense. Life is harsher than what you think, Maddie, especially when you are a young woman in London."

Maddie rose from her armchair and bit her inner cheek not to cry. "I'll prove you wrong, Mother."

"We'll see." Mother didn't look at her.

She shuffled out, keeping her back straight and her chest thrust out. But when she entered her room, she sagged against the closed door. She allowed herself a moment to shake with anger and fear before striding towards her painting corner. She pulled the curtains, letting the morning sunlight in.

The painting set on the easel showed a couple dancing in the middle of a meadow blossoming with buttercups and forget-me-nots. Lots of bright colours on the front contrasted with the shadows in the background, creating a well-balanced—in her opinion—shade throughout the canvas. Weeks upon weeks of work. Corrections upon corrections. Tears, sweat, and blood. Would they be worth it?

"Maddie?" Verity's voice came muffled from the other side of the door.

Maddie pinched her cheeks, not wanting to alarm her sister with her pallor. Although she probably didn't look pale but red with anger. "Yes, come in."

Verity slipped inside with a soft swish of velvet. She, Maddie, and their mother had the same looks, but where Mother's mouth was constantly pressed in a harsh line of disappointment, Verity's was soft and warm.

"I heard voices." Verity walked over to her. "Well, Mother's voice. Is something the matter?"

Maddie took out her paintbrushes and colours before turning the canvas towards the light. "We had an argument. Nothing unusual. I want to meet Mrs. Blanchet when she comes to London, and Mother believes it's a waste of time." She shrugged, pretending she didn't care. "But I want to meet Mrs. Blanchet anyway because, if she likes my style, she's going to help me receive a fellowship for the Royal Women's Academy of Arts."

"Good Lord." Verity clamped her hands over her mouth. "This is fantastic news. I knew your talent would be recognised sooner or later."

"Thank you." Maddie faced the window, blinking away more tears. "Besides, this painting only needs a few more layers. Then it'll be ready to be shown to Mrs. Blanchet whether Mother likes it or not." She couldn't completely remove the hurt from her voice.

"Maddie." Verity took her hand. She opened her mouth to say something but then remained silent, smiling at the painting. "It's beautiful. I'm sure Mrs. Blanchet will be impressed."

Maddie tilted her head to have a better look at the leaves in the background. The river still needed a retouch, but the sky and the hills had a dramatic flair she approved of.

"I hope."

"What's that ghastly plant covering your window?" Verity opened the window, causing the long green stems to tremble. "Why didn't you ask the gardener to pull it off?"

"Don't touch it, please." Maddie locked the window again.

"The plant grew weeks ago. I guess it has its roots somewhere in the gutter. Anyway, it creates the perfect light, especially in the afternoon. Leave it be. The golden flowers are so pretty."

"I'll leave you to work, then." Verity bussed her sister's cheek. "I'll ask Cook to have your lunch served here if you want to."

Maddie smiled. Verity knew her so well. "And dinner. It's going to be a long week."

two

HECTOR'S DREAM TO achieve notoriety at the Royal Botanical Society had become true, and that was the problem.

He'd meant to become famous for his scientific achievements, not because the other scientists considered him the laughingstock of England. Famous for the wrong reasons. How undignified from a scientific point of view. How humiliating from a personal one.

He couldn't even enjoy his daily walk through Hyde Park, so annoyed he was.

"Hector, for heaven's sake, stop brooding." Robert nudged him with the pommel of his Malacca walking stick.

Apparently, walking sticks were all the rage at the moment even among young gentlemen. Not that Hector cared about his brother's fashion choices.

"And stop staring at the pavement," Robert said. "We took this walk to lift your mood, not to ruin mine."

Hector raked a hand through his hair. "I apologise, but three rejection letters in one day! It's more than my mood can take."

Every inch the duke, Robert touched his hat as they walked

past a couple of smiling ladies. His blond strands of hair brushed against his jaw. The tree canopies in Hyde Park swayed in the gentle breeze carrying the fresh scent of the flowers of *Lonicera periclymenum*, or honeysuckles as people, who weren't plagued by an obsession for botany, called them. Hector preferred the name of 'luscious woodbine' that Shakespeare had used. Flowers had such pretty names; one wouldn't believe how brutal botanists could be.

"What happened this time?" Robert asked, smiling at another lady who bobbed a quick curtsy.

"I informed the scientists of the Royal Botanical Society that I found a rare specimen of golden pimpernel. It's so rare that the discovery, once confirmed, would be sensational. My name would end up in the most prestigious journals. Oxford University would ask me to make a speech." He clenched a fist. "But the scientists of the society demanded proof."

Robert came to an abrupt halt on the gravel path, one hand behind his back. "How dare they! Scientists demanding evidence? What will ever happen next? Physicians requiring to visit a patient before producing a diagnosis? Oh, in what times do we live?"

Hector couldn't suppress a smile. "Fair point. I didn't express myself appropriately. See, the golden pimpernel is so rare it was considered extinct in Great Britain. It's a precious, delicate species. When I found it, I didn't want to rip the plant and destroy it just to take a sample to the society. I thought it'd be barbaric. I wished for a member of the society to come with me to the place where I spotted the plant, but no one agreed. They said having found a golden pimpernel in London was impossible. Everyone laughed at me, calling me deluded."

"Bring the plant to them then." Robert shrugged. "Can't you simply take a small sample?"

Yes, that was the problem. Hector twisted the hem of his jacket. "Ahem, I can't seem to find the right spot any longer. It was in a corner of Hyde Park, of all places, but either the gardeners ripped it up, or the plant died, or my memory isn't good. I was so excited when I found the plant I didn't think to mark the spot. Poor judgement on my part, but in my defence, I thought Hyde Park was small enough to allow me to find the plant easily again. I was wrong."

"If you found one, you'll find another. It's a matter of time." Robert resumed walking, his thick eyebrows drawn together.

As they exited the busy park, Hector gave another long look around, searching for the infamous plant. The noise of the carriages and hansom cabs filled the silence between them as Hector pondered what to say to his brother. No, *how* to tell his brother about his latest decision.

"I don't have time." He raised his voice to overcome the yells of a hawker selling the new issues of *The Times*. "I hoped the society would accept me as one of their members about to join Mr. von Humboldt's next expedition to South America. It's a unique opportunity."

"And when exactly did you plan to tell me that?" Robert came to another sudden stop. His polished leather shoes screeched on the wet pavement.

Hector rubbed the back of his neck. "Mother knew it. The expedition will start in a few months, but I must present my application for the journey within two days or they won't consider me." He shrugged. "Impossible."

"Why didn't you tell me? And for how long would you be gone? Isn't the trip dangerous?"

Hector leant against the red-brick wall behind him, not caring about the thin layer of coal dust covering every inch of London. From aristocratic mansions to humble homes, the soot showed no mercy. There was some justice in that.

"You're always so busy, and you need not worry about my safety because obviously, I'm not going anywhere."

"I'm never too busy for you." Robert sounded hurt, which hurt Hector in turn. "And I do worry about you."

Hector nodded, ignoring the knot in his throat.

"I want to support your career as a scientist, but unless you talk to me, I can't help you." Robert patted Hector's shoulder. "I'm not like Father. My ducal duties will never come before my family," he said in a gentle tone that cracked something in Hector's chest.

Hector gazed around to avoid meeting Robert's concerned blue eyes. "I don't want to interfere with your..." The rest of the sentence died a swift, merciless death in his mouth as he gazed up.

A fresh, luscious, living specimen of golden pimpernel literally covered the window on the first level of the house in front of him. The small golden flowers gleamed in the sunlight as if teasing him. Through the cascade of fluttering leaves, he caught a glimpse of someone painting.

"By Jove." Why had he lost hope? How foolish of him.

"What is it?" Robert gazed around. "Anarchists? Another riot? Or worse, a match-making mama?"

Hector laughed. "The golden pimpernel. *Anagallis pratensis*. Over there. It's the largest specimen I've ever seen."

A shiver went through him. Oh, he wouldn't make the same mistake twice. He would both cut a sample and then drag one of the sceptical botanists here. The spot was easy to find. Those pompous scientists would have no choice but to welcome him in the society and apologise.

He'd go to South America and see the Amazonian Forest. All those species unknown to humanity. Knowledge. He'd contribute to the advancement of science. Many scientists claimed that in the Amazon there were plants with extraordinary medicinal properties. Plants that could treat a fever or heal an infection in a matter of days. Oh, to be the one to discover a plant that could cure consumption—a strong hand wrapped around his arm and tugged.

"Hector, what are you doing?" Robert said, stepping in front of him. His tall hat bobbed.

Wasn't it obvious? "I need the plant." Only at that moment, he realised he was halfway to the front door.

"And what do you plan to do exactly? Knock on the door and ask to take it?"

"It'll take a moment."

Robert's hat slipped down his eyes as he frowned. "These people don't know you. Knocking on a door without being introduced is not the appropriate way to intrude into a respectable house."

"As opposed to a disreputable one?" Hector glanced at the window again.

The breeze shuffled the leaves, offering him a better view of the room. A lady was working on a canvas, but he couldn't see what she was painting from where he stood.

Robert exhaled. "No, not even in a disreputable house should we arrive unannounced. Let's return home. I shall send a card to the inhabitants of this house and make a formal request for a meeting, explaining the situation."

Formal request? Card? Meeting? "But Robert, it'll take days to arrange a visit."

"Don't be ridiculous." Robert pierced him with a penetrating glare. "I must follow the rules, Brother. I don't want to end up in the scandal sheet for everyone's entertainment."

"The application for the expedition expires tomorrow afternoon. By then, I have to take a sample of the plant to the society, convince the botanists to accept me, and present the application. Not even your ducal state will speed the matter." He pointed at the unreachable plant. So close, so distant.

"I'm sure everything will be fine." Robert kept his hand firmly clasped on Hector's arm. "I'll write a letter as soon as I learn who lives in this house. I'll do my best to speed up the process. I'm sure a meeting will be arranged in a couple of hours."

"Robert, please."

"Will you trust me? I know what I'm doing."

Hector's shoulders sagged with his exhale. "All right."

So more delay then. Reluctantly, he let his brother lead him away from his golden dream. As he cast one last glance at the window, the lady stared at him. A red spot stained the tip of her nose. She wielded a paintbrush as if it were a sword. Good Lord, those eyes. They were two emerald pools currently glaring at him.

He averted his gaze lest she think he was a degenerate. Maybe he was. He might not be as observant regarding etiquette as his brother was, but he wouldn't delay his dream. He'd wait a few hours for a reply. If the green-eyed lady didn't answer by the time the sun had set, he'd snatch his plant and take hold of his future.

HECTOR PACED as the crimson light of the sunset crept over London like bloody fingers. Hours had passed from the moment Robert had sent an urgent missive to the house of the golden pimpernel, and no answer had come from the green-eyed lady. He'd checked for an answer every ten minutes, galloping down the stairs and making enough noise to earn a reprimand from his mother. Drinking tea had done nothing to calm him but had increased his need for the water closet. Reading a book hadn't distracted him from the anxiety. The library usually never failed to soothe his nerves. But today, even the ticking of the grandfather clock bothered him.

"Hector?" Robert appeared on the threshold of the library door, seemingly out of thin air. Or maybe he'd been there for a while. "Don't you want to have dinner with us?"

"No, thank you." He raked a hand through his hair.

"For heaven's sake, stop fretting and eat something."

"My stomach is churning. I can't possibly eat anything."

Robert put a hand on the knob. "They will answer. I sent a formal letter, with the stamp of the Duke of Blackburn."

"Maybe they don't care about the fact you're a duke. Not

everyone gives a damn about your position." He regretted the words the moment they left his stupid mouth.

Robert's fingers closed around the knob. He worked his jaw and fiddled with the knot of his silk cravat. "Very well."

"Robert, I'm sorry. I didn't mean to sound so bitter."

"No, it's all right." Robert raised a hand. "I'll tell Daniels to set something aside for you in case you change your mind." He closed the door, leaving Hector alone with his guilt.

"I'm sorry," he whispered in the silent library.

In his defence, an expedition founded by Sir Alexander von Humboldt happened once in a lifetime. He couldn't miss the opportunity to work side-by-side with the most renowned scientists in the world. Botanists, zoologists, and even anthropologists would join the expedition. Hector had to be on that ship.

Dusk overcame the sunset. Shadows flickered in the glow from the gas street lights. The grandfather clock struck nine.

Enough. Hector was tired of waiting. A dream required action to be realised, and he was too restless to be optimistic. He rushed upstairs, careful not to let the wooden steps squeak under his weight. He rummaged through his room in search of a few tools. Judging by how long it took him to find his satchel, Robert was right about Hector's lack of organisation. Oh, lawk. He'd searched for that book on Irish mosses for weeks. Who would have guessed it'd ended up behind the stove? And where was his coat? Not in the wardrobe; it was full of dried plants for his herbarium. Never mind. No coat.

Twenty minutes later, armed with a glass jar and a knife, he sneaked out of the house. He couldn't sleep anyway. What was the point of tossing and turning in the bed, worrying about a trip that could happen if he only did something? He'd cut a sample of the plant and return home as quietly as a thief, and Robert would be none the wiser. Then he'd wait for the damn reply and play the role of the perfect gentleman, drink tea, and discuss the weather with the green-eyed lady. Maybe ask her to see her painting. Everyone would be happy.

But tonight was for grabbing his dream by the throat. It shouldn't be difficult. The brick wall around the lady's house would offer an easy way to climb to the first-floor window. A cut, and done! A few months from now, he'd be onboard the *Observatory*, staring at the sea and chatting with other scientists about Dr. Darwin's latest articles. He'd return to England enriched by knowledge and strengthened by experience. The botanists of the Royal Society would apologise for the poor way they'd treated him. Not that he cared about their apology. Science was all that mattered.

He couldn't contain his impatience as he hurried along the empty pavement. The smell of burning wood and smoke lingered in the night air with the ever-present stink of horse dung. Police constables might present a problem if he was caught climbing the wall of a house, but the whole deed shouldn't require more than a few minutes.

He stopped in front of the house and cast a reverent gaze on the plant. His moment of awe was ruined by the yellow light pouring out of the window. The lady painter was still at work at this time of night. Painting had to be an obsession for her.

Well, he shouldn't judge. Never mind. He'd be discretion itself. He had no intention of waiting. He'd waited enough.

After he searched the street where the long shadows of the trees crept, he pulled up his scarf to cover his face and stole to the wall on his tiptoes. Now that he stood right under the window, the golden pimpernel didn't seem so close, but the ivy plant covering the wall could be used as a rope. He wiped his sweaty hands on his trousers and grabbed the thick stems. When he hauled himself up, he rested the tip of his boots on the bricks. The surface was slippery with London's humidity, and he dropped a good foot.

"Damn." He gritted his teeth, wishing he had Robert's brawny physique.

Mayhap, he should start boxing as his brother did every week at the gentlemen's club. It would improve his physical strength to trek through the Amazonian Forest.

He pulled himself up again. His arms quivered with the effort. Definitely, he'd underestimated the difficulty of the climb and overestimated his strength. At least the light from the window gave him a good view of where he put his hands. He had to reach the plant's root to take a sample that wouldn't wilt and die in an hour, which meant climbing all the way up to the gutter. Not an easy task, but he was up to it.

Moving to the right, lest the lady see him and start shouting, he advanced up one inch at a time. Sweat dampened his neck, and his legs shook so hard he feared he might fall at any moment. Another inch up. More sweat. Hellfire. His knees almost buckled.

He let out a growl. And there it was. The golden pimpernel. His breath came out in quick pants both from the exertion and the excitement. The delicate petals were wrapped tightly around themselves against the night's chill. From the bedroom, muffled, angry mutters came. The lady argued about something.

Holding himself with one hand, he slid the other into his satchel to take the knife. He smiled. Another minute or two and he would have his fresh sample of golden pimpernel. Glory was a few inches away.

Everything was going according to plan.

three

THE INSISTENT, SCRAPING noise coming from the window made Maddie pause mid-stroke with the paintbrush. Was a rat climbing the wall? Who knew what creatures might be nestled in the plant? Perhaps she should cut it or move it away from the window. She waited. No noise came.

The good light had disappeared with the sunset, but she'd almost finished for today. She took a step away from the canvas and admired her work. Her heavy eyelids seemed to drop against her will, but she couldn't stop smiling. The painting needed a few final touches. A brighter colour there, a few black lines here. But the view was there. The gentle hills, the mist, and the river created a pleasant but unobtrusive background. The focus remained on the couple dancing among the flowers. The lady's dress was caught in the middle of twirling around her legs, and the gentleman's jacket was fluttering up.

Maddie's first idea had been to draw them naked in a Hades and Persephone's depiction. But alas, Mother would have never allowed her that.

What would Mrs. Blanchet say? Hopefully, she'd see the passion Maddie felt every time she picked up a paintbrush and—

what was that noise again? It came from above the window while earlier it'd come from below it. The scratching sound sent a chill down her back. It had to be an intruder. A rat couldn't make so much noise. Unless it was a very large rat. She almost preferred an intruder to a giant rat. Some said the rats along the Thames grew bigger than the normal urban rats and that they were spreading throughout the city. She didn't want to be the one to prove the rumour right.

Another loud screech jolted her. Blimey. What was it?

She stretched out an arm towards the window but didn't have time to open it before the deafening sound of glass shattering came. The window exploded. Something large and dark smashed through it and shoved her back with the strength of a rugby player tackling an adversary. She cried out as her back hit the floor hard and a searing pain slashed through her hand. The agony cut off her breath and the scream about to burst out of her mouth. On top of that, some type of fabric, a jacket perhaps, covered her face. She couldn't see anything.

"I'm sorry," a masculine voice said close to her ear.

The man scrambled to his feet amid the noise of glass shards being smashed under his weight. The moment he rose, the thing covering her face lifted too, revealing the disaster in front of her. Wood splinters, broken glass, and leaves littered her room. Debris covered even her vanity and bed.

Maddie lay on the floor, unable to speak. What had happened?

"I...I didn't mean to hurt you. Miss?" The tall blond man crouched next to her. His blue eyes flared wide as he stared at her. "Are you all right? Oh, God. You're bleeding."

She closed her eyes and kept down the wave of nausea threatening to overcome her. When her mind calmed, she sat upright but in doing so, she put her right hand down on the floor and a new shot of pain made her whimper. A sharp piece of glass was buried deep in her palm. A shock of stillness went through her. The shard caught the light, enhancing the ruby drops of blood on the glass.

"Let me help." Strands of blond hair tumbled down the man's sharp cheeks when he removed his flat hat. He reached out for her injured hand.

"Don't touch me!" Maddie scurried away from him, smashing more glass underneath her.

He held up his hands. "I mean no harm."

"You mean no harm? Look at me!" She raised her injured hand that throbbed and swelled. A hysterical laugh shook through her.

He rubbed his forehead, paling. "It was an accident."

The door to her bedroom was flung open, and footsteps thudded from behind her.

"Maddie, what happened?" Verity crouched next to her sister, her long braid falling over her shoulder. "Maddie!"

"What is the meaning of this?" Father said at the same time as Mother screamed, clutching her shawl around her shoulders.

The man kept his hands up, gazing away from Verity and Mother in their nightgowns. "I'm not a thief. It was an accident."

As he stepped away from Maddie, she had a full view of her bedroom and understood the extension of the disaster. She forgot about the pain in her hand and about the fright. Even her father's rant and her mother's complaints became a muffled, distant noise. All the air was punched out of her lungs with a single sharp breath.

Her painting had been slashed by the glass and the broken wooden frame of the window. The river had been cut in two by a splinter, and the dancing couple had been ripped apart. The gentleman didn't hold the lady's hand any longer. Even worse, the turpentine must have dropped on the canvas because a corner of the painting melted like tears from a rainbow.

Weeks of work. All her dreams. All her plans. Gone. Vanished. Destroyed.

The intense agony tearing her apart cut her so deeply she couldn't even howl, although an insistent ring buzzed in her ears. If she was about to faint, she wouldn't oppose any resistance. Unconsciousness sounded like a jolly good idea now.

Voices echoed around her. The man talked, gesturing at the window and shaking his head. Everyone talked. Verity supported Maddie's injured hand, blathering something about calling their physician, but Maddie couldn't focus on anything aside from the paint smearing across her shattered dream.

Sitting in the armchair, Maddie cradled her bandaged hand. A blazing log fire roared in the hearth, and the gas lamps and candles spread a warm atmosphere. It'd be cosy and comfortable if not for the throb in her palm and the tangible tension in the room.

The family physician had been summoned from Harley Street, the glass shard had been removed, and the wound promptly stitched. But the pain in both her hand and chest remained. The ointment the physician had applied to the wound smelled like vinegar, and the numbing pain potion had left a sour taste in her mouth. But somehow, she didn't care about any of that. It was as if she witnessed her own downfall as an observer, watching her life crumble with a sense of helplessness.

Now she was in the sitting room with her assailant, her parents, Verity, and a very agitated young constable who blushed so fiercely she wouldn't be surprised if he passed out. In the midst of the utter chaos following the destruction of her window and life, no one had properly interrogated the intruder who, to his credit, hadn't tried to flee. Maddie's mother had never stopped talking, but Maddie couldn't tell about what.

"Please, madam." The constable dabbed his forehead with a handkerchief, cutting off Maddie's mother. "Let me ask a few questions to the gentleman."

"Gentleman?" Her mother tilted her chin up. "He's an intruder."

"My name is Lord Hector Wentworth," her assailant said in

the tone of someone whose patience was wearing thin. That made two of them.

Tall and gangly, he had the refined manners and cultured speech of a lord and the sapphire eyes of a perfect spring sky; it was a peculiar colour, not quite blue and with a hint of violet. She would love to replicate it once she came out of her catatonic state.

Not that any of Lord Wentworth's striking features changed the fact he'd attacked her, broken her window, destroyed her precious painting, and injured her hand. The hand she used to paint. Her mind was a jumble of incoherent thoughts. One moment, she wondered if her hand would allow her to paint any time soon. The next, she pondered if she could have a nice cup of tea, perhaps with an oat biscuit. No, her stomach roiled at the thought of food, but a cup of tea would be wonderful.

"Wentworth?" Mother asked. Her dressing gown covered her from chin to toe, but even in a garment that made her look tinier and shorter than she was, she didn't lose her commanding aura. "Are you a relative of Robert Wentworth, the Duke of Black-burn?" Her voice acquired a sudden sweet note that even Maddie in her confused state couldn't miss.

Hector nodded several times, his curly golden hair bouncing over his face. "I'm his brother, actually. Please send for him. He will vouch for me."

Duke, earl, prince, king. Who cared? Maddie slouched back in the armchair. She didn't care who the man was, but her mother apparently did because she smiled and ordered the constable to call this duke.

"What were you doing in my sister's bedroom?" Verity asked, holding Maddie's good hand.

Hector twisted his flat hat with his restless fingers. "There's this rare plant covering Miss Madeline's window." He paused to inhale. "It's an extremely rare species, believed to be extinct, and I wanted a sample to take to the Royal Botanical Society. But when I reached the gutter where the plant had its root, I tripped and smashed through the window. It was breaking the window or falling to my death." He rushed to Maddie and took a knee in front of her, startling her. His unique eyes widened, and the light from the fire was reflected in them. Really peculiar colour.

"Miss, I swear I'm sorry. I didn't mean to hurt you. It was an accident." He was so lean his Adam's apple was particularly prominent.

In a tiny corner of her mind, she found his large eyes, strong jaw, and straight nose worthy of being captured in a painting. He'd be a great model for a Greek god or an angel, although she knew better. The man was no angel.

But then his words sank. A plant. The entire disaster had happened because of a stupid vegetable. She snatched her hand out of Verity's, her chest rising and falling quickly.

"Why didn't you simply ask?" she hissed.

He blinked as if the possibility of asking had never crossed his mind. "I couldn't wait. See, I needed a sample of the plant in order to apply for the expedition financed by none other than Sir Alexander von Humboldt. It's a one-year-long trip to the Amazon with a team of selected scientists. An opportunity I couldn't miss."

"Oh, Lord." Maddie stifled a sob, the first since the incident. Her state of numbness was fading, and it wasn't a good thing. "You should have asked. I would have given you the whole stupid plant." She cried, unable to hold back the tears. "Th-there was no need to break m-my window." And wreck her life.

"By Jove, Wentworth." Maddie's father plonked down onto his chair. "My daughter is right. A simple inquiry would have sufficed."

"My brother sent a letter," Hector said. "Haven't you received it?"

Verity trapped her bottom lip between her teeth. "I saw a letter and took it to the parlour, but I forgot about it and didn't mention it to anyone. I'm sorry. Was it important?"

"The letter was a formal request to take a sample," Hector said in a resigned tone. "You didn't answer, and I was in a hurry. It's not an excuse, but I was eager to get the plant."

Obviously. Maddie shook her head.

Her mother waved a hand. "But the window can be repaired and Madeline's hand will heal. Nothing irreparable happened."

More tears poured out of Maddie's eyes. She disagreed. The damage was irreparable because she couldn't finish a new painting in a matter of days even if her hand hadn't been injured. Aside from sketches and a few other canvases that weren't halfway ready to be shown to Mrs. Blanchet, she didn't have anything complete. Her fellowship? Gone, like the colours melting on her painting. She glared at her mother who glared back as if challenging her to contradict her.

Verity hugged Maddie. "Mother. Maddie lost her painting and her hand is wounded."

"I'm so sorry," Hector kept saying.

"A pastime," Mother said. "Nothing more."

The words were nothing new for Maddie, but maybe because she was so fragile at the moment, they cut deeper than the glass shard. How could her mother be so dismissive of something bringing so much joy to her daughter? And Maddie's hand hurt!

Her father stomped a fist on his polished desk. "Catherine, please. Don't you see how distraught Maddie is?"

Her mother shrugged. "Reality and dreams are two different things. The sooner we learn this lesson, the better."

Hector scowled and opened his mouth, but didn't say anything.

There was more bickering between her parents, Verity whispering that everything would be all right, and footsteps thundering around her. Maddie mentally went through her half-finished canvases in the hope of finding something she could present to Mrs. Blanchet.

Voices sounded from downstairs. The door opened, and the maid said something she didn't care to understand. When Maddie wiped her face, a man she'd never seen before stood in front of her. From his fair hair and peculiar blue eyes, she guessed he was Hector's brother, the darn duke. Where Hector was all angular shapes and raw beauty, the Duke if Blackburn had a certain softness to his features that made him less harsh but less intriguing as well. Even his eyes, even though of an intense blue, didn't hold the determined quality Hector's had.

The duke took in the scene, pausing on Maddie and his brother.

"What is the meaning of this?" he asked Hector.

"Your Grace." Mother's voice lost her high-pitched tone completely. "Thank you for coming here." She curtsied.

"Robert." Hector hung his head, not pleading with his brother for help while Maddie's father recounted the incident.

The more she heard the story of the incident, the more bizarre it sounded.

Whenever Father turned angry about Hector's abrupt intrusion, Mother would intervene with a kind word, reminding everyone Hector had meant no harm. He should still be held accountable for his actions, in Maddie's opinion. Not that anyone asked for it.

The duke listened in stoic silence. The only sign the tale upset him was the ticking tendon in his neck. When her parents finished talking over each other, he narrowed his eyes to slits as he regarded his brother.

The duke's teeth flashed. "Hector, we'll talk about what you did later." He bowed to Maddie. "Miss Debenham, I wish to express my deepest and most sincere apologies for tonight's incident. My brother is an overeager scientist who didn't mean any harm, although he triumphantly succeeded anyway."

"Nothing serious happened." Mother smiled, tugging at her long braid.

Oh, not again! "Excuse me?" Maddie stood up on shaky legs.

"Nothing serious? My painting is ruined. My hand is injured. And my window doesn't exist anymore."

Hector tortured his hat again, his cheeks turning a deep crimson. No, she wouldn't feel pity for him...all right. She did pity him a little. He was obviously sorry for what he'd done, but the rage boiling inside her had to vent somewhere. The duke shook his head in consternation, but Mother pressed her lips in a flat line.

"For heaven's sake, Maddie. A silly painting is nothing." Mother pressed two fingers to her temples. "And your hand will heal. No harm done."

"Mother." The single word came out strangled. "My painting...the academy...Mrs. Blanchet..."

"Academy?" Hector and the duke asked together, turning towards her.

She let out a strangled noise.

Verity wrapped an arm around Maddie's shaking shoulders. She seemed unable to leave Maddie alone.

"That painting would have granted my sister a place in the Royal Women's Academy of Arts. Mrs. Blanchet herself was supposed to inspect the painting and help her find a fellowship. Now..." She rubbed Maddie's shoulder. "With the painting destroyed and her hand injured, it seems unlikely her dream will come true."

"I won't allow that." Hector paled, twisting his hat so tightly to rip the fabric. "Miss Debenham, I will make amends. I promise no matter what, I'll help you."

The honesty ringing in his voice struck a chord within her. His calm determination soothed her anger. At that moment, she could believe he'd find a solution and help her get a fellowship. Who knew? His brother was a duke. Perhaps not everything was lost.

"Thank you," she said, staring into his intense gaze.

A spark of hope kindled in her chest as he bowed his head.

"I don't deserve your gratitude, miss."

A fire burned in the depths of his gaze. His brother lacked that fire, which wasn't necessarily a bad thing. If she had to guess, she'd say Hector was the fighter while his brother was the diplomat. Although she wouldn't want to be at the receiving end of the duke's angry gaze when he'd glowered at his brother. The duke and his brother were going to have a loud conversation tonight.

Mother shifted her weight, her lips pressing together. A chill shuddered through Maddie. She knew her mother too well. Mother was plotting something. To her credit, Mother always did her best to turn a terrible situation to her advantage. The problem was she didn't care if someone got hurt in the process.

"Your Grace," Mother said, smiling too sweetly for the smile to be real. "Perhaps we should discuss a solution in private tomorrow." She put a hand on Maddie's shoulder. "It's late and my daughter is tired."

Maddie pushed her mother's hand away, earning a pointed glare from her. The last thing Mother was concerned about was Maddie's fatigue. She needed time to plot.

"I understand." The duke bowed. Hector copied him. "As my brother said, we'll be happy to help. I'm sure we'll find an arrangement that will satisfy Miss Debenham and compensate her for her loss."

Hector shot her a pleading glance, and some of her anger petered out. Maybe she was too tired and sad, but she couldn't find in her heart to be angry with him anymore. She still thought the whole incident could have been avoided if he'd been more considerate and less reckless. But he showed sincere concern and regret. She had to take that into account. Besides, she was too tired to stay angry.

She wanted to curl up in her bed—after she removed the glass shards from it—and forget the world for a few hours.

four

HECTOR BRACED HIMSELF for his brother's wrath once they were alone in their sitting room. But the onslaught of fury—fury he deserved—never came.

Robert dropped himself onto the plush Italian sofa Mother was so fond of and sighed. He'd dispensed with his jacket, and his silk waistcoat stretched over his tense body.

Hector shifted his weight from one foot to another next to the fireplace that was so large he could stand in it. He almost wished to be sucked into the dark chimney and come out when the nightmare was over. Yes, it'd be a cowardly thing to do.

Still clenching his hat, he took a tentative step forward after his brother didn't utter a word. "Robert, I didn't mean for any of this to happen."

Robert rubbed the bridge of his nose and the wrinkled spot between his eyebrows. "Didn't I ask you to wait?" His tone was calm. In a way, it would have been better if he'd shouted.

"You did."

"Why didn't you listen?" Exasperation radiated from Robert in waves.

Hector went through all the possible answers but couldn't find one strong enough to make an argument with. All the answers were true—he was too eager; he needed the plant immediately; he was running out of time—but they sounded hollow now.

So, he simply said, "I made a huge mistake."

"No. That's not the point." Robert rose, and even though Hector was taller, his figure demanded obedience. "The point is, you have no respect for the work I do."

"That's not true."

"You mock the duties of a duke, considering them beneath your obsessive pursuit of science and knowledge." Robert's voice remained low but sharp. "You don't trust my word and don't respect me because you think you're better than I am."

"For God's sake." Hector was the first to lose his temper and tossed his hat on the sofa. "This is rubbish. I have only respect for what you do."

"No. If you had, you would have listened to me." Robert bared his teeth. "The lives of many people depend on my work." He thumped a fist against his chest. "Entire families count on me doing my job and protecting their interests from greedy politicians, to have a job and food on their tables. I must take care of my tenants, their houses, the land, and their trades while arguing at the House of Lords with old barons who are too scared of losing their privileges to change anything." Passion burned in his voice. "I'm not complaining. I have accepted the burden of the dukedom. But it's a job full of responsibilities, and if I make one mistake, someone might starve or lose their home."

Hector ground his teeth. There was some truth in Robert's words. Hector wasn't concerned of his brother's important documents and meetings, the endless chatter about the law or the necessity to be on friendly terms with the people in power, even with those he despised. Hypocrisy and double standards weren't Hector's idea of a good life. And yes, dammit, science was more important to him than signing papers.

"I never asked to be a duke." Robert loosened the knot of his cravat. "I'd rather have a simple job and take care only of our ship-ment company. But no. The title and the damn responsibility are all mine."

"It's not my fault, though."

"I didn't mean that." Robert fired him a glare that shook him. "I've never forced you to get involved. I left you free to follow your interests, and you repay me with mistrust and deceit."

Hellfire. Put like that, Hector sounded like the worst scoundrel of the century.

"Never sneak behind my back, especially after I explicitly told you to let me handle it." Even Robert shook now.

"I'm sorry," Hector said again, aware of how useless those words sounded.

Robert pointed at the door. "Get out now. I'm glad you have your plant. I hope it's worth it."

Tears burning his eyes, Hector left the room. In one night, he'd managed to hurt a poor woman, destroy her dream, make a fool out of himself, and even ruin his relationship with his brother.

~

THREE MONTHS later

HECTOR HELD the bouquet of roses harder as he waited to talk to Maddie.

His footsteps echoed in the hallway of Debenham House—a pretty townhouse with dark wooden floors and brocade curtains that made him think of a library. He knew the house intimately by now. At least the hallway and the ground-floor parlour where he met Maddie whenever he could and whenever she felt so inclined. He knew her bedroom after having worked with the builders to repair the window. Robert had insisted on Hector joining the constructors as part of his repenting process, and Hector had wholeheartedly agreed.

Doing some physical work to repair the damage he'd done had helped assuage his own guilt. A little. It'd also given him the opportunity to learn a few things about Maddie. Her passion for painting matched his obsession for botany if the piles of remarkable sketches, unfinished canvases, and colours in her bedroom were any indications. Even if she were a bad artist—and she wasn't—he'd admire her hard work and resilience. The way she captured a person's emotion in a sketch had him in shivers.

But if he was going to be honest, the fact she was such a great painter made his guilt even harder to process. He'd ruined the future of the next Turner. His sin was inexcusable. Unforgivable. But today, he'd make amends and take his responsibility as Robert did. Today, he was going to propose to Maddie and spend the rest of his life helping her. It was the right thing to do.

Three months had passed since the fateful, stupid incident, and many things had changed. Some not for the better. Not that he could complain. He'd got his damn plant, and now he was a fully respected member of the Royal Botanical Society, although the victory hadn't brought him any joy. But for Maddie, the past months had been a nightmare.

"Lord Wentworth?" the maid called him, interrupting his brooding. "Miss Madeline will receive you in the parlour."

"Thank you." He shuffled forward, his heart pounding faster in a combination of guilt, anticipation, and sorrow.

He knew what he was going to see, but the sight of her pale and gaunt face never failed to steal his breath. She was reclining on a chaise lounge with a thick quilt covering her up to her chin. Her clouded emerald eyes appeared bigger in her thin face. The flowers he'd sent her in the past days were scattered around in vases on the mantelpiece, low table, and windowsills. But the roses couldn't cover her sweet lavender perfume. He could pick it easily among the other scents.

He removed his tall hat and bowed, glad to be wearing one of his best afternoon suits. Not to show off his wealth. He wanted to make an effort for her.

"Ma'am." He turned towards Mrs. Debenham who worked at her needlework in the armchair next to the fireplace.

She graciously nodded. "Lord Wentworth."

He had to admit she was a stunning woman—although Maddie's beauty was warmer and more angelic—but there was a coldness about Mrs. Debenham's manners that reminded him of the politicians he'd met during one of Robert's formal dinners. Not necessarily malicious, but it left him wary and tense.

He focused on Maddie. "Miss Madeline, how are you today?"

She coughed. The harsh sound caused her frail shoulders to shake violently. When she finished coughing, she exhaled, closing her eyes for a moment. "Dr. Wilton said I'm improving. The infection is finally receding."

She didn't look any better to him.

He placed the flowers on a table but didn't get nearer to her. The door was open, and her mother was present, but he'd behave as a perfect gentleman should. He had to. It was likely too late for that since a gentleman shouldn't climb a wall at night and above all shouldn't deceive his own brother, but he was learning from his mistakes.

"And your hand?" he asked.

Mrs. Debenham gazed up from her work. She smiled only when she noticed he glanced at her.

Maddie coughed again. "I have to say I'm not particularly thrilled about the use of bromine. It killed the infection, but it's so painful that I fainted yesterday. My hand and arm burn after each application. I shouldn't complain, though. It could be worse."

Yes, she could be dead because of the infection. Because of him.

She lifted her bandaged hand. It was with effort he didn't wince at her incredibly swollen hand. It was nearly the size of an orange. Since she'd lost weight, her hand looked disproportionately big compared to the rest of her body. Still, her hand was indeed swollen.

The cut had got infected. The infection had brought a high fever, and the fever had forced Maddie to a bed for weeks amid excruciating pain and a constant risk for her life. For a few days, Hector had feared for her, cursing himself to hell. If she'd died, it would have been his fault.

Robert had interceded on her behalf with the academy, but in the poor state Maddie was now, she couldn't present her work, attend the classes, nor could she paint. Who knew for how long? A complete disaster.

He swallowed past the lump of guilt lodged in his throat. "I'm so sorry."

She coughed in her handkerchief. "Lord Wentworth, you've apologised enough. I've come to terms with my fate. To be honest, I'm just happy to be alive at this point." Despite her words, her eyelashes fluttered down, and a corner of her mouth pulled up in a bitter smile. "Before doing anything else, I must get better. I didn't realise how important and precious my good health was until it was taken from me." She fiddled with her handkerchief. "I won't take it for granted ever again."

Lord, she was so strong. He'd be in tatters.

"Miss Madeline." He couldn't stand the distance between them and took her good hand gently, his deep admiration for her propelling him forwards.

"Lord Wentworth!" Mrs. Debenham lowered her work. "Please."

"I apologise." He reluctantly released Maddie's cold hand. In the past weeks, she'd been either too hot or too cold. "I deeply admire your courage, miss. In your situation, I would probably despair all day. Your strength is impressive." He had to stop himself from saying he was sorry again.

She flashed a weak but genuine smile. "Thank you for your

praise. Praises don't come my way often." She threw a brief glance at her mother. The gesture was so quick Hector wasn't sure it'd happened. "I'm too exhausted to think, be angry with anyone, or even despair. That's a positive thing about the situation, I guess. You and His Grace have been of great help to me."

"I beg to differ."

While she'd been bedridden, he'd been accepted to be part of the expedition. Although he hadn't applied to it after the incident. Hell, he hadn't even taken the golden pimpernel to the society. But the rumour about the incident had spread. Words about Hector having found a rare plant had reached the Royal Botanical Society, and the botanists had questioned him relentlessly. His discovery of the golden pimpernel had created such an uproar in the scientific world the organiser of the expedition had begged him to join them. Hector hadn't answered yet. Oh, he wanted to accept but didn't deserve it.

"Nonsense." Her voice sounded small and fragile. It killed him. "You and the duke have saved my life. We couldn't have afforded Dr. Wilton's fees if it hadn't been for your—"

"Madeline!" Mrs. Debenham's voice rang sharply. "Talking about money with a gentleman is most vulgar."

A flush crept over Maddie's face. A flare of anger at Mrs. Debenham burned the back of his mouth.

"Ma'am," he said to the older lady. "I kindly request permission to speak to Miss Madeline alone."

Mrs. Debenham arched her dark eyebrows. "For what reason, may I ask?"

"I'd like to discuss a personal matter with her and I promise on my honour"—or what was left of it—"that I will behave as a perfect gentleman."

Mrs. Debenham opened her mouth, but Maddie cut her off. "Please Mother. Besides, what could possibly happen? I'm a corpse, for all intents and purposes, cold and stiff."

"Please, Miss Madeline, don't speak about yourself in those

terms," he said at the same time as Mrs. Debenham said, "You've become so vulgar."

Maddie exhaled. "I guess having almost met my maker changed me, Mother."

"All right." Mrs. Debenham rose, muttering under her breath. "But the door remains open, Lord Wentworth."

He bowed. "As you wish, ma'am." He waited for the lady to leave the room before inching closer to Maddie.

"What is it?" As she propped herself up, the blanket slipped down a few inches, revealing her protruding collarbone.

Every time he noticed a sign of her frailty, he wanted to slap himself. "Miss Madeline, I must speak my mind."

"Please do." She tried to sit further upright but winced.

"Let me." He laid his hat on a table and hurried to help her.

When he slid his arm around her waist, the bones in her rib cage touched his palm. She was so frail, all because of him. But he was going to take care of her from now on.

He inhaled her sweet lavender scent and made sure the pillows were behind her back.

For a brief moment, he met her gaze, and her eyes held him captive with their brightness. It was as if she begged him not to hurt her again. A cold pang sliced through his chest. He finally understood what Robert had meant the night of the incident when he'd made his speech about ducal responsibilities. He was ready to pay for what he'd done and be a man Robert would be proud to call his brother.

"What did you want to tell me?" she asked, averting her gaze.

He cleared his throat and straightened. "I thought a lot about what I did and the weight of my responsibility towards you."

She narrowed her gaze, but didn't say anything.

"I am lucky enough to be a man of means. My brother holds the title, but I receive a generous allowance that would provide for you more than handsomely."

"Lord Wentworth." Her voice was so low and fragile he

couldn't understand if she was shocked or delightfully surprised. "What are you talking about?"

"I speak without the consent of your honourable father because I wanted to pay you respect and know your opinion on the matter before making a formal request."

Her lips parted, and a deliciously healthy blush blossomed in her cheeks. "Just so we're perfectly clear, are you proposing a marriage?"

"I am." He took a deep breath and waited for her answer.

She tugged the cover up, her blush intensifying. "I deeply thank you for your attention and I feel humbled and honoured by your proposal, but I must decline it."

Blazes. It shouldn't hurt so much, but the stab piercing his chest knocked the air out of his lungs. "May I ask why you declined my offer?" Even his voice sounded odd to his own ears.

"You want to marry me out of pity. I want to marry for affection," she said, reclining on the pillows.

"Not pity," he protested, squaring his shoulders. "Quite the opposite. I think you're one of the strongest persons I've ever met. I do not pity you. I admire you."

"It's duty then. Your sense of responsibility. Guilt." She shook her head. "I don't wish you to be tied to me forever only because you think I'm your responsibility. Duty, pity, and responsibility aren't good foundations for a long, happy marriage."

"You'll forgive my bluntness, Miss Madeline, but I'm the reason you're currently lying on that chaise, weak and ill. I ruined your chances of being accepted into the academy. I owe you a dream."

"That's what I mean." She pointed a finger at him. "While I agree the incident had its sad consequences for me and that you caused it, I don't want you to feel obliged to marry me. You took care of me in the past weeks without me being your wife."

"But a marriage would protect you from further unpleasant situations. You'll be free to pursue your passion." He glanced at the armchair where Mrs. Debenham had sat. "I would always support your dream of being a painter."

She let out a soft chuckle that turned into a cough. "Lord Wentworth, you don't have to bind yourself to me forever to protect me. I appreciate the thought, but I want to marry someone I love and who loves me, not someone who feels trapped by guilt for an unfortunate incident and tries to make himself feel better."

His face heated with emotion. "I don't wish to marry you to make myself feel better."

She raised her eyebrows. "Be honest with me and yourself."

He couldn't speak because some of what she'd said was true. He did mean to marry her because he believed it was his duty as a gentleman and a decent human being. And yes, he wanted to get rid of his sense of guilt.

But in the past weeks, while they'd talked to each other and come to know each other better, he'd also discovered she was clever and sensible, strong and witty, pretty and delightful. He liked her. He liked her emerald eyes, pink lips, rare smiles, and the way she stood up for herself. Was it love? He hadn't the foggiest. Not yet maybe? But weren't some marriages based on less than mutual respect? She was a gentlemen's daughter. Her father wasn't titled but was a gentleman. They were well-matched. Maybe she didn't like him at all. If that was the case, there was no hope for him.

"Please, Lord Wentworth." She coughed in her handkerchief. "Don't think I don't appreciate you. But a marriage would be a mistake for both of us. This is my choice."

"And I will respect it." He bowed and took his hat, hoping to hide his disappointment. "I understand. I won't importune you further, but I hope you'll allow me to visit you in the future. Please."

She flushed again. "By all means, yes. I..." She waved around. "I love the flowers."

Ouch. Another stab to his chest, but he took it like a gentleman.

"And your company," she hurried to say, but he recognised a hasty attempt to repair the damage when he was at the receiving end of it. "Please come back."

"Thank you."

"Besides," she said in a high-pitched tone, "aren't you about to leave for South America?"

He frowned. "No. I haven't agreed to join the expedition. I wasn't planning to. May I ask you how you know about it?"

"His Grace came here the other day to inquire about my health, and while we were chatting, he told me the Royal Botanical Society insisted that you go. You were right about how precious the plant was. You've realised your dream."

Was she trying to get rid of him for good? Was he being too obnoxious and suffocating? Bugger, he had no idea. "I'm not sure I should go."

"But it's your dream. Why wouldn't you go? Oh, Lord Wentworth." She huffed and coughed. "Don't tell me you want to stay here for me because you feel guilty."

"I *am* guilty. I don't deserve the opportunity to realise my dream while I destroyed yours."

Her lips pressed tightly in a fashion reminiscent of her mother. "At least one of us will be happy and fulfil their dreams."

"Miss Madeline—"

"Lord Wentworth, honestly." She exhaled. "Your consideration is admirable, but I don't want you to become a martyr out of guilt for my sake. You made a mistake. Yes, my opportunity to impress Mrs. Blanchet is gone, but thank heavens I'm alive, and with a bit of luck and your family's help, I'll paint again and have my fellowship. I haven't abandoned my dream. I have never asked you to sacrifice yourself for me. I don't want you to."

"I don't want to go. You haven't improved and I don't think I should leave London whilst you aren't fully recovered."

"Remain in London and do what? Come here every day?" She propped herself up on her elbows. "You've done enough, neglecting your preparations for the trip. I'll heal, Lord Wentworth, whether you are here or not. Please go. Fulfil your dream. For both of us."

He was impressed both by her passion and the fact she managed to say all that without coughing. Still, the idea of leaving didn't bring any spark of joy to him, just a sense of hollowness.

"Would you at least agree to receive an allowance? I'm more than happy to share my allowance with you. Forever. Even after you marry." Oddly enough, the last thought caused a fresh pang to his chest. He must have said something wrong again because she stiffened.

"Your brother was kind enough to promise to help me get a recommendation for the academy and receive a fellowship since my parents don't want to support me, or at least my mother doesn't." She waved a hand as if to dismiss the subject. "My hope is to be able to support myself. I am that stubborn. I'm not proud of it, but not ashamed either. So, thank you, but I can't accept."

He swallowed his humiliation and bowed again. Apparently, his kindness, money, and company weren't required. Or maybe he really suffocated her with his attention, and she wished to see him gone.

"As usual, I wish you a quick recovery." He put his hat on and left the room, trying to look as dignified as possible.

five

A WEEK PASSED since Maddie had received her first marriage proposal, and she couldn't stop thinking about Hector despite the fact he hadn't shown himself since.

He was used to visiting her every day, even if only for a few moments. But after their last conversation, he'd kept his distance, which, she had to admit, had been partially her goal when she'd prompted him to join the expedition. Or maybe not. She wasn't sure.

She liked him, she really did. When he talked about plants and flowers, his whole face brightened, and he knew the most unusual and curious things about nature. But yes, at times during his visits, she'd wished to be left alone. Her mood had shifted from high to low during her worst days, and even though she loved her family and Hector was kind to her, she'd wanted to be left alone to cry in her bed and pity herself. Sometimes that was what she needed before flourishing again. But she refused to let him ruin his life because of his guilt. Ridiculous. If she'd agreed to marry him, years from now, he would resent her, and she'd hate it.

She sighed, glancing out of the parlour window overlooking the busy street. The trees in Hyde Park had put on new leaves that fluttered like tiny waving hands in the wind. Ladies promenaded with their friends, showing off bright coloured frocks, lace-rimmed parasols, and silk reticules. Summer filled the air with the scent of freshly mowed grass and flowers. London was so pretty in summer, so full of people. There would be art exhibitions and presentations in every gallery and theatre. She wished she could go with Verity to take a walk through the park, eat a gelato, and watch the swans in the Serpentine. Maybe sketch one of those lovely poplar trees.

She coughed in her closed fist, her throat still burning. The incident and its aftermath had ruined her life—no, that was ungrateful of her. She still could become a painter. Her dream was merely postponed. But she'd be lying if she said she didn't wish Hector had never broken through her window that night.

She didn't regret having rejected him. His offer had come from the wrong place, nothing more. He wasn't really interested in marrying her. It was his sense of duty, or worse, guilt to have pushed him to propose. Thank goodness her mother wasn't aware of the proposal. Maddie would never hear the end of it.

She grimaced as a new shot of pain travelled up her arm after yet another bromine application. The liquid stank of sulphur and burned her skin like acid, leaving her shaken and in pain. After each application, her fingers remained numb for a while and her stomach roiled with nausea. She didn't know if it was a good or a bad thing. Dr. Wilton had said the nausea was normal.

There was a quick knock on the door before it opened, and the maid entered. The servants never waited for Maddie to reply, knowing their missus couldn't raise her voice.

The maid dropped a curtsy. "The Dowager Duchess of Blackburn, is here."

The Duchess? Her almost mother-in-law. "Please let her in." Maddie struggled to sit up, wondering if her hair looked like something that had been dragged out of the Thames. She hadn't used a hot rod or ribbons in weeks.

"Miss Madeline, may I?" a sweet voice asked from the door.

Maddie coughed. "Please."

The duchess came inside in a swirl of black linen and pristine lace. She had nothing in common with her sons. Where they were all golden hair and fair eyes, she was dark-haired and with gentle brown eyes. Her beauty resembled Hector's though. Same straight nose, fine features, and natural elegance.

Maddie tried to stand up, but it was too much effort, and the bromine caused her head to spin. "Your grace." She bowed her head.

"Please don't stand up, my dear." The duchess took her good hand. "I apologise for not having come earlier."

"Do not worry, your grace. Your sons have been very kind to me."

The duchess sat on the chair next to her. Her black skirt frothed around her. "How are you? Is there anything I can do for you?"

"I'm recovering, slowly, but I'm on the mend. Your sons took very good care of me." By paying all the medical bills and even her meals.

The lady's bottom lip quivered. "I'm sorry for what happened. Hector has always been wilder than his brother. I know he might behave like a scoundrel."

Maddie smiled because Hector might be passionate when he talked about plants and ignore some rules of society, but he couldn't possibly be a scoundrel.

"I've never thought him to be one."

The duchess clenched her gloved hands in her lap. "He's so immersed and focused on his love for science that oftentimes he isn't connected with real life."

To that, Maddie had to agree. But then again, she was the same.

The duchess lowered her gaze. "I gather he proposed and you refused."

Oh, dear. What was she supposed to say? "Your grace, I

couldn't accept his proposal. He proposed out of guilt, and I can't let him feel guilty forever."

"My guess is he's trying to emulate Robert and his sense of duty, so I agree with your conclusion." Hector's mother cradled Maddie's injured hand gently in hers, stroking the bandage. "I want you to know..." Her voice cracked, and she took a deep breath. "We'll provide for you anyway. You're bedridden because of my son's foolish actions. He didn't mean to hurt you, but that's the result, and we will not shy away from our responsibilities."

That seemed to be a common theme in the Wentworth family. Now Maddie understood where Hector and Robert's sense of duty came from.

Maddie could easily shun Hector's offer of money, but refusing the dowager was another matter. "Thank you."

The maid opened the door again. "Lord Wentworth is here."

"Please send him in." Maddie pulled her quilt up to cover the part of her chest the nightgown left exposed.

Hector's mother released Maddie's hand and angled towards the door, her expression guarded as if she were ready to scold her son.

"Miss Madeline, Mother." Hector bowed and smiled at his mother.

He didn't seem surprised to see her there. His mother's presence had to be a plot to convince Maddie to accept the money.

"We were talking about you, darling," the duchess said. Whatever emotion had taken her over a moment ago was gone.

He removed his hat, letting his beautiful golden curls tumble down his jaw. "I hope the conversation was interesting." He kissed his mother's cheek tenderly, and for some reason, Maddie's throat tightened. When had the last time been when she'd kissed her mother? She couldn't remember.

"Miss Debenham agreed to accept our help." The duchess smiled.

Yes, the whole visit was an ambush to make sure Maddie

would accept their financial help. Perhaps she'd been too stubborn after all.

"When are you leaving?" Maddie asked and regretted it immediately. His ruse to convince her to accept the money had stung her a little. But since he'd won, surely it meant he was going to sail to South America, right? "You should leave soon, shouldn't you?"

He toyed with his hat as a smile tugged at a corner of his mouth. "Sir von Humboldt himself asked me to join the expedition, and well..." He shrugged, flushing a deep red. "I'd love to go."

"Then go." Maddie meant it. For him. She understood the fierce need to chase one's dream. "Please do it." A sob remained trapped in her throat. What was it? Sadness for his imminent departure? She didn't know. "I'm happy for you. I really am."

Their gazes locked, and she couldn't deny the shiver of attraction going through her as she stared at his incredible sapphire eyes. The incident had changed them both, and as absurd as it sounded, she believed for the better. She was stronger, in spirit that is, ready to fight for her dream. The incident had also formed a connection between them, a bad memory, yes, but a connection, nevertheless.

He took her good hand gently and ran his thumb over her knuckles. Another shiver caused her pulse to spike.

"Thank you, Miss Madeline. Your blessing means more to me than I could ever express." He kissed her hand, and the emotion made her dizzy.

"I will see you when you return," she whispered.

"I'd be honoured to." He released her hand when his mother cleared her throat politely. "One year from now, I'll be a famous scientist and you a famous painter. I might see you at one of your exhibitions at the National Gallery."

She laughed for the first time in weeks, a weight lifting from her chest. "Lord Wentworth, I believe we have a deal."

six
Eight years later

O N THE DECK of the *Steamship Empress*, Maddie wondered why the sky there, in the middle of the ocean and so close to The Bahamas, had a peculiar azure quality England's sky lacked.

Even the clouds curled and twisted to form fluffy puffs with the most outrageous shapes. That cloud running overhead had the shape of two lovers entwined together. Their arms and legs were clearly visible, and they kissed in a fashion that made her lips tingle. Or maybe it was her wicked mind to conjure up such debauched images. She blamed the weeks spent in Nassau where everything from the culture, nature, and people vibrated with life and colour.

She had to thank Aunt Anne for the trip. Her aunt had married a Bahamian and invited Maddie, Verity, and her mother to spend a few weeks across the pond. She wouldn't mind staying with Aunt Anne permanently and walking along the beautiful beaches of Nassau while enjoying its warm sun.

But what she loved most about the trip were the scents. Nassau had smelled of flowers, roasted meat, and fruit. On the ship, fresh, salty air that teased her appetite and restored her spirit, filling her with optimism—something she'd missed dearly in the past years.

What she didn't miss was the stuffy air in her small cabin or London's fog and the smell of burning coal and of something rotting in the Thames.

The only terrible thing about staying on a ship was there wasn't much to do aside from taking strolls along the deck— unchaperoned strolls, which was liberating—reading and playing bridge. London might be crowded and smelly at times, but it offered luscious soirées, wonderful nights at the theatres, and an endless series of art exhibitions. Two more weeks before they arrived in England. She might grow less optimistic out of boredom. Besides, what waited for her didn't thrill her. With her artistic career compromised, she agreed to be the companion of a lady friend of her mother. Who knew? She might enjoy the work.

Sitting on a wooden bench on the deck, she faced the blue expanse of the sea. Such a simply soothing view for something so vast. Oh, if she were still able to paint, she would make a grand painting out of those shades of blue. Not a day passed without her wishing to paint again.

She stretched out the fingers of her right hand to warm them up. After the stabbing incident and the infection, her hand muscles could become rather stiff, the joints would lock up, and pain would bother her for a while. Sometimes the pencil would slip out of her fingers without her conscious thought. Her physician had told her that, with months, maybe years, of long exercises that had brought her excruciating pain, she would still write and sketch. She'd tried that and yes, she could write and do some sketching, but for what purpose? She wasn't an artist anymore. She'd paid a large price the night of the incident. Back then, she hadn't known how difficult, long, and painful her rehabilitation would be. How compromised her fingers would be.

But Hector had paid a higher price.

Foam curled on the crests of the waves like the curly locks of a white puddle dog. The soft sea breeze shuffled her hair, and she inhaled deeply the scent of the sea. She squinted in the sunlight, scrutinising the horizon as strolling passengers and sailors obstructed the view of what had turned out to be Hector's grave.

Eight years ago, he'd sailed that very water to South America after she'd encouraged him to go. If only she'd known. His ship had sunk well before it'd reached its destination, caught in a storm, and Hector had died with his companions. No survivors. Another ship had witnessed the tragedy but hadn't been able to intervene. The worst naval disaster in the past decade *The Times* had called it. Her chest still clenched for him. How happy he'd been when he'd decided to go. One word from her, and he would have stayed in London. Safe and alive.

Sadness caught her as she imagined being thrown into the angry sea in the middle of a storm with waves several stories tall, thunder, and squalls. Had he died quickly? Had he suffered? How frightened had he been? She shivered in the warm air and rubbed her arms.

She opened her sketch book and started drawing his face or what she remembered of him. His straight nose, cleft chin, and thick eyelashes. But other details eluded her memory, like his charming smile. Its slightly sinful quality was difficult to capture. She winced as her fingers stiffened, sweat dampening her forehead. Not that she ever finished a sketch these days. She'd start, get frustrated, and stop.

"There you are." In a froth of pink satin and under a pretty parasol, Verity sat next to her. She peered at her sketching book, and her smile vanished. "You're thinking about poor Hector again."

"This trip makes me think of him a lot." She sketched his hair. He'd had long, curly hair the colour of spun gold. But between her patchy memory and her trembling fingers, the lines never quite came as she wished and missed the softness of his hair. "I thought you were taking a nap."

Verity huffed. "Mother felt sick again. When she finally fell asleep, I left her cabin. I needed a bit of fresh air."

As Maddie's fingers struggled to draw the fine details of an eye, she fought the urge to throw the pencil and the sketchbook into the sea. Her fingers refused to move the way she wanted, freezing over the paper. No wonder the academy rejected her, despite the help from the late Duke of Blackburn.

Back in those days, she'd underestimated the struggle of her recovery. The infection hadn't been the problem, but its effects on her body had stayed. Her heart had broken when she'd realised her hand was no longer as functional as she'd wished. No more delicate sfumato or subtle strokes of the paintbrush for her. The committee of the academy hadn't been impressed by her work. No amount of exercise had given her fingers the flexibility an artist needed.

"Don't be too sad." Verity closed her parasol and faced the sun. The sunlight had turned her skin a lovely golden shade Mother found horrible but Maddie loved. "Tragedies happen. It's not your fault. Everyone knows Hector wanted to go."

Maddie sighed. She was both sad for him and for herself, if she was going to be honest. Cramps took hold of her fingers, and she set the pencil aside. The disappointment never failed to hurt her. She guessed she mourned the death of her dream. Better to gaze at the sea and the—she straightened, forgetting about the sketch.

The foam she'd admired earlier didn't seem to be foam at all but a...blanket? A flag? Whatever it was, the piece of fabric flapped in the breeze. The waves rhythmically hid it from view, but there was no mistaking the fact it was something human made. She craned her neck. The piece of fabric was attached to a pole or something similar. Another wave lifted it, and wooden planks tied by ropes came into view, along with what looked like a body.

A gasp tore out of her as she shot up, the sketch pad falling to the floor. "It's a raft."

"What is it?" Verity stood up as well, shielding her eyes with a hand.

"Over there. It's a raft." She clamped her hands over her mouth. "Good Lord. There's a person on that raft."

Verity cried out. "I don't remember what we are supposed to do or say when a person drops into the sea."

She gave her sister a gentle shove. "Go find a sailor. I'll keep an eye on the raft in case the current drags it away."

Grabbing a fistful of her skirts, Verity ran away. "Ring the alarm as well. It's right over there," she tossed over her shoulder.

Right. The alarm. Staring at the raft dangerously floating up and down, Maddie pulled the chain of the alarm hanging on the wall. A deafening, high-pitched ring sounded, making her wince. She couldn't tell if the raft sailed away from the ship or closer. Passengers came to abrupt stops as the alarm ripped the quiet afternoon.

"What is it?" a woman asked.

"Are we sinking?" another cried.

Maddie waved them away. "Move, move. I must see the raft."

She squeezed herself through the small crowd gathering on the deck and grabbed the handrail, searching the waves. She sagged in relief when she spotted the raft. Definitely closer.

"Maddie, Maddie!" Verity returned with two sailors at her heels and another one came from the other side of the deck.

Before they asked any questions, Maddie pointed at the raft. "There's a raft over there."

A mutter spread through the passengers as more people stared at the spot she was pointing to. The sailors leant over the rail, craning their necks.

"Man overboard!" one of them shouted.

Other sailors repeated the yell from somewhere, and soon the shout "man overboard" echoed around her.

Three long rings followed by three long blasts bellowed from behind her. Gosh, they were loud. A metallic groan resounded as the ship slowed and came to a halt.

She grimaced but didn't dare to close her eyes so as not to lose contact with the raft. Footsteps thundered against the polished wood of the deck. More orders were yelled and repeated until a lifeboat was dropped into the sea with a few sailors on board.

Gripping the rail with both hands, Maddie breathed heavily. People pressed against her from every side. Minutes passed, and the boat seemed miles away from the raft. In fact, it looked like it wasn't moving at all.

Why did it take so long to cover the short distance? The boat floated up and down with the waves, disappearing from view. She rolled her bottom lip between her teeth and scratched the glossy surface of the rail. For God's sake, couldn't they speed up and row faster? The sun would set before those sailors reached the raft. What if the person wasn't dead and needed medical attention?

"Quick, quick," she muttered under her breath.

The wind picked up speed, raising the water. Great. Now both the boat and the raft weren't visible, hidden by the growing waves. Maddie shifted her weight and bit her lips. No one panicked, so probably she overreacted. The sailors next to her seemed perfectly calm, as if the situation were normal.

A few passengers had lost interest and left, returning to their game of pétanque, while she dug her fingers into her palms. A wave lowered, and the boat swept into view again. But was it sailing towards the raft or the ship? Bother. Nothing made sense in the sea. She could have sworn the raft had been barely a few yards away.

She released a breath when the boat appeared again. There was no mistaking the direction. It rowed towards the ship, and she spotted a slumped figure among the sailors. Lord, they got him.

The commotion returned to the deck. The passengers talked in excited tones and pointed at the boat. The raft floated up and down, empty. She swatted the anonymous hand of one of the pointing people away from her field of vision.

Faster. Faster.

When the boat was close to the hull, she leant over the railing, rising on her tiptoes. A man, wrapped in one of the blankets of the ship company, lay on the boat. Aside from a leonine mane of dark-blond hair, she couldn't see anything. It took another good half an hour for the boat to approach the hull and for the sailors to haul it up with ropes.

"Give them space." A sailor urged the passengers back until he formed a wide circle of space.

She stepped away, clasping her hands together.

"My goodness," Verity said next to her.

Blimey. Maddie hadn't realised Verity stood so close to her.

"He needs a doctor," one of the sailors shouted. "The man is alive."

Alive. The tension lifted from her shoulders.

Now that he was closer, she could see the man clenched a bundle in his arms and when a sailor tried to take it from him, he growled, his tanned skin wrinkling under the curtain of his hair and thick beard.

"I'm a doctor!" A short man hurried forwards, opening a path through the crowd. "Out of my way."

Maddie tried to see what was going on, but too many people were gathered on the deck. The doctor exchanged a few words with the sailors. She stretched her neck to catch a glimpse of the castaway.

As the man was carried away by the sailors, she lingered after the passengers lost interest again. Alive. How could anyone survive on a raft in the middle of the ocean? What had happened to him?

The wind carried the torn page of her sketchbook with Hector's face to her. She snatched it before it fell into the sea.

seven

A BED. A proper, soft bed was under Hector's sore body. Not the rough pallet made of palm leaves he'd slept in for the past few years. He wasn't sure how many. Unless he was wrong in his calculation, it should be eight years since the damn storm had sunk the *Observatory*.

He blinked his eyes open. They hurt after two weeks spent on the raft under the glaring sun. Everything hurt.

Someone had found him. It wasn't a hallucination induced by a sunstroke and exhaustion. A ship had found him. At least he hadn't been wrong about his calculation on the ships' journeys across the ocean. He'd hoped one of the ships sailing in front of the island where he'd been stranded would have spotted him.

After his sight adjusted to the blissfully dimly lit room, he gazed around. Yes, he was in a cabin, all dark wood and pristine floor. Polished wooden wainscoting covered the walls of the cabin, giving him a sense of calm. The pungent smell of carbolic acid and paraffin teased his nostrils. He touched the area around him, savouring the softness of the bedsheets and their scent of soap. But where was his book? Panic seized him.

He bolted upright, wincing as his back muscles shot pain

through him. He couldn't see his precious diary anywhere. There was a cabinet with a lamp on its top, a narrow wardrobe, a water basin, and...there. He sagged against the pillow when he spotted his bundle in a corner. Hopefully, no one had touched it.

He breathed the stuffy air in and out. It was the first time in years that stale air had filled his lungs. The porthole showed only a portion of the sea, a small, deceitful portion because the sea wasn't the placid giant the view portrayed. It was a sleeping monster, ready to swallow lives without mercy.

Somehow, he wore a clean white shirt and a pair of breeches. The fabric felt soft on his hardened skin since he hadn't worn any clothes for a long time. He propped himself up on his elbows, grimacing at the pain stinging his body. Then he waited. But no emotion, tears, or shudders came.

He'd dreamt of the day he'd be rescued, even cried, thinking about the moment he would be found. He'd even prepared a speech to thank whoever had spotted him in the sea. On those occasions, a storm of emotions had raged in his chest. Relief, gratitude, and happiness. But now? Nothing. Only mild curiosity at the ship and her destination.

He raised his calloused hands. His thick skin was dark against the white bedsheets. He didn't even shiver. A void of sensations lay in his heart. He felt...nothing. And how disturbing was that? Had the sea robbed him of his humanity, too?

After the storm and the sinking, he'd awakened on a beach, surrounded by dead sailors, broken equipment, and flotsam. At that time, he hadn't felt anything either. Just annoyance at his absurd situation. The nervous breakdown had come later when he'd fully realised he was alone on a deserted island and that no one was going to search for him.

A new breakdown would arrive soon, he guessed. It was a matter of time. Hopefully. What was a man without his emotions?

He jolted when the door swung inward and a short man entered. Hector bared his teeth, an instinctive reaction he didn't want to control at the moment. The man stilled and raised a hand. The skin around his brown eyes wrinkled when he smiled.

"Good day, sir. I'm Dr. Landon. I'm the physician who has been attending to your health since you were rescued."

Hector didn't say anything, too stunned to talk. He hadn't heard a human voice in years and wasn't sure what to make of it now.

Dr. Landon fiddled with his small hands. "You've been asleep for three days."

Hector said nothing. Oddly enough, his brain fixated on examining the doctor's dark waistcoat. So different from the waistcoats Hector used to wear. The neckline was low, and there were only three buttons on the front. Why was he paying attention to fashion?

"May I check your pulse?" the doctor asked.

A dozen questions piled up in Hector's mind, but still his tongue refused to move and let him speak.

The doctor came closer, seemingly unaffected by Hector's silence. "You're on board the *Steamship Empress*, sailing from Nassau to Southampton. We're due to arrive in less than two weeks if the weather remains fair."

His breath hitched. England. Home. His mother. His brother. The thought caused a painful tightness in his chest. His family had to be distraught over his supposed death. He'd missed them so much.

The doctor sat on a stool next to the bed. "May I?" He waited, but since Hector didn't move or speak, he reached out for Hector's wrist.

On pure instinct, Hector recoiled and moved to a corner of the bed. Why? He hadn't the foggiest idea. The doctor wasn't one of those dangerous primates that had attacked him on many an occasion.

"What is your name?" the doctor asked, withdrawing his probing hand, but still smiling.

Hector opened his mouth, but his throat was sore, and only a raspy noise came out.

"Oh, right. Wait." The doctor poured him a glass of water and handed it to him. "Here. You were dehydrated when we found you, but not as much as I'd expected. My guess is you had some provisions with you on the raft."

Hector gulped down the water, closing his eyes at its fresh passage in his throat. He nodded.

The doctor beamed. "Ah, so you understand English. Good. I was starting to think you didn't speak my language. Are you an Englishman?"

Hector nodded again, drinking more.

"Your throat is fine, by the way. Just a bit dry. What is your name, lad?"

He swallowed a couple of times, feeling a burning scratch in the back of his mouth. "He-Hector," he croaked out. "Hector Wen-Wentworth."

Dr. Landon stilled, his cheeks paling. "Hector Wentworth? The Duke of Blackburn?"

Hector swallowed again. "My brother, Robert, is the duke." His voice sounded all raspy and low.

"Good Lord." The doctor removed his rounded glasses and rubbed the bridge of his nose. "But Lord Hector Wentworth...his ship sank eight years ago."

"So she did. I sank with her."

Dr. Landon's mouth dropped open. "How did you survive?"

Hector brushed a lock of hair from his face. "Luck. I'm not sure."

"Lucky, I'd say. Lucky a woman on the ship spotted you."

"A woman spotted me?" he asked, since he didn't know what to say to the doctor's astonishment.

"Yes." The doctor put his glasses back on, but they couldn't hide the odd look in his eyes. "She was on the deck when she saw the raft and raised the alarm."

Blazes. That woman had saved his life. "I want to see her."

Dr. Landon scratched his chin and poured more water in Hector's glass, studying him as if he were a rare beast. Maybe he was.

"It can be arranged."

THE NEWS that a mysterious blond man had been recovered from the sea was whispered, muttered, and discussed in detail everywhere Maddie went.

From the dining hall to the main deck, her name was on everyone's lips. Her role in the finding of the raft had been greatly exaggerated by the gossip. In one of the versions she'd heard, she'd dived into the sea and single-handedly saved the man. In another, she'd suffered from a hysterical crisis and fainted on the deck.

She'd also heard another, more disturbing tale. A few people believed the castaway might be a passenger of the *Observatory*, perhaps even Hector. There hadn't been any other sunk ships since then. It was logical to assume one of the passengers on the *Observatory* might be the castaway.

But Hector couldn't be the man on the raft, could he? The survivor was unconscious as he'd been for the last three days, and Dr. Landon had firmly forbidden anyone from approaching him. But if the rescued man was Hector, she wanted to talk to him. Still, how could he be? Eight years had passed. His ship had been swallowed by the sea. Where had he been all that time? But if it was him...just the possibility sent her heart into a frenzy and started a flutter in her chest. Hector alive. She couldn't even fathom the huge meaning of the news.

She was strolling along the deck, twisting her sketchbook with her stiff fingers, when Dr. Landon rushed over to her. The chain of his pocket watch bounced up and down as he ran.

"Miss Debenham. Miss, I need a word." His reddened face glistened with sweat, which he dried with a handkerchief.

Oh, no. She came to an abrupt stop. Had something happened to the survivor?

"Doctor, is something the matter?"

"Miss Debenham," he said, dabbing at his face with the handkerchief again. "I apologise if I'm being so straightforward, but my patient, who claims to be the presumed dead Lord Hector Wentworth—"

"Excuse me?" She tottered on her legs.

"Yes, yes. I know it sounds impossible." Dr. Landon loosened the collar of his shirt. "But he claims to be he. Did you know Lord Wentworth?"

"I did." Oh, Lord. She'd never suffered from seasickness, but now seemed a good moment to start to.

"Well enough that you would recognise him?" The doctor gave her a pointed look.

"Yes. I think I can."

"Good. He wishes to see the woman who spotted his raft."

"Me?" She was eager to see him too, but she hadn't expected him to care.

"Yes. He wants to meet the lady who saved him."

She didn't have to think about it. "By all means, let's go."

As he led her below deck, she shoved people aside in her hurry to see the castaway. The passageway in that part of the ship was narrower than the one in her area. Two people could barely squeeze through together.

"I must warn you," Dr. Landon said, "he's easily startled, and his appearance is rather wild. He didn't let me check his pulse or cut his hair. His hand is swollen. He must have hit it hard somewhere." He paused in front of a door. "It'd be extremely helpful if you'd be able to tell me if the man is indeed Lord Wentworth."

"All right." She nodded, fiddling with her sketchbook.

Dr. Landon went to open the door but paused again, and she barely contained a frustrated groan.

The doctor opened the door and peered inside. "Not to worry, lad. It's me with the lady who found you."

Maddie rose on her tiptoes to see past the doctor but couldn't catch a glimpse of the cabin. No answer came, but the doctor entered all the same. She followed him, holding her breath.

The doctor stretched out an arm towards her. "This is Miss Madeline Debenham."

A tall, strapping man stood in front of the porthole but spun around when the doctor introduced her. She remained still, studying the castaway. He towered a good foot and half over her. When the sailors had dragged him inside, she hadn't appreciated how tall, broad, and brawny he was. His shirt was scandalously half-buttoned, leaving a portion of his muscled chest bare. The skin had a dark, golden-brown tint that enhanced the gold in his long, long hair falling well past his shoulders. She'd never seen a body so perfectly sculpted, as if Michelangelo had just finished adding the final touches.

Between his thick beard and his unruly hair, his face was hidden, but his eyes...Lord, his eyes were the most intense sapphire she'd ever seen, fringed by long gold eyelashes. She'd unsuccessfully tried to replicate the elusive shade of his irises for a long time. There was no doubt.

"Hector," she whispered, forgetting to address him properly.

He drew in a breath that lifted his chest, but he didn't say anything.

"Is it really you?" She found it hard to believe it. Aside from his startling eyes, he didn't resemble the lanky, young man who'd brought her flowers and visited her every day. If anything, the blond giant looked like a pirate ready to slit her throat. She placed a trembling hand right there as she regarded him. "Do you remember me?"

"Maddie." His voice didn't sound like Hector's but was all

rough and deep. But then again, his voice must have changed in eight years, as the rest of his body. The fact he'd used her short name with a sweet tone hadn't escaped her notice. "Of course I remember you." His gaze dipped to her hand. "I hurt you. I broke your window and destroyed your painting. I could never forget that horrible night."

"Heavens." Maddie dropped her sketchbook. "You are Lord Hector Wentworth."

"Oh, Lord." Dr. Landon propped his hand on the table as if he needed something to support him.

Maddie took her time, regarding Hector, trying to find more similarities with the man she remembered. The problem was that he regarded her as well. His intense stare burned with an emotion she couldn't place, and it distracted her.

"We thought you died in the storm." Relief and happiness choked her, and she couldn't suppress a sob.

"For a while, so did I." He didn't say anything else. His right hand was bandaged, but the gauze couldn't hide the swollen skin underneath.

"How did you survive?" she asked.

The doctor perked up.

Hector sat on the bed and stared at his big hands for a few moments before answering. "I don't remember much about the sinking. There was a storm. Thunder. Waves taller than London's buildings. Then a crack as if the ship split. I hit my head and lost consciousness. When I woke up, I was lying on a beach. I guessed a current had dragged me to an island. It was uninhabited. There were many species of birds, fish, and even edible plants. And primates. Aggressive primates." He gritted his teeth when he said the last words.

"Primates?" she asked.

"Animals similar to monkeys. Similar to us." He stared at his hands again.

Maddie copied the doctor and leant against the wall, needing support.

"You lived on the island for eight years?" the doctor asked, his glasses slipping down his nose.

Hector didn't gaze up. "My knowledge of plants helped me survive. The majority of species were new to me, but I identified the Families and went from there." He paused to drink a glass of water. "Flotsam from the ship proved to be precious too. I found knives, wood, and even blankets. With time, I learnt to hunt, fish, and which plants I could eat."

"This is most extraordinary." Maddie took the chair in front of him, since her legs weakened. "Like Robinson Crusoe."

Hector raised his gaze to her, and the flicker of a smile graced his lips. She couldn't be sure though with his wild beard.

"How did you leave the island?" she asked.

Hector lowered his gaze again. "I could see the ships from the island when the weather was good and the sea calm. They were in the distance. But they never saw me even though I lit a bonfire several feet tall. It took me time to understand the ships had a schedule. I saw them only during a precise period of the year and always on the same spot. So I built a raft." He breathed hard now, his muscles swelling under his shirt. "I was terrified to leave the island. The currents were too strong for me. They shoved me away from the ship I wanted to intercept. I was so scared. The ship seemed so far away. The sea started to become rough." He shook, his broad shoulders quivering. Sobs tore out of him. "I can't believe I survived. I thought I was going to die. The sea was terrifying." His pupils dilated, and his cracked lips parted.

A lump swelled in her throat at his pain. "It's all right." Maddie took his hand, feeling his hard skin and strong fingers. "You don't have to tell us everything now. We're just glad you're here safe."

He stopped shaking. His eyes flared wide with a feral glint as he stared at her hand over his.

Good gracious. Had she stunned him with her boldness? Hurt him? She went to remove her hand, but he held it in an almost painful grip as if he were desperate for the contact. Lord, his fingers were strong indeed. He could break a person's neck with them. A shiver slithered down her back, but she wasn't sure it was only fear.

He released her abruptly, and she inched her hand back. He spied on her from underneath his fringe like a predator waiting to lunge at his prey.

"How do you feel today?" the doctor asked after a moment of charged silence.

Hector didn't reply.

"Lad." Dr. Landon reached out, but Hector bolted back with such speed to make her jolt.

"I want Madeline to cut my hair and beard," he said in a gruff tone.

She tilted her head, not sure she'd heard him correctly. "Excuse me?"

He stared at her. "Cut my hair and beard." An order.

"Lord Wentworth." Dr. Landon straightened his glasses. "I may be patient with you, but you do not speak to a lady that way. You do not order her around."

"Dr. Landon," Maddie said, never taking her gaze off Hector, "it doesn't matter."

She'd be rude too after eight years surrounded by monkeys.

"It does, miss. I don't mind being mistreated, but a lady is a different matter. I believe we might need to remind Lord Wentworth of how we behave in civilised society." The doctor pinned him with a glare holding all the outrage of a British gentleman.

"You're right, Doctor." Hector blinked, his shoulders sagging. "Please, Maddie. My hand is injured. Would you help me?"

Maddie's cheeks warmed under his scrutiny, and he seemed so lost she wanted to hug him. "But I've never cut...oh, well. I'll do it."

eight

MADDIE HELD THE sharp, shiny pair of scissors in her bad hand, wondering if she should have Verity cut Hector's hair. He'd survived eight years alone on a wild island. She didn't want to be the one who killed him with scissors on a ship on his return trip to civilisation. Her mother and Verity didn't help. Mother, grey from the seasickness, couldn't stop staring at Hector as if he were a circus freak, and Verity seemed scared to death of him.

But Maddie wished to be alone with Hector. Her mother and sister were intruding into a private moment, as absurd as it sounded.

He sat stiffly on the chair, chin up and eyes scanning the cabin. His long hair almost reached his waist and fell in golden curls over his back. He must have washed it that morning because it smelled of verbena and shone with a glossy hue.

"I'll start now," she said, trying the scissors.

He didn't say anything.

But she needed to hear him. "Hector, I—"

"Just cut it, Madeline." Her mother waved a dismissive hand. "Stop this fuss."

"It's not a fuss. I want to be sure he knows what's about to happen."

Mother's gaze travelled skywards. Verity gave Maddie an encouraging nod.

"You may cut," Hector said.

"All right." Maddie cut the first lock, needing to apply more strength than she imagined. The severed curl dropped to the floor in a glitter of gold and copper.

Mother raised her eyebrows. "Good gracious, Lord Wentworth. Why don't you wear something appropriate?"

Hector didn't reply, closing his fists on his thighs. Maddie kept cutting his hair, careful not to graze his skin. The more she cut, the more his strong neck became visible. She appreciated the hard tendons and roped muscles twitching under the skin. Her fingers itched to draw them. Would she be able to capture the life pulsating in his thick veins? She doubted it, but blazes if the challenge didn't tickle her.

"It's rude not to answer one's question." Mother folded her hands in her lap.

"Leave him be, Mother," Verity said, peering at Hector's half-naked chest with an interest her betrothed wouldn't like.

Mother huffed. "His manners are barbaric."

"Mother!" Maddie and Verity chorused.

Mother pressed her lips together but thankfully didn't say anything.

Maddie cut through the thick mane until his hair was at a fashionable length right below his strong jaw. Perhaps the curls needed to be straightened here and there, but overall, they looked more decent. He watched his hair fall around him but again didn't show any interest.

"Done." She brushed a few curls from his shoulder, holding back a gasp when she inadvertently slipped her hand inside his shirt.

It wasn't her fault if he kept his shirt half-unbuttoned and the fabric became loose around his neck. Her fingers skimmed over hard muscles and smooth skin. For s split moment, she wished she could explore more, but she was lucky that Mother was distracted by Verity when the incident occurred. She slid her hand out of his shirt, but Hector turned towards her, his chest rising with his deep inhalation, and his pupils dilating again.

"Apologies," she whispered.

Was he flushing? She couldn't tell. Between his tanned skin and the beard, it was difficult to see his face, but the visible skin had blushed red for a moment. Heavens, she behaved wantonly with him, touching him when he didn't expect it.

"Don't apologise," he whispered back before staring ahead.

She took her time preparing the bowl of warm water. Shaving him would be trickier than cutting his hair, and she would need to stand quite close to him, which wasn't an explanation for her suddenly fast heartbeat.

"I'll cut the beard now," she said, standing in front of him. "After I shorten it, it's probably better if you ask Dr. Landon to use the razor." She let out a nervous laugh for no reason, but Hector didn't even smile. Oh, well. "I once cut my father's beard when he broke two fingers."

Verity nodded. "A client at the bank got furious and closed Father's fingers in a drawer, smashing them. How horrible for him. Although Father admitted the man had a good reason to be angry since the bank refused—"

"Verity, shush!" Mother chided her.

Maddie stroked the beard, finding it surprisingly soft, and cut a big chunk. The curls fell over his shirt, and she fought the urge to brush them off. Lord, she was becoming a degenerate, and the fact he kept his trusting gaze on her didn't help. Gentlemen didn't stare at ladies with his intensity. Such a shame.

"It'll be such a shock for you to return home." Mother's smile didn't hold any kindness.

Hector didn't acknowledge her, but Maddie shot her a warning glare, which her mother promptly ignored.

"It'll take some time," Verity said. "But I'm sure Lord Wentworth will be all right once he's reunited with his...ahem, friends and peers."

Maddie cut another chunk, hoping Hector didn't ask Verity questions about his family. Clumsy of her to mention it.

Mother turned on her chair to glance at Verity. "What are you talking about, silly girl? His whole family is dead."

Verity gasped, clamping her hands over her mouth.

"Mother!" Maddie lowered the scissors and stomped a foot on the floor.

Hector whipped his head up. "Dead? How?" His expectant face radiated too much trust.

"Lord Wentworth, we didn't tell you, but it happened—" Maddie couldn't finish the sentence. Her mother cut her off.

"For God's sake. Your brother died of a fever, and your mother killed herself. She isn't even buried in holy ground."

Hector's mouth dropped open as his breath seemed to get stuck in his rising chest. He didn't even blink.

"Mother, enough!" Maddie's voice thundered in the cabin.

She shook so hard the scissors slipped out of her hand. How could her mother be so cruel? Controlling her daughters was one thing, but destroying a man's hope was quite another.

Mother straightened as if she were the one who had been attacked. "It's true and someone ought to tell him. It's his right to know the truth." She dabbed her forehead with her handkerchief. "Would you have let him believe that he would see his family once in London?" She tsked. "Now, that's cruel."

Maddie folded her arms over her chest. "I would have told him in a kinder fashion."

"So, is it true?" He shivered, and goosebumps pebbled his skin.

She drew in a breath. "I'm so sorry."

Hector's fists clenched so tightly she worried he might punch her mother. "Get out," he gritted out.

"Your manners—" Mother started.

As he shoved himself up to his feet, the stool was knocked backwards. The cut strands of hair fell softly to the floor. "Get out!" he roared. "All of you."

Maddie grabbed her mother's elbow and dragged her out as Verity held the door open for them.

"Oh, my goodness." Verity shut the door behind them once they were in the passageway.

"Let me go." Mother shrugged herself free from Maddie's grip. "What is the matter with you?"

"With me?" Maddie's voice shook with anger. "How could you be so cruel to that poor man? There was no reason, none, to hurt him the way you did. He's barely recovered from the shock of having been rescued, and you overwhelmed him with horrible news."

Verity shook her head. "Mother, honestly."

Mother didn't flinch. She tugged at the shawl around her shoulders and lifted her chin. "He's a barbarian. A creature." She pointed a finger at Hector's cabin. "Didn't you see how he behaves? He has no courtesy, no decency, and his mind is probably irreversibly damaged."

"Since when are you an expert physician?" Maddie said. Although she wondered if Hector's mind would remain troubled forever. "You should apologise."

"To him?" Mother huffed. "I'd rather feel sick for another month." She turned around and hurried away.

Angry tears burned Maddie's eyes as she stifled the instinct of yelling at her mother and making a scene. "How could she have done that? Blathering out about Hector's family with no respect for him."

Verity wrapped an arm around her shoulders. "Sometimes, I do wonder how she produced us."

"She destroyed him as if he hadn't been through enough already." She'd become accustomed to her mother's mean behaviour, but watching her cruelty hurt someone as vulnerable as Hector was at the moment cut her deeply. "I must apologise." She put a hand on the knob, but Verity stopped her.

"Listen, let's wait a while. Then you'll visit Lord Wentworth again and see how he's doing. He needs a moment of peace. I think we should give it to him. He's probably less interested in our apology than in dealing with his pain."

Maddie stooped her shoulders. "Very wise words. And I'm the older one."

Verity smiled. "Let's have a cup of tea." She started leading Maddie away. "No, forget tea. I want one of those hot cocoa cups with whipped cream and cinnamon on top."

Maddie rested her head on her sister's shoulder. "You also have the best ideas."

She started down the passageway when the noise of broken furniture came from the cabin.

nine

DEAD? DEAD? HOW could they be dead?

Hector punched the wall, ignoring the pain burning his knuckles. In fact, he welcomed it. His mother and his brother couldn't be dead. He tossed the table across the room, finding satisfaction in the loud crack of the wood as it hit the wall. What was the point of going back home if the home was empty? He smashed the porcelain basin on the floor, splashing water everywhere. He punched the wall again until blood trickled down his wrist. All those years, he'd been worried sick about his mother and brother, thinking about their pain. For what?

Someone touched his shoulder, and he spun around, ready to yell to leave him alone. All his wrath vanished the moment he stared at a pale, wide-eyed Maddie. She held up her hands, her chest rising and falling quickly.

"Hector," she whispered.

He opened his fist and stepped away from her, ashamed of having scared her. "I'm sorry."

"I called you, but you didn't hear me." A quiver went through her.

He shoved aside the porcelain shards lest he hurt her again. The outburst hadn't soothed the sorrow in his chest, but he didn't feel the need to smash something anymore.

Maddie crouched and started to gather the wooden splinters and the shards.

"No." He regretted his tone when she jolted. Curse his temper. "I'll do it. It's my fault, and you might get hurt."

Verity was watching them from the threshold, seemingly petrified. He cleaned up the room and dried the floor with a towel while Maddie stood in a corner. He'd terrified the only person he didn't want to scare. Great.

"You'd better leave," he said, gathering the pieces of broken wood.

"You're bleeding."

"It's nothing."

"We'll call Dr. Landon." Verity waved her sister closer. "Come, Maddie."

"But he needs help."

"I'm sure Lord Wentworth wants a moment alone, don't you, Lord Wentworth?" Verity reached out to take her sister's hand.

"Yes, I do." He sat on the floor in the middle of the chaos. Why had he lost his temper? He didn't know or care.

"Will you be all right?" Maddie asked.

"Don't worry about me. I'll be fine."

Maddie paused on the threshold before Verity pulled her out of the cabin. And he was alone with his ghosts.

HECTOR SAT ON THE STOOL, waiting for Maddie to return. After he'd cleaned up his cabin and Dr. Landon had changed the bandage on his hand, he'd asked him to call her and bring everything necessary to shave him. He was calm now, but refused to let anyone inside. No more strangers. The last thing he wanted was to receive more bad news about England. He couldn't avoid bad news, but he needed time to handle his grief. Right now, his emotional numbness protected him from hurting. Mostly. But another blow would shatter him.

A soft knock came from the door. "Lord Wentworth? Hector? It's me, Maddie."

For a moment, he simply stared at the door before remembering people waited for him to speak after knocking. "Come in."

She inched the door inwards and slipped inside, pale and shivering. "How are you?"

It was a simple question, one that people constantly asked each other without being actually interested in the answer. But to him, the answer wasn't so simple. Too much had happened to him in a short time. He still couldn't believe he'd left the island or that he was alive. How could he come to terms with the fact his family was dead when the thought of seeing his mother and brother again had sustained him through his darkest moments? They were the reason he was alive. He'd been tempted to give up many times. But they were dead, and he was alive. What nonsense.

He shrugged. "I'm not sure." He raked a hand through his hair. "I'm sorry if I frightened you. It wasn't my intention."

"I know." She shut the door and fiddled with her hands. She hadn't changed much in eight years aside from regaining her healthy pink complexion and growing more curves. She looked more beautiful than he remembered. "I have no words to express how sorry I am for what my mother said."

It was done, and while the news had been brutal, he had to know the truth. "Cut..." He cleared his throat, remembering what Dr. Landon had told him about manners. "Would you please finish cutting my beard?"

He had no idea why having his hair and beard trimmed was so important. But a choking sensation gripped him every time his tangled curls fell over his eyes. It was like being caught in one of those vines growing on the island. The first time the long, spiky stems had taken hold of him, he'd panicked. He hated the feeling of having something wrapped around him.

She stopped fidgeting, surprise showing on her parted lips. "Of course."

"Was I polite enough?" He didn't want to be rude to her.

It was amazing how he'd forgotten about etiquette. The rules that had been hammered into his mind by his parents and tutors made no sense now.

"A perfect gentleman." Her voice shook.

As she gathered what she needed to shave him, she didn't gaze at him. Had he done something wrong? Hell. He couldn't tell anymore. Had society always been so complicated?

"I should apologise for having yelled as well." He wasn't sorry about his outburst, but he was sorry about having scared her.

"Don't you apologise." She balled a hand on her hip. "I perfectly understand your reaction. It's my mother I struggle to understand. No, you don't have to apologise. She should."

Right. So, she wasn't angry with him. "Why are you upset then?"

"I feel sorry for you." She placed the new water basin on the nightstand. "And guilty for what happened."

He didn't know what to say, so remained silent while she finished getting ready. After a few minutes, she got to work on his beard. He remained still on the stool as Maddie cut the longest portion.

The soft brush of her gentle fingers against the skin of his neck was both stunning and painful. Her touch was the best remedy for the wave of agony threatening to assault him. No one had touched him in eight years, and every time she brushed her fingers against his skin, a jolt of sensation went through him.

"What is the worn book you always keep with you?" she asked, focusing on his chin.

"I recorded my days on the island on a register I recovered from the flotsam. I took notes on the plants and animals I saw. Hopefully, it has some scientific value."

As she worked with the scissors, her fine eyebrows drew together and the tip of her pink tongue stuck out between her lips, starting a turmoil inside him. He lowered his gaze.

A jagged scar crossed the palm of her right hand. Her fingers were slightly skewed with one joint protruding to the side. How much damage had he inflicted upon her? The last time he'd seen her, her hand had been bandaged. He had no idea the glass shard had ruined her hand so badly.

"It's done." She straightened, studying his face. "Now the razor. Although I must warn you. I'm not an expert. Are you sure you don't want me to ask Dr. Landon to do it?"

"I don't know him, but I trust you."

Her cheeks flushed the same colour as her lips. "All right. Let me know if I scratch you." She poured hot water into the basin from a heavy-looking flask.

He didn't say anything. Although he found people seemed displeased when he remained silent. If he had nothing to add, why bother to speak?

She sat in front of him and applied a wet, hot towel to his face. The smell of soap wafted from it.

"How did it happen?" he asked. "My brother." He had to force himself to keep his voice steady.

Maddie lowered the towel. "When your ship sank, His Grace financed an expedition to find you."

"Robert?" He sucked in a breath. Robert had organised an expedition for him. Had he sailed close to the island?

"Yes. He didn't believe you were dead, despite the fact there was little hope you might be alive. The wreckage washed over the shores of The Bahamas, and there were witnesses, sailors on another ship, who described how the *Observatory* had been ripped in two by the waves." She paused, making herself busy with brushing off his cut hair from her skirt. "Unfortunately, your brother contracted a disease while arranging a search party in The Bahamas. Some said it was yellow fever, others war fever. He died in Nassau a few days after his arrival."

He was glad she paused again because he needed a moment to collect himself. It would have been just like Robert to search for him. Hector could easily picture Robert's determined expression as he'd boarded the ship to sail across the Atlantic. Only to die. For him. Hector's throat tightened as the numbness that had shielded him faded and the emotions that had been trapped somewhere in his chest erupted. He didn't care about his composure. He let out a sob as tears smarted his eyes. The only reason why he didn't let himself cry with abandon was because he needed to hear more.

Maddie touched his hand, and the usual shock of sensation shuddered through his body, sobering him.

He inhaled deeply, tasting his salty tears on his lips. "My mother?"

"Your mother," Maddie said softly, releasing a breath. "She couldn't cope with the pain of losing both her sons. It was too much for her." She took his clenched hand in hers. The contact was enough to help him breathe more easily. "She wouldn't eat. She couldn't sleep. So, she acquired the habit of taking a sleeping draught at night. One night, she took too much." Her fingers closed around his. If she found his rough, hard-skinned hands disgusting, she didn't show it. "The physician wasn't sure if the overdose happened on purpose or not. She'd become more distracted and detached from reality with each passing day. The possibility she made a mistake is strong since she didn't want the help of a maid. But he didn't exclude the possibility that she'd done it consciously either."

"Then why isn't she buried in consecrated ground in my family's crypt?" He gripped her hand in turn, but when she winced, he eased his grip. He had to learn to dose his strength. Among other things.

"Your cousin, Quentin Wentworth, now the Duke of Blackburn, didn't believe your mother should be buried in holy ground." Her voice lowered. "He believed she'd taken her life."

"Quentin." He barely knew him and had vague memories of a cousin who lived outside London. Not that it mattered now.

"I'm sorry for how my mother told you. It's inexcusable." Maddie inched closer. "She spouts gossip without caring about the consequences. Or maybe she knows perfectly well what she's doing. Both options are awful."

He said nothing, focusing on their joined hands. Mother. She should be buried in the family crypt next to Father as she'd wanted. A pang sliced through his chest so strongly he couldn't breathe. His inner turmoil was a stark contrast with the angelic vision of Maddie, who looked so ethereal in a dark-green gown matching her eyes.

She smelled of lavender and cleanliness, of peace and harmony. Her pink skin radiated softness, making him painfully aware of his wild state and shattered mind, and he wasn't even sure why he noticed her dress now. If it was an unconscious attempt at reining in his grief, it didn't work.

He couldn't stop himself and started crying, not bothering to hide his face. Returning to London seemed such a monumental task, harder than surviving on the island. How could he pick up the pieces of his life, be normal again, and bury his mother where she belonged? How could he deal with the strange people around him, people he didn't understand anymore, when he found it hard to leave his cabin?

Maddie wrapped her arms around him. His first instinct was to stiffen and pull away from her. But her scent and softness calmed the panic rising within him. He let her hold him as he cried on her shoulder. If he was going to be honest, the pain of having lost his family wasn't the only reason he was upset. He was scared of returning to London, almost as scared as after he'd woken up on the island. Once again, he faced the unknown.

She caressed his hair while whispering something he didn't

understand. He wasn't sure for how long he cried, but when he straightened and wiped his face with his shirtsleeve, his neck muscles were strained by the awkward position he'd been in. He didn't feel better, but at least could control himself.

She handed him her handkerchief. "I'm sure your cousin will be happy to see you."

He dried his eyes and said nothing. Although she seemed to wait for him to talk since she stared at him with her large eyes full of compassion.

"Would you like me to leave?" she asked, already rising. "I can shave your beard another time."

He shook his head and tilted his chin up, exposing his neck. "Please," he croaked out. "Unless you want to leave."

"No, I'm happy to stay."

She put the hot towel on his face again. Every time her fingers brushed against his cheeks, his heart flipped. He'd forgotten what it meant to hold someone's hand or feel someone's heat. When the doctor visited him, it was with an effort that he kept himself from flinching. But Maddie's touch brought him a sense of peace.

A crease appeared between her eyebrows as she spread the shaving cream on his face. Ah, the sweet sensation of the soft, soapy cream. Its minty scent tickled his nostrils.

"Stay still. I don't want to cut you." She took the sharp razor. "Let's hope the ship doesn't decide to jolt right now." She chuckled nervously, but fell silent when he didn't laugh.

He did as he was told as she gently passed the blade over his neck and cheek. She was close enough he could see the tips of her black eyelashes curling up and overlapping. The layer of face cream she wore couldn't hide the red tint of her cheeks and nose. Likely, the tropical sun had burned her delicate skin. It had taken him months to grow a thick hide resistant to the sun and the insect bites. During the first weeks, his body had been itching and burning. No earrings hung from her small earlobes. He wanted to touch them to see if they were as velvety as they looked.

"No earrings," he said as she shaved his chin.

She paused. "My earrings? Oh, I stopped wearing them when...a long time ago. I found them impractical. I don't have any regrets to be honest. One less thing to worry about."

She washed the razor into the bowl of water. The foam spread on the surface, releasing its fragrance.

"What happened a long time ago?"

"Nothing that matters."

"I want to know."

Perhaps his tone was too harsh because her emerald gaze flashed for a moment. He ought to learn good manners again.

She continued shaving him. "After I healed from the infection, I found it difficult doing a few tasks, including putting my earrings on. Some types of earrings require the use of both hands to close the clip. Anyway, my fingers were clumsy, and I ended up either hurting myself or dropping the earrings. I could have asked for help, but I wanted to practise with my right fingers. Wasted time. I grew angry and impatient. So, I stopped wearing them."

When she focused, as she was doing now, she acquired a more mature expression. Her lips were the same colour as those berries he'd eaten on the island. He wondered if her lips tasted the same. He remembered her beauty, but somehow, he rediscovered it now, and it stunned him.

"You're absolutely beautiful," he said in all honesty, because it was true.

Her reaction didn't make any sense though. She blushed fiercely to the roots of her hair and averted her gaze.

"Lord Wentworth, we're alone in your cabin." She withdrew her hands and cleaned the blade, her hands shaking.

What did the fact they were alone have to do with anything? "I'm not saying you're beautiful because I haven't seen a woman in years. I genuinely believe you're stunningly beautiful. Your sister is pretty too, but your more mature beauty strikes me harder. You're almost painful to look at, like the sun." What had he said now?

Why did she fret and blush? Her breath hitched. "Have I said something wrong?"

She wiped her hands on the towel and took the bowl. "I need more water."

She moved towards the door, but he took her wrist, jolting her. The bowl dropped to the floor, spilling the soapy water around and soaking the floor again.

"Bother." She crouched to wipe the water.

"I'm sorry." He cursed himself for his lack of control and knelt next to her. He helped wipe the water, but she waved him away.

"Don't you worry."

"Why are you upset?" He could understand being upset if someone had lied to her. But he spoke the truth.

She exhaled. "Lord Wentworth—"

"Hector."

Another exhale. "Usually, gentlemen aren't so straightforward when talking to a lady. Men don't pay direct compliments to women in such a candid fashion. Surely, you remember that."

"Someone else must have told you how beautiful you are." He was confused. He'd broken a rule. He understood it. But if the rule was stupid, did it matter?

"No. No one." She shoved to her feet, holding the bowl and marched out of the cabin.

He wiped his face with a fresh towel, failing to understand her sudden change of mood. But then again, he failed to understand a great many things.

ten

WHY WAS MADDIE so angry? She didn't know. As she waited for one of the members of the naval staff to bring her more warm water from the kitchen, she paced along the passageway. The truth was...the truth was no one had ever told her she was beautiful. Certainly not with Hector's honesty and intensity. All right. It wasn't completely true. Verity had told her she was pretty many times. Her father had often complimented her grace and eyes. But they were family. Their opinions didn't count. Although her mother had told her she was too plain to be beautiful, and Maddie had believed her. Why did her mother's opinion count then? She should disregard it as well.

She waved a hand as if to fend off those thoughts. But then there was Mr. Hillebrand, a not-so-gentle gentleman whom she'd danced with and who had told her she possessed the grace of a bison. He'd added he knew what he was talking about because he'd been to the Americas and seen the wild beasts running free through the prairie. How rude. All because, before his comment, she'd stomped on his feet once or twice, no more than thrice, and kicked his knee, accidentally, of course. And she'd been barely involved in the incident with the crystal bowl of lemonade that had ended up on his head. She wasn't a great dancer. So what? Lots of ladies couldn't dance.

And then there was Mr. Clarke who, unbidden, had pointed out that her lips were too full and her hair too dark for his liking. And her Aunt Cornelia claimed Verity was the only beauty in the family, which Maddie believed. But Aunt Anne had told her she was as beautiful as Calypso, whatever that meant. Still, it sounded nice.

Oh, why was she fussing about nothing? Besides, poor Hector had been separated from civilization for years. He must have forgotten his manners, and she didn't care about her beauty or grace. She was happy with the way she looked, but Hector's honesty had shaken her deeply. Because he really thought she was a stunner.

"Miss." The steward handed her the flask of water. "Be careful. It's very hot."

"Thank you." She had to push down her nervous energy not to slosh the water around as she walked to Hector's cabin.

She would finish shaving him, then leave without engaging in more conversation with him. Not because she didn't want to talk to him, but every time they talked, one of them ended up upset.

She didn't bother knocking...and regretted it. Sort of. A gasp left her as she found him wearing only a pair of tight breeches and nothing else. All the sharp ridges of his well-defined muscles were on display. There were a lot of them. She'd seen muscles like his only in the anatomy books she used for drawing, and those naked bodies didn't cause her chest to flutter with some odd emotion.

He turned towards her. His dark-golden hair bobbed over his hard jaw in soft curls, enhancing his strong neck. Without the long hair and beard, his features shone in all their beauty. Good Lord. Her mouth grew dry. He was utterly handsome. As her gaze roamed over his strong pectoral muscles and lowered—only for an artistic appreciation of his male body—she gasped again. His torso showed the hardship of his life on the island. There were burnt spots and scars, bumped edges and marks of different sizes. And goodness, those legs. So thick they stretched the fabric to its limit. Drawing him would be wonderful, especially naked. Again, for artistic purposes.

"I didn't think you would return," he said, seemingly oblivious to the fact he stood almost naked in front of a lady while alone in his cabin.

She would become the most scandalous woman in London in a moment, should this encounter be known to the ton. A part of her found the possibility disturbingly alluring.

She returned her wandering gaze to his stunning eyes. "I wanted to finish shaving your beard." Although his short beard enhanced his masculine beauty and made him look like a dashing pirate.

He sat on the chair and tilted his head back, exposing his Adam's apple. His hair fell back, and she wished she could immortalise his beauty as he stayed in that position with the sunlight glowing from behind him. She didn't know why his pose—not at all gentleman-like—struck a chord deep within her. A tingle started in parts of her body that had no business tingling, and she wasn't talking only about her fingers itching to draw him. All of a sudden, being close to him and attending to his face caused her breath to come out more quickly.

She took her time shaving him because she wanted to do a good job and because she wasn't an expert barber. No, not because she enjoyed the closeness to him.

She ran the razor over his square jaw, sharp cheeks, and cleft chin, heavily aware of the flex of his powerful muscles and the heady scent of his skin.

"I apologise if I said something wrong earlier," he said as she wiped the shaving cream off his neck. "But I don't understand why you were upset."

"We live in a world made of rules. Breaking them confuses us."

She'd better step away from him. "Gentlemen shouldn't be so honest when complimenting a lady."

He trapped his bottom lip between his teeth, causing her to almost drop the razor. "Yes, but it's a stupid rule, and it was only you and me."

Oh, dear. Being alone with him was another problem.

"And you *are* beautiful," he said as if making a point.

She had to change the subject before she did something stupid and...and...kissed him. "How did you get all those scars?"

"This one." He touched a long scar right under his nipple and she hoped she wasn't blushing. "Is from the night of the storm. I don't remember what hurt me. When I regained consciousness on the beach, I had this cut. The others are from various attempts at hunting, fishing, building a shelter, or leaving the island. I'm lucky none of them became infected. I believe the seawater and a plant I used to clean the wounds had a role in it. Others are from my fights with the primates."

"Did they attack you often?"

He lifted a shoulder. "At first, yes. I think they saw me as a rival or trespasser. Then only during certain months when they reproduced. The mating could go on for hours. The males fought fiercely to conquer a female."

"Oh." Her face flamed again.

He talked about those matters with such nonchalance she couldn't stop herself from blushing.

More scars crisscrossed his abdomen like thin silver lines. Her chest constricted for him. She had one not particularly thick scar, but the pain still bothered her. She couldn't imagine being cut repeatedly while having no medical assistance and needing to provide for herself.

"The burn?" she asked, shaving a spot under his ear.

He smiled, watching her from underneath the blond curtains of his curls. It was the first time she'd seen him smile. It transformed his whole body from handsome to angelic. Or maybe devilish. She had still to make up her mind. His beauty was too ruthless and intense to belong to heaven, but too ethereal to belong to hell.

"My first fire," he said, touching the burnt skin. "I learnt to be more careful when handling a burning log rather quickly. In that instance, the seawater was sheer torture."

"You were so brave."

His smile disappeared. "No. I was desperate. Desperate people have nothing to lose. Brave people do."

Even his stare, so intense and piercing, wouldn't be considered proper in polite society, but Lord, if it didn't make her shiver.

The horn signalling the lunch would be served hooted, breaking the moment.

She straightened her bodice. "You should dress. People will think you're rude if they see you half-undressed."

"I don't care about what people do or don't think about me." His tone wasn't reproachful, merely honest.

She cleaned the razor. "My reputation would be damaged. I shouldn't be here alone with an undressed gentleman."

That caught his attention. "That's another matter." He slid the shirt on, alas, failing to look less enticing. "The fabric chafes my skin. I'm not used to wearing clothes and the sun wasn't gentle on me when I was on the raft."

"Oh, right." She rubbed the bridge of her nose. "So silly of me not to think about that."

"Not silly at all." He fell silent. The spark of vitality was gone, replaced by a scowl as if she had offended him.

She put away the razor and admired her work. A light stubble darkened a few spots on his face, but overall, he looked clean. Who was she fooling? He was devastatingly charming, with the right balance of ruthlessness and decency.

"Would you like something to eat? Come with me to the dining hall?" she asked because she had one too many inappropriate thoughts on a man who needed to recover from a dreadful ordeal.

He shook his head. "I'm not hungry and I'm not ready yet to leave the cabin. Too many people."

She could relate. "Would you like me to bring you something to read?"

"Read?" His whole face brightened, almost in a childish manner. "Yes. Anything. Everything. All you can find."

She laughed. His enthusiasm was contagious. "I'll be back with a newspaper and some books."

"Thank you." He took her fingers in a surprisingly gentle grip. "For everything."

A tingle started from her fingers, ran up her arm, went down, and stopped with a throb in her lower abdomen. Good gracious.

"You're welcome."

When he released her hand, a sense of loss weighed her down, which was ridiculous.

As she walked towards her cabin, she rubbed her forehead. Every conversation with Hector was unpredictable. She ought to remember his past before commenting on his manners. In a way, he behaved like a child, who was unaware of the rules of propriety, but at the same time, he definitely was no child. Not at all. He was all manly man. Oh, bother.

When she entered her cabin, Verity was sprawled on the narrow bed, reading Ernest's letters. The man had sent Verity letters every day during their stay at The Bahamas. Her brow furrowed as she focused on the pages as if trying to solve a riddle.

Maddie read from over Verity's shoulder. "Reading Ernest's letters again?"

"Bah!" Verity jolted, clenching the letters to her rising chest. She exhaled and sagged back into her pillow. "It's you."

"You didn't hear me." She searched the room for her books. Which one would Hector be interested in reading? "You should know those letters by heart now."

"It's their inner meanings I'm trying to decipher," she whispered. "It's harder than it seems."

Maddie picked up *The Scandalous Life of Lady Barlow*. Would he like a romantic story? Or rather, would she combust at the thought of him reading some of the most improper passages? Yes, she would. But she'd brought only romantic novels. There should be that mystery book somewhere.

"What inner meanings?" she asked, rummaging through her trunk. She'd take her sketchbook and a piece of charcoal just in case she needed them.

Verity waved her closer, glancing at the door. "You know Mother reads our letters."

Yes, she was aware of it. She nodded.

Verity blushed, showing her one of the letters. "Ernest and I have a little trick to communicate intimate things without Mother knowing it." She pointed at the top line of the letter where Ernest had written the date and the time of day. "Look at these numbers here. Do you see anything peculiar?"

Maddie narrowed her gaze. "Not really. Date and time. A bit unusual to add the time of day, but Ernest is a bit unusual. In the most charming way," she added quickly when Verity opened her mouth.

"Well, if you look closer, you'll notice there's a tiny blotch of ink on the number five."

Maddie brought the letter up to take a better look. "It's barely visible."

"Yes, but it means the number five is the key."

"The key?"

Verity flushed again, her eyes brightening. "Read the letter but only one word every five."

Maddie did as she was told, skimming Ernest's elegant writing. "My...dear...I...wish..."

"Shush!" Verity glanced at the door again. "In your head, you ninny."

"All right." Chuckling, Maddie started reading.

I wish to lift your skirt and dip my head between your—

"My goodness!" Maddie stopped reading. "Verity."

Her sister had the good sense to blush. "The letters aren't all like that one. Unfortunately. Sometimes he simply expresses his deep feelings for me and what he'd like to do once we're married." She wiggled her eyebrows. "Isn't it an intriguing reading though?"

A laugh burst out of Maddie. "It is. By all means, the man is passionate and quite...anatomical."

Verity giggled. "Don't tell Mama."

"I won't. Do you reply in the same fashion?"

She sighed. "I have to. I can't lie about my desires. You know, my name means 'truth' and his name means 'sincere.' We're made for one another."

Maddie put down the letter. She would always blush when she saw one of Ernest's letters from now on. "How did you create this code?"

"We didn't, really. Do you remember Miss Annabelle Fanshaw?"

"Vaguely. Isn't she the one who started a scandal with her very low-necked dress when she was a debutante?"

"Yes. I met her at my weekly piano concert, and we became friends. Almost. She told me about this code. She uses to send secret messages to her lovers, too." Verity lowered her voice again.

"Lovers?"

"She's a woman who knows what she wants." Verity gathered the letters, her features tightening. "A woman who isn't afraid to get it." She cleared her throat. "Annabelle introduced me to some of her friends. They believe in expressing their desires freely. They say there's nothing wrong about seeking physical pleasure."

Maddie paused her search, worried about the serious tone the conversation had taken. "Did something happen with Annabelle? Did she make you uncomfortable? One of her friends, perhaps?"

Verity paled, but her distress lasted a moment. "No, of course not." She waved a dismissive hand. "Don't mind me. I'm simply having trouble deciphering Ernest's latest. There are too many blotches."

Nodding, Maddie grabbed her sketchbook and a few past copies of *The Times*. "If you need to talk, let me know."

"I'm fine." She eyed Maddie. "Are you going somewhere?"

"Lord Wentworth's cabin. He asked me to bring him something to read."

Verity turned serious. "How's he faring after Mother was so terrible to him?"

"He's heartbroken. I think he's scared of returning home." She toyed with a corner of the newspaper.

"I would be as well. Do you think Mother was right when she said he isn't right in his mind?"

Maddie thought about her conversation about propriety with him. "No, I think he's one of the sanest people I've ever met."

"What about his body?"

Maddie clutched the newspapers against her chest. Guilt caused her to fidget. "His body?"

Verity nodded. "Does he have any physical damage?"

A vision of Hector standing half-naked in front of her flashed across Maddie's mind. "No. I believe he's more than fine."

eleven

NOT TO CATCH Hector shirtless again—alas, society and its rules—Maddie knocked on his door. "Lord Wentworth? It's me."

"Come in," came his deep voice.

He was fully clothed. Unfortunately. No, she meant luckily. Yes, luckily.

"I've brought you some newspapers," she said. "They aren't fresh from the press, but I thought you might be interested in knowing what's happening in London right now."

He nodded, causing his curls to fall over his cheeks. Maybe she should cut his hair again. He was far too attractive...or wild with those luscious curls. Or a pomade perhaps to tame them. No, it'd be a pity.

"How is your skin?" she asked. "Still sore?"

He nodded.

"We should ask Dr. Landon to give you a lotion."

"We." A corner of his mouth pulled up. "Thank you."

She paused shuffling the newspapers. "For what?"

"To include yourself in my predicament."

"Oh." She shifted her weight. "I want to help you."

"Thank you." He took one of the newspapers from her hand with reverence as if she handed him the crown jewels. He opened it and stared at the pictures. "Amazing. The pictures are better than I remember." He flipped through the pages, inching closer to them. "Very detailed."

"The press made progress." She grinned, enjoying his outburst of enthusiasm.

"Who's the prime minister?"

"Lord Salisbury. Again. Funny how some things change, and others stay the same."

"Indeed." Hector raised his eyebrows, focusing on an article. "The Irish are protesting."

"They are. My father says the parliament should have followed Gladstone's example when he was prime minister and granted financial independence to the Irish farmers who—" She fell silent, surprised by her own boldness. There was something about Hector that pulled out the rebel within her. "I'm sorry."

He lowered the newspaper, frowning. "What for?"

"Gentlemen don't usually enjoy hearing me talk about politics. Mother says I'm too opinionated, and no one is interested in what I have to say."

His frown deepened. "I am. What were you saying about Gladstone?"

She rolled her bottom lip between her teeth, but stopped when Hector stared at her with too much intensity. She felt his stare all over her body. "He proposed to grant the Irish financial independence from the crown, which would mean fewer taxes and more equality for them. But the current parliament and prime minister are stricter than Gladstone. They think the government should tighten the sanctions on the Irish."

He was utterly focused on her. "And what's your opinion?"

"I think it's poppycock. The government should support the Irish instead of punishing them. Repression will only lead to more riots."

"I don't know all the facts, but I agree with you." He skimmed through the pages again. "Robert was interested in politics. I confess I never paid much attention to the House of Lords or took his duties seriously." He dropped himself onto the bed, even though she was still standing. But she didn't mind. "Would you read it for me, please? I'm not used to reading anymore. My head hurts."

"My pleasure." She took the newspaper and sat in front of him.

She read the political column, then the humorous one. She skipped the sport column because who would ever care about a cricket game that lasted days, for crying out loud? By the time she finished the scandal sheet where the wanton adventures of a certain Miss F had caused an outrage in London, Hector was asleep, breathing softly.

She lowered the newspaper. Sunlight streamed through the porthole and created a golden halo around him. With his head reclined over his arm and his shirt open in the front, he looked indeed like an angel who was taking a nap. His sculpted lips were parted, and a curly lock of hair caressed the tip of his chin. She couldn't resist.

She took her sketchbook and a piece of charcoal and started drawing him. Her stiff hand couldn't catch the softness of his hair and the harshness of his jaw properly, but if she worked slowly, the lines almost obeyed her. She held her breath as the charcoal traced the lines of his closed eyes, the eyelashes, and his straight nose. When her fingers hurt, she paused to flex them, determined to carry on before he moved from his lovely position.

The light changed quickly as the sun set, but she captured the shadows on his cheeks and chin before the twilight fell over the ship. Oh, his neck was a study in tendons and muscles, and what was visible of his chest was all taut skin and ridges. She'd never paid attention to men's Adam's apples, but Lord, his was delectable.

Dusk crept through the cabin. She turned on a lamp to keep

drawing. Thank goodness he didn't move. The way darkness fell abruptly at sea both startled and fascinated her. London was always full of light. She'd never experienced complete darkness as on the ship. The darkness made her sketching more intimate, like a secret.

Her sketch couldn't do justice to the nuances of his features, harsh in some places and soft in others, but on the bright side, she'd drawn for longer than usual. Normally, she'd stop sketching after a few minutes. Having a living model and being worried about the light were good motivators to keep going.

She was drawing the shadows in his hair when he blinked his eyes open. She paused like a thief caught red-handed. Neither of them talked. They stared at each other—he, with the glow from the lamp dancing in his eyes, she, still drawing him with her gaze, caressing his lines.

"Are you drawing me?" he asked, remaining in his reclined position.

She nodded, not trusting her voice.

"Why?"

She swallowed past the knot in her throat. "You're beautiful."

He lowered his gaze as if embarrassed, which was ironic, considering he'd started the whole 'be honest' affair. He rose from the bed, uncoiling his large physique. A little tremor went down her back as he approached her. He tilted his head to take a look at her work.

She handed him the sketch. "Here."

He studied it for a few moments, brushing a curl from his face. "Is this how you see me?"

"What do you mean?"

"Beautiful, fair, and angelic?"

"An artist's job isn't to reproduce the real world. It's to extract the hidden spirit from a scene or a person according to the artist's sensitivity." And yes, he was that beautiful, fair, and angelic.

He trapped his bottom lip between his teeth, and she wished to have drawn that pose.

"I haven't seen my reflection in a mirror in years," he said in a low voice.

"Goodness me." She rose and searched the cabinets. Every cabin had at least one hand mirror somewhere. She pushed aside bottles of tonic Dr. Landon must have left for Hector and found a round mirror. "Here."

He hesitated before taking it, but when he did, his fingers brushed against hers.

"Thank you." He took a deep breath before peering at his reflection.

Maddie waited for his reaction. He frowned and tilted his head, his features tightening. Perhaps it'd been a bad idea. She shouldn't have—he burst out laughing, a full, warm laugh that made her laugh with him. The happy sound lifted a weight off her chest.

He put the mirror down. "I think I prefer your sketch."

"You don't see what I see."

A corner of his mouth pulled up. "That's something we have in common. You don't see what I see either."

Touché.

He picked up the sketch again and studied it until his smile vanished.

"What are you thinking?" she asked, worried he might not like her style.

"You stole something from me."

"No." She clamped a hand over her chest. "I didn't touch anything."

He chuckled again. "I mean with this drawing. You took a moment from me and captured it on the page. A little piece of my soul."

"Oh." She'd never thought about it. He was right. She'd caught his image without asking him first. "I'm sorry."

"Don't be. I didn't mean it as a reproach." He smiled at the sketch again. "You're talented."

Another compliment. Pity she didn't know what to do with it.

He lowered the sketch. "Did you attend the academy?"

After all those years, the answer to that question still stung. "No. Your brother was kind enough to intercede for me with the director, but my hand took a long time to recover." She stretched out her fingers. "Even now, my fingers are stiff and don't follow my orders. Then your brother left..."

"I see." A shadow crossed his face. "I'm sorry. Didn't you receive your allowance?"

"The new duke didn't think I needed it, and I agreed," she hurried to add when he opened his mouth. "My hand was useless. What was the point of taking his money?"

"The allowance was established by my brother." He scowled. "Quentin should have honoured it."

She should change the subject lest he become angry. "On top of that, something rather peculiar happened to Mrs. Blanchet. One of her most appreciated paintings, *The Lady of the Lake*, was stolen from her London's townhouse. She organised a dinner party, and one of her guests somehow sneaked the precious painting out. Gosh, she was furious. She couldn't believe one of her guests had dared to steal from her. I didn't feel it was right to approach her and ask her for help after the incident. To this day, no one knows where *The Lady of the Lake* is. It was an unfortunate circumstance even for me, indirectly. It's life." She shrugged.

He kept frowning.

Bother, she'd made him sad again. "I can't give you the piece of your soul back, but is there something I can do to make amends for my pilfering?"

A hint of a smile touched his lips. "There's something."

"Ask away."

"May I hold your hand?" He was so honest she was always surprised by his direct manners.

"Please." Why not? She'd seen him nearly naked and stolen a piece of his soul. Giving him her hand to hold was a small price to pay. In fact, it was no sacrifice at all.

He put aside the sketchbook and took her hand gently. He drew in a breath as he stared at her small hand in his with awe. Her skin tingled when he traced her knuckles with a gentle finger.

"So delicate. Soft. I know it sounds odd, but holding your hand gives me a sense of peace."

She swallowed. "Not odd at all."

He scowled at the scar. "This is my fault," he said in a low voice. "I remember that night. I thought about it many times. I ruined your career, your life, and your dream."

"No, it's the past. It doesn't matter." She shivered as a phantom pain went through her.

He touched the curve of the scar, his brow furrowing. "Climbing to your window was my first mistake. I shouldn't have taken that plant. I shouldn't have left. My brother and my mother would be alive if I'd stayed."

A riot of sensations burst within her. His touch was pleasant, but his words stirred the ugly beast of sorrow in her chest. "I encouraged you to go."

"I wanted to." He inhaled a shaky breath, stroking the scar. "If I hadn't been so stupidly obsessed with my travel, my family would be alive today, and you'd be a famous painter."

"Exploring was your dream." She closed her other hand over his, feeling him shake. "You couldn't have known what was going to happen. Don't torture yourself with what could have been. I did that, and it didn't make me feel any better."

"But what I did made me who I am now." He squeezed her hand gently. "I don't know how to build my life in England again or how to make amends to you. And my family is dead. What am I going to do? I am the cause of so much pain. Including my own." He sounded so scared she couldn't keep her distance.

She ran her fingers through his hair. "It'll take time, but you'll be happy again."

He leant against her touch. "I swear on my honour I'll do everything I can to repay the damage I inflicted upon you since Robert couldn't help you because of me."

This time, she didn't protest. If making amends was the reason he needed to build his life again, then she'd let it do it. Besides, he didn't have anything else to grasp at the moment. Helping her was the only thread of his former life left.

He released her hand slowly and drew in a deep breath. "I'd like to take a walk. Do you think the deck is crowded?"

"The passengers should be in the dining hall now. Are you sure you're ready?"

"If I can't face the people on a ship, how can I face London? How can I help you?" He paled. "Would you come with me?"

"Yes." She brushed his knuckles. "We'll face the crowd together."

twelve

WHEN MADDIE HAD said she was ready to face the crowd with Hector, she'd meant it. But she wondered if he was ready. He'd stepped outside the cabin only to stand in the passageway.

She took his jacket from the chair and joined him. "You should probably wear this. You know, propriety and all that."

She handed him the jacket, worried he might refuse. But he slid it on without a word. Still, he didn't move.

"There's nothing to fear." She hooked her arm through his. "I'll take you to the main deck. If it's too crowded, we'll return here."

"I'm ready, and I've had enough of my cabin. I need some fresh air."

He was barefoot, but she hadn't seen any pair of shoes in his cabin. Oh, well. At least he wasn't half-naked.

A man threw a sideways glance at Hector as they walked down the passageway. Another muttered something as they brushed past him. A couple of ladies gasped. Perhaps Hector's hair, bare feet, and general sense of wildness were too much for those people who weren't used to seeing him every day. Thank goodness he didn't make a scene. His muscles tensed, and he slowed his pace, but he didn't panic or reply to the whispers.

He gripped her arm a tad too tightly though. His gaze followed every person they met along the passageway. He even stopped and craned his neck to stare at an attendant who hurried his pace once he realised Hector was focused on him.

"Hector." She nudged him so he'd stop staring. "What are you doing?"

He blinked. "I'm curious. The uniform of that man is so sparkling white."

"Yes, but please don't stare at people. It looks like you want to murder someone."

"But they stare at me." He arched an eyebrow.

"That's true." She led him on. "But I think the best strategy is to ignore them."

He nodded solemnly, as if she'd revealed to him the meaning of the universe.

"None of them are as brave as you are. I wouldn't have lasted five minutes on the island. I can't even swim." She let out a nervous chuckle.

"You should learn. You never know."

"Fair point well made."

The salty, humid breeze blowing from the sea thickened the air when they stepped onto the deck. The stars cast their silver light over the ship, more brightly than in London where the smoke and street lamps hid the sky. She hadn't realised it was so late, perhaps well past dinner. Goosebumps pebbled her skin as the chilly wind picked up speed. He released a long breath, and his posture slouched.

He tilted his head back and stared at the stars. "I lived there."

"Where?" She searched the dark horizon.

"Among the stars."

She wasn't sure she'd heard correctly. "What do you mean?"

"There were so many stars shining over the island. Often, I

slept outside of the shelter I'd built just to stare at the stars. The island was so dark that, when I lay down and watched the stars, it was like being there among them. I was surrounded by starlight. Peace. All my worries disappeared. It was my moment of freedom in the prison that was the island." He lowered his gaze. "I wished to die so many times that the thought became a constant presence. I wanted to dissolve myself in the starlight."

"Hector." She took his hands as a knot tied in her throat for all the pain he'd endured. "You're safe now."

"The stars saved me. Literally. By watching them, I understood where I was. They showed me the way." He held her hands, turning towards her. "The way to you. And you found me." He brought her hand up and kissed it. His soft lips brushed against her knuckles before placing a gentle kiss on the scar.

Oh, dear. Her knees weakened. A moment ago, she'd been sad. Now she was a quivering mess. Too many emotions. The sweetness of the kiss sent a delicious shiver down her back. Perhaps she was a wanton woman or Verity's secret letters had affected her, but her body tingled with sensation, even though he kissed her hand reverently rather than decadently. The kiss was one made of gratitude, not lust.

Still, she couldn't deny the sliver of pleasure going through her or the sudden throb between her thighs. For some reason, her mind conjured up the memory of his marriage proposal. Should she bring it up? No, it would be rude, and why did she think about it to start with? Because the other option was to think about his half-naked body. Or about his courage, honesty, and kind heart. He was too many good things all together.

"What are you doing?" Mother's voice rent the calm night with its sharpness like a strident note in a beautiful song.

Maddie snatched her hand out of Hector's grip. He didn't flinch but scowled at her mother and shifted in front of Maddie as if to protect her.

"Madeline, are you behaving wantonly with this individual?"

Mother's cheeks, pale from her sickness, gave her a spectral look that only added a layer of menace to her tense figure.

"Of course not, Mother." Maddie brushed a lock of her hair from her heated face. "Lord Wentworth is a perfect gentleman."

"Kissing your hand in such fashion while alone with you?" She fired a glance at Hector.

He hunched his broad shoulders. "I'll leave you then, Miss Madeline, Mrs. Debenham. Good night."

"Hector, wait!" Maddie took his hand.

He flashed a shy smile. "Your mother is right. It's late. You shouldn't be with me. I'll see you tomorrow. Perhaps we can have tea in the dining hall."

"If you want to."

"Thank you for your time. It means a lot to me." He slid his hand out of hers, a lingering sadness in his manners.

She watched him heading below deck, an ache spreading through her chest. "Why are you so cruel to him?" she asked once alone with the termagant.

"Why are you so kind to him? He made you a cripple, destroyed your room, disappeared, and then had the brilliant idea to return and behave like a beast. He's nothing but a savage." Mother added three 's' to the last word.

"Mother!" Maddie balled her fists, tired of her mother's rudeness. And her mother claimed to be a decent lady?

"I'm concerned about you." Mother grabbed the railing. "I gave you plenty of freedom, and you repay me by behaving recklessly. He's dangerous."

"Not as dangerous as you are," Maddie said.

Mother shook her head. "How can you not see he's a beast?"

"Honestly. There's a beast on this ship. But it's not him." She started to walk away, but her mother grabbed her arm.

"I don't want you to spend time with him." Mother bared her teeth.

She shrugged her arm free. "He needs compassion, and I was

the one who spotted his raft. I'm also the only person he knows and trusts on this ship. I will not leave him alone in a moment like this."

"He isn't your responsibility."

Maddie resumed walking. "As I'm not yours, and thank goodness for that."

∼

MADDIE REGRETTED HAVING AGREED to take tea with Hector the next day. But he had insisted, saying he needed to become accustomed to people again, and she couldn't disagree on that point.

She wished he had returned to his cabin though. Not because he didn't wear any shoes again, nor a waistcoat. She didn't mind it, although she hated the odd and curious glances the passengers threw at him and the constant whispers echoing around them. What bothered her was the fact he was easily startled, jolting on his chair every time someone laughed too loudly or dropped a cup on the saucer. His chest heaved. His gaze kept sweeping through the hall and the pristine round tables as if he searched for an escape.

Not to mention her mother sniffed and arched her eyebrows at everything he did, covering her mouth with her perfumed silk handkerchief. She hadn't been happy about having tea with Hector, but Maddie had refused to listen to her.

The sunlight shone on the white floor and the crystal chandeliers, casting dozens of colours on Hector's hair. It would be wonderful to paint him. If the moment weren't charged with tension, she'd enjoy her bergamot tea. The lemony scent alone soothed her nerves.

Verity exchanged a glance with her as Hector started again when a waiter rushed past them.

"Lord Wentworth, perhaps you wish to return to your cabin?" Verity asked.

Hector gripped his cup of tea with both hands so strongly Maddie worried he might break it. "No."

Her mother huffed. "Such manners."

Maddie compressed her lips. "Lord Wentworth spent years alone. The fact he doesn't like a crowd is perfectly understandable." She also hated speaking in his stead as if he weren't there. But the urge to protect him was too strong to be ignored, and despite what Mother said, he was too much of a gentleman to tell her off.

"You're right," Verity said cheerfully. "I can't imagine spending years alone. It must have been so incredibly hard for you, Lord Wentworth."

"I wasn't alone," he muttered, staring at his tea.

"You weren't alone?" Mother asked, lowering her cup. "Who else was on the island?"

"Thomas." He ran a trembling hand over his face. "He was my friend. I talked to him all the time. It helped not to forget my language. I was worried it could happen."

Maddie pondered his answer. He'd said the island was deserted aside from animals. If he talked about Thomas in the same manner as the stars, then Thomas was probably a tree.

"Where's Thomas now?" she asked.

"I left him behind." He raised his gaze, and the pain echoing in its depths hurt her. "I had to. He couldn't come with me."

"Good heaven." Mother placed a hand on her throat where the white lace of her shirt covered her neck. "You left a man on that forsaken island? Your supposed friend? Another survivor? By all means, that's horrible."

Maddie ignored her, having a hunch. "Is Thomas a man?"

Hector's expression softened when he turned to her. "A bird. I don't know what species, but he had the most flamboyant plumage and—"

Mother's laughter cut him off. "A bird? You're so upset about a chicken. Oh, good gracious. And it was your friend? You talked to it?"

"Mother," Maddie and Verity hissed together.

She waved dismissively, wiping a tear of laughter. "Oh, please. This is the most ridiculous thing I've ever heard. Bethlehem Hospital should be Lord Wentworth's home. A bird." She snickered again. "What nonsense."

"I apologise, Maddie." Hector scraped his chair and rose. "I think I'll return to my cabin."

Maddie tossed her napkin on the table and stood up. "Hector, please don't leave."

He shook his head. "Enjoy your tea. I'm sorry." He strode across the room among mutters and whispers.

"Mother." Maddie suppressed an unladylike comment. "I cannot believe you could be so rude to him."

"He isn't human." She giggled. "Perhaps he's a bird too."

Anger burned the back of Maddie's throat. How she wished to see her mother's smug smile vanish. "Don't forget he's the Duke of Blackburn," she said in a rush.

She didn't know why she bragged about Hector's title. Perhaps because peerage was something her mother appreciated, and, gosh, she wanted to sting her. If Mother didn't care about treating Hector horribly, she'd probably care about mistreating a duke.

Mother stopped laughing. "Quentin Wentworth is the current Duke of Blackburn."

Maddie gripped the edge of the table. "He's Hector's cousin. He inherited the title only because Hector was already pronounced dead when Robert died. But once Hector is back, he is the direct heir."

Actually, she had no idea if it was true. Once Hector was proclaimed alive again, why wouldn't he inherit the title belonging to his family?

"Doubtful such an animal could be accepted as a duke." Her

mother opened her mouth to say something else, but Maddie didn't wait for her reply.

Satisfied to have shut her mother up, she hurried out of the dining hall and along the passageway, chasing Hector. He marched towards his cabin, stepping aside every time he met someone.

"Hector." She took his arm, and he stopped. "I'm so sorry."

He didn't turn around.

"Hector." She stepped in front of him.

His eyes were a storm of sorrow. He seemed so lost her throat tightened with a lump of emotion. As more passengers walked past, she held his hand and led him to his cabin. His pain didn't need more witnesses.

Once they were inside his cabin, she faced him. "I've always known my mother was cruel, but I keep discovering new layers of her depravity."

"Am I insane?" he whispered. Tears hung on his eyelashes. "Did the island damage my brain?"

"No." She cupped his cheeks, following an instinct that came straight from her heart. "Don't listen to my mother. She's the insane one. Tell me about Thomas." She stroked his face. "Tell me everything about him."

He rubbed his chest, his gaze lost. "Thomas was my friend. I spent days with him. I gave him pieces of fruit he'd eat from my hand. He would perch on a tree next to me when I chopped wood or on my shoulder when I searched the forest for berries. At first, he didn't trust me, but then he sought my company as much as I did his. The decision to leave him on the island broke my heart. Talking to him kept me alive. It made me feel better. I needed him, and I left him behind." His voice broke.

She hugged him, and he shivered. "You did the right thing. He would have died on the raft, and even if he survived, he would have died in London, so far from his warm climate. Taking him with you would have been unkind. You proved to be selfless by letting him go. Now he's happy on his island."

"I feel like I'm going mad." He shook with each breath.

"No, you aren't." She held him, although he didn't lean against her. He'd crush her otherwise.

"I should have stayed on the island."

"No. You did the right thing." She took his face again, needing to see his eyes. "You were brave to leave, and I'm glad we've found each other again."

He wiped his face with the sleeve of his jacket. "You're the only ray of sunlight in my life. If you weren't here now, I don't know what would happen to me." He was too honest to be a member of London's ton.

"You're strong, Hector. Don't doubt it. And you aren't mad or a savage. When we're in London, I'll be by your side whenever you need me."

Yes, she made a huge commitment while she didn't know anything about helping a castaway deal with society. But she wouldn't leave him alone.

He turned serious. "I don't want to cause you trouble. In a few days, I've caused you to argue with your mother more than once."

She chuckled. "Trust me, you aren't the cause of my constant arguing with my mother. It's a natural occurrence."

He laughed, and gosh, the deep, warm sound was intoxicating. "What if the people in London agree with your mother? I don't want to be locked up in a hospital."

"We won't allow that." She hitched a breath when he brushed his lips against her inner wrist.

He froze as if realising what he'd done, but she didn't withdraw her hand and he didn't step away from her.

"You should leave," he whispered.

"I don't want to."

He kissed her wrist again, keeping his stare on her face. A fierce longing burst within her with such strength she tottered on her feet.

"Do you want me to stop?" he asked, brushing his lips against her skin again.

"No." There was no hesitation in her voice.

He dipped his head and paused one inch from her mouth. His warmth reached her already heated skin and caused her lips to burn. She could easily slip her hand out of his and leave, but she wouldn't. She edged closer to him, feeling as if she stood on the top of a cliff, ready to plunge into the sea below.

Only a veil of air separated their mouths until he inched further and kissed her. The softness of his lips caused her inner muscles to clench with a sudden ache. It was the gentlest of kisses, merely a brush, but the effect within her was far from gentle.

He moved his mouth over hers slowly, and she let him, closing her eyes to focus only on the sweet sensations overwhelming her. He cupped her cheek and ran the rough pad of his thumb over the curve of her jaw. Oh, the shivers. She wilted. What would she do if he deepened the kiss? No one had ever touched her with such reverence and passion at the same time. She wanted to explore his mouth with her tongue and his body with her hands, but she didn't dare ruin the moment by doing something too bold. Before she could savour the kiss further, he pulled back, his cheeks blushing a deep crimson.

"I'm sorry." He passed a hand over his face, horror widening his eyes.

"Don't be. I liked it." Was she blushing too? Because her cheeks were on fire.

"I shouldn't have taken such liberty." His words came out in a rush.

"I'm glad you did."

He held her with desperation, and right then and there, she vowed to protect him.

thirteen

T HE CLOSER THE *Steamship Empress* sailed to Southampton, the more Hector's stomach roiled with anxiety. Maddie had convinced him to wear a few garments borrowed from...he wasn't sure. Anyway, he wore a greatcoat, a pair of socks, and shoes against the cold wind blowing from England, but he'd refused to wear a waistcoat and a cravat.

The shirt already constricted his chest, and the greatcoat felt heavy on his shoulders. Not to mention the shoes squeezing his feet. Had shoes always been so uncomfortable? He didn't want another layer constricting him.

He gripped the railing as a light fog swirled over the grey sea. The sky was no longer a bright shade of blue, and the air had lost its warmth. Even the fresh scent of the sea had dissolved, replaced by a combination of the smells of burning coal and oil engines.

When Maddie moved closer to him, he released his grip on the rail. In a dark-blue dress and capelet adorned with silver flowers, she was shrouded in starlight. His mood lifted. She'd offered to be close to him once in London, but he'd already taken too much from her. He didn't want to become a burden. And Lord, he'd kissed her. Perhaps he was as uncivilised as her mother said.

She brushed a dark strand of hair from her rosy cheek and smiled. The sight rent him asunder as a dark desire seized him, causing a sensation to explode below. How could she have let him kiss her?

"I'm sorry." He fought the urge to take her hand. "I behaved beastly with you."

"You didn't." The colour of dawn blossomed on her cheeks. "I enjoyed the kiss," she said so low he would have missed the words if he weren't focused on her.

Enjoyed the kiss? The world tilted. "I thought you were being nice."

She nodded, her eyelashes fluttering down. "We agreed to tell each other the truth."

Would she let him kiss her again? The possibility sent his pulse spiking. The question died on his tongue when an attendant announced they were about to dock. A cold sliver of dread put out the fire of his desire. He turned towards the coast. England. He was so close. Yet so distant.

He took her hand and cursed inwardly when she was startled by his brusque gesture. Damn. He had to learn to be gentle again.

"Sorry," they said together.

She smiled, and his chest became lighter, his head cleared, and the sky wasn't so grey after all.

"Do you think I'm going to meet my cousin soon?" Fear rose in his chest, and the urge to escape nearly overwhelmed him. He needed her help to face London's society, at least at the beginning. "I promise I won't bother you any further after I meet him. I don't want you to feel obliged to be with me. I'll manage, somehow."

She parted her lovely lips, but whatever she was about to say was cut off by her mother.

"Madeline would love to come with you," Mrs. Debenham said. Her hands were tucked in a fluffy muff, and for once, she didn't glare at him but smiled. "She'll help you in every possible fashion she can. Will you not, darling?"

He didn't care about whatever reason had brought Mrs. Debenham to show kindness to him, but as long as Maddie was with him, he was happy. He waited for Maddie's answer expectantly.

"Just so we are clear, I don't think I need anyone's permission." Her gaze was on fire. "I'll be with you, Lord Wentworth, as I promised."

"If you want to." He kept holding her hand, but opened his fingers in case he was trapping her. "I understand it's not easy to deal with me."

Her expression softened. "I want to deal with you, and you won't scare me away. Besides, I'm used to dealing with a worse lot than you."

He could breathe again, except the air was thick and heavy with the smell of coal. England was close.

Verity joined them, the tip of her nose reddened by the cold. "Are you excited to see London again, Lord Wentworth?"

"I'm afraid not."

The ship took an hour to dock at Southampton, but to him, it seemed a matter of minutes. Time flowed differently outside of the island. On the island, a day was as long as a year. On the ship, everything happened quickly. Everyone was in a rush. London would be worse. The passengers disembarked in a steady flow, talking excitedly.

Mrs. Debenham handed Verity a few guineas and patted her shoulder. "Hurry."

"Where is she supposed to hurry?" Maddie asked in a sharp tone.

"I'll go ahead and send a wire to the duke." Holding her hat, Verity rushed towards the stairs.

Quentin. His cousin. Hector hadn't seen him in well over a decade. Goosebumps covered his skin as if icy shards pricked it. Maddie narrowed her gaze over her mother who kept smiling.

"Lord Wentworth." Dr. Landon approached him and removed his hat.

Hector bowed his head in greeting.

"I have a practice on Harley Street. Please don't hesitate to contact me should you need me."

"Thank you for your help, doctor." Hector shook his hand. "You've been very kind."

"I'm glad I helped." Dr. Landon held Hector's hand. "I'm sure you'll be all right in London. Just remember that manners maketh man." He released Hector's hand and bowed to Maddie and Mrs. Debenham before strolling away.

Hector exhaled. Great. If manners made a man, who was he?

People chatted, laughed, and carried their luggage among sailors and attendants. He waited for the deck to be almost empty before heading for the flight of stairs that would allow him to walk again on British soil.

"Ready?" Maddie asked.

"Do I have a choice?"

"Not really." She hooked her arm through his. "But I'll be with you. We'll share this moment."

With Maddie at his arm, he left the ship on unsteady legs. The last time he'd been to Southampton, he'd embarked aboard the *Observatory* in a troubled state. The thought of leaving Maddie sick and pale behind had tormented him. But he'd be lying if he said he hadn't been hopeful and excited as well, looking forward to studying the Amazonian Forest. Now he wasn't either hopeful or excited.

"We're going to take a train to London," Maddie said, steering him away from the crowd.

He scowled when a group of passengers ran past him, causing him to stiffen. The noise of dozens of voices, footsteps, and horses made his pulse go faster and his ears buzz.

Ladies in colourful frocks and hats chatted or waved their hands to the passengers. People hugged each other and cried their welcomes or goodbyes. Someone played an accordion somewhere, and a small dog barked as its mistress held it in her arms.

So many smells, not all of them pleasant. The ladies' perfumes mingled with the scent of roasted meat from the street vendors and coal from the ships. A shine of humidity glistened on the cobble-stones, and he nearly slipped. He jolted when a ship let out a piercing hoot. His brain couldn't deal with all the colours and the sounds, but he searched the crowd for Robert all the same. Having left the island seemed like a terrible idea. England was too much. A choking sensation gripped him.

"Hector." Maddie gently tugged at his arm and led him to the station. "This way. Ignore the crowd."

He held her arm harder when a pair of tall men strode close to them, but she didn't seem worried. His thoughts piled up in his mind so quickly he couldn't keep up with them.

So many people. How would he pay for the train? Horses everywhere. Was that a seagull? He shouldn't have had breakfast.

Verity bought the tickets, or so Maddie told him. He couldn't keep his focus on her, too distracted by the overwhelming crowd. Only her arm anchored him to the ground. If she let him go, he'd float away with his thoughts like a kite.

"We're nearly there." She helped him down a flight of marble stairs stained by grease and oil.

He kept being distracted by people and sounds, almost tumbling down the stairs. So much for being independent.

Panting, Verity joined them. "The message has been sent. Hopefully, the duke will receive it before we arrive."

He calmed down when he finally sat in the carriage and opened his coat. The plush seat smelled of worn leather, a pleasant change from the stink of coal. Maddie sat in front of him with her mother and sister. His stomach flipped when the train jerked forwards and sped up. The train's loud whistle pierced his eardrums. He ought to calm himself. As the train raced towards London, the red-brick houses of Southampton disappeared behind a curve, replaced by green fields gleaming with dew.

"What are you planning to do once in London?" Mrs. Debenham asked. "You'll have a lot to do with your title to reinstate."

When she smiled, her similarity with her daughters was striking but for one thing. Verity's and Maddie's smiles were warm and genuine. Mrs. Debenham's was strained and calculated.

"Mother," Maddie said in a harsh tone.

Hector peeled his gaze off the window. "I don't understand."

Mrs. Debenham patted his hand, causing him to stiffen. "You're going to be a duke soon. Isn't that thrilling?"

Maddie glared at her mother. "Is this the right moment?"

Verity shook her head, muttering under her breath.

"No time like the present," Mrs. Debenham said.

Hector didn't answer. He had no idea what she meant.

"Well?" she prompted. "The Duke of Blackburn will be surprised to see you, even more surprised to know he isn't the duke any longer."

"Mother, you're impossible." Maddie acquired the fierce light she always had when she defended him.

He liked it. He liked her passion and determination. He liked *her*.

"Quentin is the duke," Hector said, puzzled by the whole conversation. He only wanted to watch the English countryside and think about nothing.

"Bless him." Mrs. Debenham tilted her head. "He's your cousin. You're the direct heir, now alive, and the only Wentworth who should be the duke. The title and the estate should go to you."

Maddie shook her head. "Please don't mind my mother, Lord Wentworth. She talks nonsense."

"Silly girl." Mrs. Debenham pressed her lips in a flat line. "Titles aren't nonsense, especially ducal titles."

Hector slouched back on the seat and watched the landscape stream past him. Green hills spread across the land covered with trees and barley fields. So much green. So much space. No more endless blue and water. Only firm land. He still had to decide if the idea excited or terrified him. In a few hours, he'd sleep in his bed. Be in his house. Eat food he hadn't hunted or gathered. How was he going to fill his days?

The door to the compartment was pulled open, and he moved before he could reason on his actions. He shot to his feet and flexed his knees in the stance he'd taken many times to wield his pointed stick to defend himself. A startled train attendant stepped back.

Maddie stood up and placed a hand on Hector's arm. "Everything is all right, Lord Wentworth. It's the attendant."

Breathing hard, Hector sat down again as the man talked with the ladies and checked their tickets. His heart beat more easily when Maddie sat next to him in a swish of blue velvet. She peered at his face with her big, concerned eyes.

"We're about to arrive in London," she said.

He nodded.

"Do you wish to go to your house in London, where your cousin now resides, or do you want to find another accommodation?"

No, he didn't want a new place. "My house."

"Very well." She squeezed his hand briefly. "Be ready for the city. London might be scary."

If Southampton was noisy, London was positively boisterous. An oppressive sensation lodged in his throat the moment he stepped out of the station. The chaos hurt his senses, overwhelmed by too many voices, colours, and smells. Hawkers yelled about the last issue of *The Londoner*. The smell of fried fish mingled with that of burning coal. People jostled each other along the platform in their hurry to reach a train. He had to step aside not to be hit by a rushing boy. If Maddie didn't lead him through the crowd, he would wander aimlessly, distracted and scared by all the things happening at the same time around him.

Even in the carriage, he couldn't filter out the rowdy noises and the flashes of colour from the people promenading along the pavement. Hell, the air was so thick he could barely breathe. A thin layer of coal dust covered everything from the white walls of the townhouses in Kensington to the faces of the street vendors.

He loosened the collar of his shirt. If those people spoke English, he couldn't tell. The words and the clunking of the carriages became one big noise buzzing in his ears. Mrs. Debenham and Verity talked about Verity's betrothed and the preparation for her wedding, thankfully not paying attention to him.

Maddie touched his hand from across the carriage. "Too much?"

He nodded, wishing he could hold her.

"Does the city look familiar?"

He forced himself to gaze outside. So many carriages, so many people, and so many houses. In eight years, more buildings had risen where there'd only been a patch of land. The gentlemen wore sleek coats and shiny hats he didn't remember having ever seen before. The ladies had tighter skirts and smaller bustles, and there seemed to be more streets than a city would ever need. Piles of horse dung covered the cobbles. That hadn't changed. He winced as a street hawker yelled about the latest copy of the *Illustrated London News*.

"Everything looks different. Bigger. More crowded," he said.

"That's your house." Mrs. Debenham pointed at the huge, three-story red-brick house surrounded by a wrought-iron fence. "Do you remember it?"

The evergreen bushes of privet had grown a few feet and had been trimmed in an unusual, squared shape his mother wouldn't approve of. The white curtains had been swapped with grey ones; another change his mother would frown upon. But aside from these differences, the building was the same.

His pulse spiked and he half-expected to see Robert coming out of the front door in one of his impeccable dark suits and tall hats. A knot of sadness was stuck in his throat. Mother wouldn't be reading a book next to the fireplace while she waited to welcome him and kiss his cheek, complaining about how thin he was. No one was waiting for him.

He stayed in the carriage, letting the ladies go out first.

"Gentlemen should go out first and help the ladies," Mrs. Debenham said in a forcibly patient tone.

"Don't worry about that, Hector." Maddie waved him out.

He inched out and lingered on the pavement.

"It'll be a shock for your cousin," Maddie said.

"And for me as well."

"Verity and I will wait here." Mrs. Debenham stepped aside to let Hector pass. "It's a family moment, after all."

Not really.

As he walked towards the door with Maddie, he gazed up at the towering building. It was home but not quite so. Heartbeat thudding in his ears, he knocked on the door. Moments passed. His hands became clammy. The door was swung open, and an unfamiliar man came into view.

He cast frowned at him. "May I help you?"

Hector took a deep breath. "This is Miss Madeline Debenham, and I'm Hector Wentworth, the duke's cousin. I wish to see him."

"His Grace's cousin? Lord Hector Wentworth is dead." The man inched the door closed.

"Lord Wentworth was pronounced dead after his ship sank into the ocean." Maddie gently pushed the door again. "He was rescued from the sea recently."

The man frowned, and Hector couldn't blame him. He could hardly believe the tale himself.

"Please, may we see the duke?" Maddie said, almost getting inside. "We sent a wire his grace should have received."

"My lord." The butler stepped aside. "I'll call his grace imme-diately."

She showed them to the room where his mother had enjoyed reading and receiving her guests.

A weight pressed against his chest when he entered the room. Mother's favourite armchair had been moved next to the window, and the antimacassar was missing. The Persian carpet, where he and Robert had played with their train sets, was gone, replaced by a dull dark rug. Even the scent had changed. No longer flowery like his mother's perfume, but woodsy. He ran a hand over the back of the silk sofa, the only original piece of furniture. Tea and coffee stains marred the precious fabric. Mother would be outraged.

Maddie put her hand over his. "How are you? Do you want to come here another day? I'm sure my parents won't object if you stay with us for a while."

He pressed his lips together and shook his head. "Nothing feels like home, but I want to stay here."

He wouldn't impose upon Maddie. He needed her, yes, but he wouldn't tire her. He paced around the room and paused next to an ugly painting radiating depression.

Maddie shook her head. "What a horrible painting...I'm sorry."

"No, please. I was thinking the same. I've never seen it before and I'm most curious to know your opinion."

She assumed the adorable expression she always wore when she focused on something. "It's so ugly it could be used as a weapon. The landscape is dull, painted with lazy, weak strokes that have no depth or tension. Too many strokes. Less is more. Look at those leaves. They're all over the place. The colours haven't been mixed properly. See those strikes?" She pointed at a few thick green lines. "An amateur, if you ask me, and not even a particularly creative one. Who would want such a painting in their own house? I'll get depressed by viewing it."

He smiled, releasing some of the tension. "I agree with your assessment."

A delicious pink crept over her cheeks. "Thank you."

Voices coming from the corridor interrupted his contemplation of the painting. Footsteps thudded. His name was mentioned. Maddie stepped next to him as if ready to shield him from whoever entered the parlour.

The door opened, and his cousin swept into view, holding a crumpled piece of paper. He was taller than Hector remembered, but even so, Hector towered over him. Quentin's dark hair was neatly styled, but a rebel strand fell over his forehead. The fabric of his dark suit shone with the hue only good quality clothes had. The straight nose and large blue eyes were similar to Robert's, but aside from that, he had little in common with the rest of the Wentworths. His facial muscles contracted with an emotion that could be either anger or surprise.

"Your Grace. You'll probably remember me. I'm Miss Madeline Debenham." Maddie curtsied, breaking the awkward moment. "I'm sorry for the intrusion. I believe you received a wire from Southampton about the incredible news that your cousin Hector, thought dead, had been rescued alive."

The duke blinked. He glanced at the piece of paper then at Hector. Holding open the door, the butler stood behind Quentin and other members of the household staff were grouped together while some rose on tiptoes to glance past him and into the room. Whispers and worried looks were exchanged.

"I did receive a wire, but I thought it was a joke." Quentin peered at Hector with an intensity making Hector uncomfortable.

"It's not a joke. It's me, Quentin." Hector straightened, ignoring his starched shirt chafing his skin. "I was stranded on an island for years. The ship, on which Miss Madeline sailed back to England, found me."

"Hector." Quentin stepped closer, his pale-blue eyes fixating on him. "I can't believe it. You must tell me everything."

"Your grace." Maddie bowed her head. "Lord Wentworth has been through some harsh days. The physician, who was on board the *Steamship Empress*, recommends that he rest."

"Of course." Quentin crushed the message and tossed it in the fireplace, keeping his gaze on Hector. The flames flashed brightly as they devoured the paper. "Miss Debenham, thank you for seeing Hector home. Cousin, this is where you belong." He spread his arms as if to embrace Hector, who shifted away from him.

Quentin's face stiffened. "Welcome home, Cousin. I'm eager to hear everything about your extraordinary adventure. I'll have a room ready for you immediately. What a bizarre day."

"I'll leave you then." Maddie curtsied again. "Lord Wentworth, we'll see each other soon." She lingered, her lips parting ever so slightly.

Don't leave me. He bit down the plea. He'd survived alone for years. He wouldn't force Maddie to look after him. He waited for her to add something, but she curtsied again.

"Good day."

"Thank you." A sharp sensation chilled him as she walked out of the parlour. The farther she went, the less he could breathe. The servants' chatter receded to a dull noise, and the light dimmed. Only his own pulse pounded loud and clear in his temples. "Maddie!"

She came to an abrupt halt. "Yes?"

He reminded himself he didn't want to be a burden. So he bowed his head. "I'll see you soon."

fourteen

HECTOR'S THROAT BURNED from the endless talking he'd done in the past hours.

Quentin had asked him dozens of questions about the storm and his life on the island, about how he'd been rescued and what he remembered of his life in London before the tragedy. He'd inquired about some personal events of the family, things only a Wentworth could know. Likely, he tried to understand if Hector was an impostor. Funny, but Hector wondered the same thing about his cousin.

Hector had answered with brief replies, and yet, his throat burned. He rubbed his forehead, exhaustion weighing him down. "Enough questions. I need to sleep."

Quentin's smile tightened for a moment. "You must be tired. Your room should be ready. Jones will take good care of you."

An ache pounded against Hector's temples when the butler showed him to his bed chamber. Not the one he'd occupied years ago but a guest room at the end of the corridor. He didn't recognise the house. The ground floor was the same, but Quentin had apparently renovated the other two floors, bringing down walls to create a large suite for himself and changing the white wainscoting with brown panels. Even the white doors had been replaced with dark ones. The result was an oppressive, dim surroundings.

His small guest room was an improvement compared to his shelter or even the cabin on the *Empress*. But knowing that Quentin was asleep in the room that had belonged to his parents started an itch along his skin. Not even Robert had dared take the master bedroom, despite Mother's insistence. He'd wanted to let her stay in the main bed chamber she'd shared for more than fifty years with her beloved husband. Yes, Mother was dead, and Quentin wasn't her son. But Hector couldn't help the wave of annoyance overtaking him.

"Do you have any luggage, sir?" Jones asked, the tip of his nose tilting up.

"Only my satchel." With his precious book.

Jones eyed the satchel as if it were a rat. "Would you want to come down to the dining hall for dinner?"

"No. I'd rather stay here." He paced around the room. It didn't take long.

"I'll have supper brought here, then." Jones bowed his way out.

Finally, Hector was alone in peace. Although London's traffic didn't allow for much peace.

He lay on the bed, staring at the gloomy ceiling. What had possessed Quentin to paint the ceiling grey in a city that was mostly grey? The sky didn't offer a better view. The clouds and smog obscured the stars. Only the city's lights blinked in and out of view through the mist. He rubbed his chest where an ache spread. Maddie's absence screamed in the room. He couldn't, wouldn't, be a burden for anyone. He'd survived on a damn island; he could survive in London.

~

EATING toast and marmalade after years of living off fruits and fish was an experience that shook Hector to his core.

Not even on the *Empress* had he tasted such delicious bread, butter, and marmalade. He ate slowly, savouring every piece, and ignored his rumbling stomach demanding to be filled quickly.

He'd given up trying to find a familiar spot in the house. Quentin made so many changes Hector hardly recognised anything. But the dining hall was mostly untouched and by far his favourite place.

His precious journal lay in front him, its worn dark cover in stark contrast to the white tablecloth. The butler had glanced at his book with horror and suggested he would be happy to toss it into the rubbish for his lordship. Rubbish?After he'd catalogued, described, and drew all the plants and animals he'd seen on the island as best as he could for those eight years. He'd been lucky to find it among the flotsam.

"No waistcoat?" Quentin asked, lowering his ironed copy of *The Times*. Just looking at him, all buttoned up in a crisp white shirt, cravat, waistcoat, and jacket made Hector nervous.

Hector shrugged. "I have no need for it."

"What about shoes and a jacket?"

Another shrug. He was hungry. He'd think about his clothing later. He was in his own house, for crying out loud. There was no one he had to impress.

Quentin raised his brow, casting a long glance at him. "Is this how you wish to present yourself?" he asked, buttering a slice of toast. "Quite inappropriate attire for a Wentworth," he added after Hector didn't say anything. "And for God's sake, what's that awful thing?" He stretched out an arm to touch the book, but Hector growled, scaring him away.

"It's mine." He scowled at Quentin from across the table.

His cousin paled, pursing his lips. "There's no need to growl like an animal. People might think you are one."

Who cared? "Why did you change the house?"

The abrupt question flustered Quentin. "Modernisation and improvements. The house has a more efficient plumbing system, and I needed more space."

"What have you done with the pieces of furniture my parents chose?" He didn't know why he was so obsessed with the house and its furniture, but the changes felt like a violation, although the plumbing might have needed to be redone.

Quentin took his time answering, stirring a teaspoon in his tea. "The furniture wasn't to my taste. I prefer a Continental style."

Right. Hector had to remind himself Quentin had believed everyone was dead. A different taste in furniture wasn't an insult...but something else was. He sipped his tea, enjoying its rich, aromatic taste before focusing his attention on his cousin.

"I heard my mother isn't buried in the family crypt next to my father and Robert."

Quentin squirmed in his tailored white suit, a colour too bright for Hector's liking, but then again, tastes and all that.

"You have to understand that the circumstances of her death were difficult. The physician, who examined her body, didn't offer a definite conclusion." Quentin fiddled with his silk ascot tie. "I had to make a decision, and with Robert's body being shipped here, a quite complicated affair if you ask me, I had too many things to take care of."

"Too many things?" Hector ate even the breadcrumbs and the few drops of marmalade on his plate before licking the butter knife clean. "I want my mother in the family crypt where she belongs, where she wanted to be buried."

The fiddling and stirring stopped. A hard glint flashed in Quentin's icy gaze. "You *want*. I understand your sentiment, Cousin, but I'm afraid you aren't in the position to make demands, much less to give me orders. I am the Duke of Blackburn. I make the decisions regarding the estate." His expression relaxed. "But I won't hold you accountable for your lack of tact. You're obviously recovering from a harrowing ordeal, and I, as the only member of your family left, have every intention of taking good care of you."

"You don't have to." Hector had never given a toss about being the one in charge, but he was talking about his mother. "I'm perfectly capable of taking care of myself. I believe I proved it these eight long years. It's my mother's resting place I'm worried about."

Quentin let out a sound halfway between a chuckle and a snort. "You have nothing to worry about."

A flare of heated anger surged to the fore. Hector slammed a fist against the white tablecloth, causing the cups to rattle in the saucers.

"I'm not the same man as I was. I won't play the propriety game with you. My mother is going to rest in the family crypt. I don't need your permission to have her moved."

He wasn't sure about that, but he'd be damned if he let Quentin stop him. On top of that, he hadn't slept well. Too many noises. Carriages driving on the cobbles, horses, partygoers returning home inebriated, and someone nearby had to own a donkey, judging by the loud brays that had jolted him. His patience wore thinner than a spider's silk.

Quentin's hands balled into tight fists. Fists that were too delicate and refined for someone who knew how to fight. Hector guessed he could knock out Quentin with a single punch if needed.

"Hector, we should leave this conversation for a later time when you're less temperamental, and—" The rest of his sentence was cut off by Jones entering the dining room.

"Sir." He bowed from the waist. "Mr. Merriweather wishes to see you immediately." Jones cast a disapproving glance at Hector. It had to be a favourite activity of his. "He has been insistent on wanting to see you now. Very insistent, your grace."

Quentin's gaze shot towards the ceiling. "Show him to the ground-floor parlour."

"Actually, sir, he wishes to see Your Grace and..." Jones

regarded Hector as if he had no idea what to do with him. "And Lord Hector."

Both Quentin and Hector scowled. Who the hell was this Merriweather?

Quentin pressed his lips together and folded his napkin neatly. "I see. Well, then, show Mr. Merriweather in." He waved dismissively, and Jones left the room.

"Who's this gentleman?" Hector asked.

"A pain in the neck. A solicitor with an opinion on everything. The worst thing our society could ever produce," Quentin said. "I'm glad I gave him the sack."

Hector scratched his chin where a stubble had grown since Maddie shaved him. Why would a solicitor want to see him?

Jones opened the door and bowed again. Hector had forgotten how many times the servants bowed. Too many.

"Your Grace, Lord Hector... Mr. Merriweather." Jones barely finished announcing the guest before a brawny, bronze-haired man strode inside, chest thrown out and shoulders squared.

Holding a leather folder for dear life, Mr. Merriweather walked into the room with long strides and came to a halt in front of Hector, not Quentin. A boyish smile stretched his wide mouth.

"Good Lord. Your Grace. It's true. You're alive." His brown eyes widened so much his eyebrows hit the hairline. "I couldn't believe the news, but I'm so glad it's true. You probably don't remember me, but we met years ago, before you left for South America."

No, Hector didn't remember the man. Back in those days, botany had been the only thing on his mind. He hadn't paid attention to anything else, certainly not to social interactions.

"Unfortunately, I don't remember you."

Mr. Merriweather didn't seem disappointed. His smile was still bright. "Do not worry, Your Grace. You might be interested to know I'm also Miss Verity Debenham's betrothed."

Hector perked up. "Miss Verity and her sister have been very kind to me."

The solicitor drew in a breath, thrusting his chest further out as if he were proud. "I have no doubt, Your Grace. Those two ladies are unique."

Indeed.

Quentin cleared his throat. "I beg your pardon, Merriweather. I *am* the duke. Stop addressing Hector as Your Grace. And why are you here? My business doesn't concern you any longer."

Mr. Merriweather straightened. His demeanour changed in a moment from pleasantly surprised to utterly aggressive. If there was one thing Hector had learnt from the primates on the island, it was to pay attention to even the smallest twitch of a facial muscle. Every tiny gesture or contraction of a muscle had a deep meaning with animals. Humans weren't different.

"I'm pleased you mentioned your title. It's the reason I'm here." Mr. Merriweather opened his leather folder and produced a few documents he laid on the table. "I stayed up all night to have these documents ready. The late duke, your cousin and Lord Hector's brother Robert..."

Hector clenched his jaw at the mention of his brother. For everyone in London, Robert had died years ago. But for him, Robert had died only a few weeks.

"The late duke left me strict instructions." Mr. Merriweather went through his documents with methodical precision until he selected a single sheet and handed it to Hector with an air of triumph.

Quentin snatched the document first, though. "What is this?"

Hector snatched the document back. "It's for me."

Another thing he'd learnt from dealing with the primates was not to cower in front of a bully. It would only make the bully stronger.

"Can you even remember how to read?" Quentin smirked. "What does the bloody document say?"

Mr. Merriweather rubbed his forehead. "If you'd allow me. Lord Robert didn't believe Lord Hector was dead. It turned out he was right." He flashed his all-teeth smile again. "Thus, before the late duke departed for his unfortunate trip to South America in search of his brother, he left me the order to help Lord Hector in his role of Duke of Blackburn in the unlucky case something horrible happened to him." He gave a final nod as if his words were the end of the conversation. "Lord Hector is here. Thus, he's the duke. The fact he went missing for a few years doesn't have any impact on the legitimacy of his title. Besides, even the Succession Law establishes the line of inheritance quite clearly. From this, you will see the late duke believed his brother would be an excellent duke."

Ignoring the sudden tightness in his chest, Hector skimmed the document. He recognised Robert's elegant signature, but the legal words had little meaning to him.

Did he want to be the duke? Go to the House of Lords and deal with aristocrats and politicians? No. He'd never wanted to be the duke. He didn't know anything about governing an estate or discussing a bill in parliament. Science was his call, not politics. But Robert's last wish was another matter. Obviously, Robert had believed Hector could lead the dukedom if something should happen to him, which hurt because during their last conversations, Hector had thought his brother had been deeply disappointed with him. How wrong he'd been.

"I believe Hector needs to be in full possession of his mental faculties to be the duke under the Righteous Bill. Am I right? We don't want insane people to hold titles. The Righteous Bill protects us from that possibility." Quentin sipped his cup of tea with a calm composure contrasting the turmoil in his gaze.

Mr. Merriweather gave a shrug. "Yes, but Lord Wentworth's sanity isn't in dispute."

"Is it not?" Quentin tilted his head towards Hector and raised his eyebrows.

Mr. Merriweather followed his gaze. The solicitor's expression hardened as he took in Hector's opened shirt, lack of shoes, and worn book.

"Hector doesn't like to wear proper clothing anymore," Quentin said.

"It chafes my skin." Hector brought up his legs and crossed them on his seat.

"He doesn't wear shoes," Quentin continued, "and he told me a bird was his best friend. Am I correct?"

Hector folded his arms over his chest. "Thomas saved my life."

"Thomas, sir?" Mr. Merriweather tilted his head.

Hector nodded. "I talked to him every day. He was a good listener, which can't be said of other people I've met."

"Except Thomas isn't a person." Quentin gave him a pointed look.

"He was to me."

"Hector also told me he lived in the stars." Quentin stirred his damn tea again.

Mr. Meriwether angled towards Hector, his eyebrows pulling together.

"You know what I meant. You're twisting my words deliberately." Hector bared his teeth. "I talked about my life on the island with Maddie, and she understood me perfectly well."

"I'm sure she did," Quentin said.

Mr. Merriweather's face didn't brighten.

"I owe Maddie my life," Hector said through clenched teeth. "And I have every intention of repaying my debt."

"And why don't we read a page of that awful book you always carry with you?" Quentin went to take Hector's book again.

Hector let out a feral growl, something he'd learnt was effective to scare the primates. "It's mine."

Mr. Merriweather inched away.

Quentin stretched out an arm towards Hector. "There. Mr. Merriweather, until you prove beyond any reasonable doubts that my cousin has the mental capability to take the responsibilities entailed by the management of a dukedom, I'll remain in my position. Thank you."

Mr. Merriweather clenched the folder against his chest. "But sir, the law—"

"You may go." Quentin's voice rose. "We don't have anything else to discuss at this stage. Jones will see you out, Mr. Merriweather," he added when the solicitor didn't move.

Mr. Merriweather offered a shallow bow, his jaw clenching. "We'll have something to discuss soon." He turned towards Hector. "Your Grace." He spun on his heels and followed the butler out of the room before Quentin could reprimand him again.

Hector wondered why the solicitor was so upset. A deep sense of justice, attachment to Robert, or something else? He read Robert's letter again. So many words to simply say he trusted Hector to take care of the dukedom and the tenants admirably.

"Don't trouble yourself with legal matters." Quentin went to take the letter, but Hector kept it out of his reach.

"Don't worry, cousin. It's no trouble at all."

fifteen

LYING IN HER bed, Maddie retouched one of the many drawings of Hector, adding more layers of shadows and light to make his striking features stand out. Not an easy task since her fingers couldn't trace all the nuances she wanted, and the more they stiffened, the angrier she became.

Some lines looked barbaric to say the least. She frowned so hard her brow muscles ached. The more she tried to be precise, the less she succeeded. How frustrating. She wanted to toss the pencil across the room. Bother. She sat upright. Another unfinished sketch. Verity always said it was a matter of practice and exercise. Maddie wasn't sure. She'd practised and exercised until her fingers had cramped, and nothing had changed. She'd given up the exercises after a few weeks instead of practising for months as the physician had suggested. Whatever. Her hand would never be the same.

"Miss?" the maid asked from the other side of the door.

"Come in." She closed the sketchbook, utterly unsatisfied with the result.

The maid inched the door open. "There's a gentleman who wishes to meet you."

Maddie shot to her feet, her pulse racing. "Lord Hector?"

They'd been separated for a couple of days, but she was eager to see him. In fact, she should visit him. She hadn't wanted to intrude into his life while he tried to get accustomed again to London, but she needed to know how he was faring.

"No, Miss. It's Mr. Merriweather. He's waiting for you in the drawing room."

Ernest wanting to see her? "Are you sure he asked for me and not Verity?"

"Yes, miss. Besides, Miss Verity is out at the moment. Her piano concert."

Oh, right. "I'll see him in a moment."

After she fixed a wayward strand of hair in her chignon, she straightened her dress and went downstairs to the drawing room. As a solicitor, Ernest's impeccable dark suit and neatly styled, bronzed hair marked him as a gentleman. A nervous one, judging by how he paced on the Oriental carpet that had cost a pretty penny. Mother would be horrified.

"Ernest." She curtsied, hoping to hide her blushing.

Since she'd read his letters to Verity, she found it hard to meet his gaze without flushing. Who would have guessed Ernest, so serious and practical, hid a passionate soul under his stiff suits?

"Maddie." He bowed, snapping his heels together. "I appreciate you receiving me immensely, even though I didn't have time to announce myself."

"You're part of the family."

"Not in this instance." He flashed a sad grin. "I'm here for business, not as your future brother but as the late duke's solicitor."

She wrung her hands together. "What is the reason for your visit?" She sat in the armchair.

"I won't take a lot of your time. I'll be gone in a minute, and I can't wait for Verity." His expression didn't soften when he mentioned his betrothed. He took the armchair in front of Maddie but remained perched on the edge. "I'll go straight to the point. Robert wasn't only my employer, but a friend. Before leaving for his fatal trip to the Americas, he left me with precise instructions should something happen that I help Lord Hector with the dukedom."

So far, nothing new. Maddie nodded, failing to understand what she had to do with the Wentworth family's legal problems.

"Quentin has no intention of surrendering the dukedom to his cousin." Ernest's voice acquired a sharp tone. "He invoked the Righteous Bill, an act approved decades ago when King George III showed signs of mental instability. Before gaining a title, the person must be deemed mentally sane by a physician."

That caught her full attention. "Mental instability? But King George III was indeed troubled. Hector isn't."

"Quentin demands I prove that Lord Hector is perfectly sane and has the mental capabilities to become the duke. The process of being reinstated as a duke requires two things." His voice sounded strained. "The first is proving Lord Hector is sane and in full possession of his mental capabilities, which implies a certificate signed by a trusted doctor. The second is finding a peer who's willing to champion Lord Wentworth before the queen."

"It sounds rather complicated." The hairs on the back of her neck stood on end. "Forgive me, but I fail to understand how I can help you. I can assure you Lord Wentworth isn't insane. He's traumatised by his experience, but who wouldn't be?"

He rubbed the bridge of his nose. "I saw Lord Hector this morning, and I couldn't help but notice he has acquired some peculiar habits during his stay on the island. He doesn't wear many clothes, for example."

"Peculiar habits?" She straightened. "He was stranded on an island for eight years, relying only on his resilience and strength to survive. It makes sense that he doesn't behave normally." Whatever normally meant.

"He considers a bird a person." He tilted his head.

Oh, Thomas. "I'm not a physician, Ernest, but I don't find it hard to believe that a person, who is completely alone, might find solace in talking to himself, or in Hector...Lord Wentworth's case, to a bird. People talk to their pets all the time. Pets are considered family. It seems perfectly normal to me."

"He also became quite aggressive when Quentin tried to take a worn, stained, book from him." Exasperation edged his voice.

"I think the book is Lord Wentworth's personal diary. It's precious to him because he recorded his whole ordeal in those pages."

"Yes but..." He exhaled. "I mean no offense. I understand Lord Hector's situation, but unless he, ahem, behaves less wildly, he'll never be considered sane enough to inherit the dukedom. I'll never find a lord who will want to be his champion, or a doctor who will certify he's sane."

Which would be a shame because she was sure Hector would make a great duke. But then again, he'd told her he didn't want to become a duke. "And?"

Ernest joined his hands as if in prayer. "Lord Hector seems particularly fond of you. I was wondering if you'd be so kind as to help him become the duke he's destined to be."

Maddie took a moment before answering. "Me? What should I do exactly?"

"Well, to put it bluntly, teach him how to behave properly, common courtesies. I can instruct him, but I'm sure he'll learn faster if you're involved. We can't expect him to find a champion if he goes around half naked or growls in that animalistic fashion. He gave me such a fright. No peer will ever agree to address the queen on his behalf. Lord Hector needs a little encouragement and someone who understands his situation to be steered in the right direction."

She worried at her bottom lip. "I believe he doesn't want to assume the title."

Ernest fixed the knot of his cravat, although it didn't need any adjustment. "He must."

"You can't force him to petition to have the title restored to him. It's his choice."

"There are things I probably should disclose to Lord Hector first behind the reasons why I think he should petition for the Duke of Blackburn. Suffice to say the dukedom is in great need of a duke who cares about his tenants and employees. Someone who's honest and with a good heart. Someone who doesn't take advantage of his position to abuse others. If Lord Hector is even slightly like his late brother, then he'd be a great duke."

The urge to defend Hector burned her from the inside out. "He is. Hector is an admirable man."

"That's what the Blackburn tenants need."

Drat. She'd never paid attention to Duke Quentin. He was often the subject of gossip, being still a bachelor. But she had no idea whether he was a trustworthy landlord or not.

"Hasn't Duke Quentin been taking care of the Hastings estate?"

Ernest rose. "As I said, I should talk with Lord Hector first. I hope you will come to the right conclusion to help his lordship adjust his return to society." He bowed, radiating sadness. "Thank you for your time. Please think about what I have told you."

"I will." She stood up as well. "But I agreed to become Lady Babineaux's companion."

Ernest shot her a pointed look as if to say, 'you're joking.' They didn't talk as she led him to the hallway, both lost in their thoughts.

She opened the door. "Pardon my curiosity, but you seem to have taken to heart the fate of the dukedom at heart."

He put his hat on. "I do, Maddie. I do. At Duke Robert's request, but he showed me great kindness when no one else did. His employees, now Duke Quentin's employees, are people in need. Had Robert been lived, he would have never allowed..." He cleared his throat. "I've talked too much. Please don't hesitate to send me a message should you convince Lord Hector to see me again. I'd like to show him something that might prompt him to make a decision. Good day. Please tell Verity I'll see her soon." He bowed again before walking away.

She shut the door and leant against it. She was more than happy to help Hector so long as he wanted to take his brother's place. But it had to be his choice.

She'd barely started to go upstairs when her mother sauntered into the hallway with a folded copy of *The Times*.

"That's an amazing opportunity for you." Her mother had the same expression as that time when Verity announced her engagement with Ernest. Mother hadn't objected only because he made nearly eight thousand pounds per year.

"I thought you were out." She couldn't completely remove the frustration from her voice.

"I returned a few moments before dear Ernest arrived."

"What opportunity?" Maddie asked, not really interested in the answer. "Have you eavesdropped on my conversation with *dear* Ernest?"

"I have." The fact Mother didn't scold her for her sauciness didn't bode well. "To make sure he behaves like a gentleman. Look." She opened the newspaper and showed it to her.

Maddie leant closer to read it. *The castaway duke: Lord Hector Wentworth returns. The future of Quentin Wentworth, Duke of Blackburn is in question. Is Lord Hector Wentworth capable of managing the dukedom of Blackburn?*

"What opportunity, Mother?" Maddie asked again.

"To be a duchess!" A crease appeared between Mother's eyebrows.

"What about Lady Babineaux?"

"Forget that old crow. When we met Lord Wentworth years ago, I didn't take him seriously. He was a young gentleman with an obsession for vegetables and about to leave for the Americas. *Pff.*

Yes, he was the brother of a duke but I hoped the duke would have proposed, but then he had the brilliant idea of chasing after his brother and ended up dying."

"Mother!" She stomped a foot on the step. "The duke tried to save his brother."

"But now Hector is going to be the Duke of Blackburn. That's a different matter. One can put up with a lot of odd behaviours when dealing with more than hundreds of thousands of pounds." She pronounced the last words clearly.

The sum stunned Maddie for a moment. Not that she cared how wealthy the Duke of Blackburn was, but Lord, hundreds of thousands of pounds?

"He likes you," Mother said, folding the newspaper. "If you spend some time with him, in a matter of months, I might call you Your Grace."

"What about what I want? What makes you think I'm ready to marry him or become a duchess?"

"He's a duke," Mother said with the tone of someone talking with a particularly slow-witted child. Even her arrogant smile vanished. She didn't add anything else. Hector's title seemed to be a good enough reason to marry him.

Maddie gripped the bannister, refusing to consider marrying Hector only for his title and money. "He isn't a just a potential duke. He's a man who needs time to recover from a seriously harrowing experience."

Mother hooked her arm through hers. "And you're going to help him as you promised."

sixteen

PEACE AT LAST. Or as much peace as a city like London could offer, which wasn't a lot.

Nestled in the top branches of the cypress tree in the garden, Hector closed his eyes and listened to the few birds flying across the sky. Their songs were all wrong compared to those he'd been used to listening to, and rather boring, to be honest.

On the island, he'd listened to the most amazing sounds made by dozens of different species of birds. Their high-pitched notes had tricked him into thinking there were humans somewhere. Their melodic songs had been so beautiful he wondered if the birds imitated Bach. Nocturnal serenades from frogs and insects had played like a concert at the Royal Albert Hall.

Here he could distinguish barely four different species, and the loud voices and thuds from the streets ruined the atmosphere. Still, staying in the tree was better than being with his cousin and bickering about how a lord was supposed to dress. Hopefully, Quentin had gone off somewhere doing ducal businesses.

Quick footsteps approached the tree, and he scoffed. If it was Quentin again or the butler, complaining about his choice of clothes, the book, or the way he spoke about the island, he would leave the house and spend the night in Hyde Park. Actually, that wasn't a bad idea. The footsteps stopped next to the tree. He peered down but couldn't see anything through the thick foliage. He jumped off the branch and landed on the ground on his bare feet.

"What the hell—" The rest of the sentence died a swift death as a feminine scream reached his ears.

Maddie stood in front of him, a hand over her rising chest. Her pretty pink hat slid an inch to the side as she jolted. "Good Lord."

"Maddie." Hell. He'd given her a fright. He wiped his clammy hands over his breeches and brushed his hair back. Why hadn't he thought to comb it? "I didn't know it was you."

She tilted her head to gaze up at the tree. The movement uncovered a few inches of her slender neck where a vein beat a fast pulse. He had to close his hands tightly not to touch her creamy skin. Or worse, plant a kiss on the tempting spot. He might have forgotten the rules of society, but he wouldn't kiss a lady without being sure she wanted to be kissed, and Maddie had already been scared by him.

"You were up there?" She pointed a finger at the tree canopy. "It's so high."

He buttoned his shirt for her sake only. "Not high at all."

"Isn't it dangerous?"

"There are no snakes. I climbed trees on the island every day, but the snakes were a problem. Many of them would avoid me, hissing indignantly after being disturbed, but sometimes, I caught a few of them off guard, and it wasn't a pleasant experience for either of us."

She paled. "Snakes?"

He nodded. "I met quite a few snakes as thick as my legs, and others that could swim."

"Swim?" She paled further.

Right. He wasn't doing a good job at reassuring her.

"Snakes are highly misunderstood creatures," he hurried to say in hopes of not worrying her further. "Many of them are very gentle and inoffensive."

"I'm not sure I'd be happy to see a snake, even an inoffensive one." She straightened her hat. "I trust you're well."

"I've missed you. I'm happy to see you again," he said to distract her from the snakes.

"So am I." She cast a quick glance over at him.

Unless he was mistaken, which was likely since he hadn't had any human contact in the past years, her gaze wasn't the same disgusted one as Quentin or the maids gave him. Or perhaps it was her artist's eye interested in him.

"Don't you feel cold?" She tugged at her velvet-rimmed cloak.

"A little, but I like it. It makes me feel...something." He must have said something inappropriate because she lowered her gaze. "Why are you upset?"

"I can only imagine how difficult it's for you to get used to London after years away from the city." She put her gloved hand on his, and his whole body tightened in anticipation. "I'm here because I need to talk to you. Shall we sit somewhere?"

The gravity in her tone distracted him from her touch.

"Of course." He dropped himself to the ground and crossed his legs, waiting for her to join him.

She burst out laughing, which he loved. From his low point of view, he could admire her slender body, lovely chin, and the way her dark curls brushed against her cheeks. So beautiful. So kind. He was lucky to have met her. He was lucky she'd found him.

"I'm sorry. I shouldn't laugh." Her shoulders shook with laughter.

"By all means, you should. You look even more lovely when you laugh." His comment sobered her in a moment. Oh, right. Gentlemen didn't compliment ladies. How silly.

"I mean, can we sit inside on a sofa or chairs? It's chilly for me here and I don't want to soil my clothes with dry leaves and mud."

She smoothed her mauve skirt. "This is one of my best dresses, and my maid works hard to keep it spotless."

"Fair enough." He sprang up to his feet, miscalculating the distance between them.

Or maybe he did it on purpose without realising it. He ended up an inch from her. So close her breasts pressed against his chest. She didn't step away, though. He drew in a breath that brought her lavender scent to him.

"I want to kiss you again." He suppressed the urge to caress her bottom lip.

She flushed but didn't move. "Where they can't see us."

He took her hand and led her behind the tall hedgerow he had so promptly disparaged a few days ago. But now he thanked Quentin and his bloody Continental taste.

She giggled when he pulled her closer to the shadows. The green plant blocked the view of the house. On the other side, the brick wall shielded them from the street. He would protect her from everything else.

She tilted her head up, her plush lips inviting. "I want to kiss you, too."

He dipped his head and kissed her, closing his eyes and thanking every angel for granting him his wish. She pressed her body against his, raising on her toes. He coiled an arm around her waist and held her up, taking her weight. Holding his breath, he parted his lips and tentatively ran the tip of his tongue over the seam of her lips. A burst of pure happiness exploded within him when she opened her mouth and welcomed him inside. The first time he'd kissed her, he hadn't dared to deepen the kiss. But now kissing her properly was a necessity.

He stroked her velvety tongue with his, hardly believing she let him do it. She sagged against him and returned the caress with a timid stroke of her tongue. No, he wasn't numb anymore. Every inch of his body was ablaze with emotion, and it wasn't only a matter of sexual arousal—although it was present, judging by the stirring in his breeches. He was...happy to kiss and hold her in his arms. The world, with its crazy rules and uncomfortable clothes, made sense when she was with him. He was bold enough to bring a hand up and brush his thumb against the underside of her breast. Even through the fabric of her coat, the soft shape of her breast was clear. She drew in a sharp breath that made him pause. Was he too bold? Loud voices from the house jolted her.

She withdrew. Yet the sensation of her closeness remained on his skin like a warm blanket.

"I'm sorry," he whispered.

"What for? You did nothing wrong." Her cheeks were the colour of ripe strawberries. Even her lips were bright red from the kiss.

He wasn't sure he hadn't done anything wrong. He wanted to give her the best kiss she'd ever experienced. Instead, his kisses were likely clumsy and boring.

"Did you enjoy it?"

She touched his hand with a delicate, gloved finger. "Very much." An emerald fire glowed in the depths of her gaze.

He wanted to kiss her again, unbutton her shirt, and kiss every inch of her skin. But even if he wasn't a proper gentleman, he knew better. They needed time.

"Let's go inside." He offered her his arm and felt a foot taller when she took it.

They walked to the house in silence. He found out people needed to fill every moment with chatter or noise. He was happy to listen to her breathing and the soft sound of her footsteps.

The maid gasped and almost dropped a carafe of water when he entered. He didn't care about her reaction. Maddie didn't gasp when she saw him and even accepted his arm. He could face the whole ton without flinching when she was at his side.

They sat down in the parlour at the same time. She narrowed her eyes at him briefly. Oh, right. Ladies first, gentlemen after. It was amazing how rules and behaviours that had been second nature for him could be forgotten. Perhaps because they didn't matter that much, especially on an island where the monkeys' idea of good manners was throwing fruit stones at him.

Maddie shifted on the chair and grimaced at the awful painting.

He should be a proper host. "Would you like a cup of tea?" He went to stand up, but she waved him down.

"I'm fine, thank you." She paused, fiddling with her reticule.

"What did you want to talk about?"

"Ernest, Mr. Merriweather, visited me and told me about claiming the title of Duke of Blackburn." She folded her hands in her lap. "Do you want to be the duke?"

The muscles in his neck tensed. "Why did he visit you?"

"Because he's my future brother-in-law and believes you might need help to find a champion."

"Help? A champion? I don't understand."

She sighed and tugged at her gloves. "May I be honest?"

"I want nothing but honesty, especially from you."

"Ernest asked me to help you get acquainted again with the rules of society and etiquette, to help you relearn how to behave so you cannot be prevented from regaining the title." She lowered her gaze. "You'll need a medical certificate attesting to your good health, especially, er, your mental health, and a lord ready to champion your cause with the queen. It's quite a lot."

"I see." He gripped the armrests, a constricting sensation tightening his chest.

He'd barely returned from eight years of constant fighting for survival, and people already wanted to drop something as complicated as a dukedom on his shoulders. But it was Robert's last wish that he takes up the title...a voice whispered in his head. Could he ignore that?

"Personally, I don't think you need to change anything about you." She raised her gaze again.

What had he said about the constricting sensation? Well, it was gone, thanks to her trust in him.

He released his grip on the armrest. "I'm not sure I want to be a duke. I don't think I'll be a good one."

"I guessed that would be your disposition, but Ernest strongly believes you'll be a great duke. So do I."

He whipped his head up. "You think I'll be a good duke?"

She nodded with energy. "I don't have any doubts. Besides, Ernest hinted at something that might persuade you to change your mind when it comes to pursuing the title." She glanced at the clock on the mantelpiece. "That's why he should be waiting for us. He said he wanted to show something, to take you somewhere."

Hell. Everything was happening too quickly. "Where?"

"I'm not sure." She regarded him again. "But you'll need shoes and a jacket. It's cold, and it's probably going to rain."

"Do you think I should go?" He hated burdening her with his problems, but she knew London's society better than he did, and he trusted her opinion.

"I do. He didn't tell me everything about why he wants you to take the title." She let out a quick chuckle. "To be honest, I'm curious. He was rather mysterious. But aside from that, I think you should consider what he has to say."

"Are you coming as well?"

"If you wish so."

Oh, yes. He nodded. "Then I'll put some shoes on."

seventeen

H ECTOR COULDN'T STOP fiddling with the collar of his starched shirt buttoned all the way up and tied by a cravat.

The constant motion of the carriage reminded him of the raft where he'd spent a couple of weeks, and he wasn't sure he liked it. If it weren't for Maddie sitting in front of him, he would have removed his clothes and climbed back in his tree, forgetting about the whole affair.

Mr. Merriweather regarded him with suspicion as if he hadn't decided yet if he could trust Hector or not. "With regard to your mother," the solicitor started.

"Yes?" Hector forgot about his blasted clothes.

"I can give you a map of the exact location of her burial." Mr. Merriweather lowered his gaze. "I'm afraid I haven't visited the communal cemetery in a while."

"Thank you." Hector flexed his fingers. "It would be most helpful."

Maddie stroked his hand. "We'll go together when you're ready."

Of course, she would say that. Did she realise how sweet and adorable she was? A warm flutter spread in his chest as he smiled at her.

"Do you remember the textile factory your family owns?" Mr. Merriweather asked, breaking the moment.

His leather folder was once again tucked under his arm, and Hector wondered how the solicitor could endure wearing such a tight waistcoat.

He had to focus on Robert and his letter not to panic just looking at the solicitor's clothes. "I do. I visited it a few times. Mother was fond of the employees and loved taking tea with them. Robert was very active in it and the other businesses, like shipping and such."

A glint of triumph flashed in Mr. Merriweather's eyes. "My grandfather was Irish," he said, with the tone of one expecting a reaction from his audience. "The majority of your textile workers are Irish. Honest, hard-working people."

Hector didn't know what to say or what he was supposed to do with the revelation.

"I didn't know of your grandfather. Did he work here in London?" Maddie asked.

"Yes. He collected the city's waste." Mr. Merriweather chuckled. "He'd be surprised to know I became a solicitor."

"Has Quentin visited the factory recently?" Hector asked.

Mr. Merriweather's face tightened. "No. I'm afraid the duke hasn't paid any attention to the factory, especially after his inquest."

"Inquest?" Maddie frowned. "I don't remember having read anything about Blackburn and an inquest."

"The police kept everything quiet by His Grace's request." Mr. Merriweather lowered his voice. "Blackburn was among Mrs. Blanchet's guests when her famous painting—"

"*The Lady of the Lake.*" Maddie's mouth hung open. "Sorry for the interruption. Please do go on."

"The night of Blanchet gathering was when the painting disappeared. Mrs. Blanchet blatantly accused Blackburn of having stolen it. But his house was searched thoroughly, and nothing has been found." The solicitor clenched his fists. "The duke was angered by the inquest and filed suit against Mrs. Blanchet to pay for the damage to his reputation." He clicked his tongue. "Mrs. Blanchet settled the dispute with an undisclosed sum."

"Heavens." Maddie slouched back in the seat. "I had no idea and you never mentioned it."

"Because until recently, the duke was my client. The client-solicitor privilege prevents me to divulge any information about my clients," Mr. Merriweather said. "Then he gave me the sack, claiming I didn't have his best interests at heart." He tilted his head right and left. "Which was true, I suppose. Anyway, I take my job seriously. I don't disclose my clients' confidential information."

"But this is Mrs. Blanchet! You could have told me." Maddie pouted, and Hector had to remind himself he wasn't supposed to kiss her in front of others. "Do you think Blackburn stole the painting?" Her whole face brightened with interest.

Mr. Merriweather shrugged. "I have no evidence, but my instinct says yes."

"Perhaps Quentin sold the painting," Hector said.

Mr. Merriweather shook his head. "Unlikely. A famous painting like that one can't be sold without leaving a trail. It's more probable the thief hid it, waiting for the price to go up and to find a private buyer. If Blackburn has *The Lady of the Lake*, it's still in his possession. Besides, many art thefts happen because the thief wishes to enjoy the object d'art and admire it in the private, although I don't think that's the case with Blackburn."

Maddie laughed. "I agree. The duke has horrible taste in art."

"And a huge debt," Mr. Merriweather said. "Allegedly."

Hector frowned. "What do you mean?"

"Before Blackburn gave me the sack, I had a look into his accounts, and even though I'm not an expert, it was clear his finances weren't in order. I can't prove it, but I suspect from what

I uncovered, the duke has a penchant for gambling." The solicitor lifted a shoulder. "As I said, I don't have any evidence. Even when I was his solicitor, I didn't have complete access to his entries, and his accountant is loyal to the duke."

The carriage stopped in front of an imposing red-brick building with tall, industrial chimneys releasing puffs of steam. Dark mould covered the walls, creeping up like a disease sprouted from the ground, and a few windows overlooking the street were broken. Potholes dug deep ruts in the cobblestones. Not as he remembered the factory. Is dilapidated state was a punch in his stomach. His mother had insisted on keeping the factory spotless, and well-insulated from the cold wind rising from the Thames to make the employees more comfortable. Robert had made sure its management had all repairs done promptly to keep the factory functioning and clean.

Mr. Merriweather watched him with a focus that gave Hector shivers. "Is it familiar?" he asked, seemingly reading Hector's mind.

"Not really." Hector winced when he climbed out of the carriage and jumped onto the cobbled street.

The shoes constricted his feet and squashed his callouses, but he didn't want to complain. Not when he was worried about the workers. He followed Mr. Merriweather to the front gate, avoiding piles of rubbish and shards of broken glass.

Maddie walked next to him. "Has it always been like this?"

"No. Years ago, it was clean and well-kept. A model for other factories.It was both my mother and Robert's pride."

As they stepped inside, a couple of workers touched their hats at their passage and smiled warmly at Mr. Merriweather.

"Good morning, everyone," the solicitor said in a loud voice. "As you must have heard, Lord Hector Wentworth, the brother of the Duke of Blackburn, is indeed alive. He's here to inspect the factory. Please continue your work. We won't be long."

Hector expected the usual mutters and whispers his introduction always started. But the workers didn't utter a sound. An acrid smell tickled his nose. Something greasy covered the floor, causing his soles to stick to it, and cold gusts swept through the hall, whistling. The noise from the spinning machines had never been so loud or braying; it was a constant hammering and strident screeches. He wasn't an expert, but something had to be wrong with those machines.

But the worst sight was the condition of the workers. Their tattered clothes hung from bony shoulders. Dirt covered gaunt faces. He'd gained more muscles on the island while hunting and fishing than these people working in a smelly factory. What struck him the most were the workers' gazes. Lost. Sad. Resigned. Hopeless.

There were young men, women, and even children with scrawny faces and frail hands covered in cuts. They bowed and curtsied at Hector's passage, their fear palpable. The name of Mr. Merriweather was muttered a few times, and the people working at the weaving machines cast bitter glances at Hector. No one said anything, though.

"I don't remember the workers being so desperate," he said when they reached the end of the hall. "When I came here with my mother and Robert, the workers would greet us with bright smiles and chat about their families. There weren't any children, and everyone wore good quality clothes. The windows were whole and shut against the cold. The floor was clean. And hellfire, there wasn't so much noise." He forgot to mind his language in front of Maddie, but she didn't wince.

"Lord." She blinked quickly, as if fending off tears.

For some reason, shame caused his heart to clench at her dismay. He hated that she witnessed the factory at its worst.

Mr. Merriweather stepped in front of him, a hard glint in his fierce stare. "My lord, I needed you to see this." He spread an arm towards the workers. "Simply describing it wouldn't have been enough. This situation started while you were away. After Blackburn took over..." He exhaled, his hands clenching on the folder.

"The new duke doesn't care about these people. His main concerns are making money and enjoying himself. He lowered the wages to a bare minimum. He forces the labourers to work long hours without further compensation. Those who fall ill, or carries a child, loses their job. These people are starving, suffering, and forced to work in miserable conditions for a handful of shillings. This is slavery, my lord."

Hector couldn't agree more. The factory wasn't what Robert had built. Maddie gazed up at him with an expectant face that destroyed him.

"There was a protesting march in November that ended up in a massacre," Mr. Merriweather said. "The journalists dubbed it Bloody Sunday. Irish workers took to the streets to protest about their work conditions and demand the release of P. M. O'Brien, one of the few politicians who did something to improve the workers' situation. As a result, he had been arrested. The protestors clashed against the police, and it was a bloodbath. Since then, Irish workers are marked as agitators and their pleas aren't taken seriously. A few of your employees were injured during Bloody Sunday, and Blackburn gave them the sack. Entire families have been ruined. My lord"—he stepped closer—"we *must* do something. These people need help. Help only you can provide. Claim your title. Help these people. Set things straight. I was one of these children. Not in this factory, but your mother helped my mother and found her a job here. Without your parents, my mother and I would be dead. What do you think is going to happen to these children?"

Maddie drew in a breath as the workers shot glances at them.

Each word shook Hector from the inside out. Robert would be appalled. His mother would be, too. Even his father would be angry about the situation. While his father hadn't been the sweetest of men, he'd always prided himself on being an exemplary employer and on having happy, productive workers who excelled in their job.

Hector rubbed his chest, watching a young woman breastfeed her child while she kept working at the weaving machine. She looked so frail he worried she might faint from exhaustion.

Maddie placed her hand on his arm. She didn't say anything though. There was no need to.

"Ernest, Hector," Maddie said after a pause. "I will agree to help Hector in any way I can if he wishes to claim his title."

He swallowed hard. "Mr. Merriweather, tell me what I must do."

eighteen

THAT NIGHT, IT wasn't the noise from the streets or the donkey that disturbed Hector's sleep, but his constant worry. The gaunt faces of those workers would appear in front of him every time he closed his eyes. His chest would tighten in worry, and shame would burn at the back of his mouth. Robert had been right. Hector hadn't cared about a duke's responsibilities or appreciated a duke's work. But now it was personal. He had to do the right thing, not only for the employees, but for his family name as well. If he wanted to honour Robert's principles, he had to take control of the dukedom.

He perked up when footsteps padded from the corridor. Quentin's voice sounded too low for Hector to understand what he said, but another voice came. Someone had to be with him. Two different sets of footsteps reached his ears, muffled by the carpet. He huffed. A lover, perhaps. He didn't care.

He rolled onto his back. Becoming a duke meant learning how to deal with politicians and solicitors. Not what he longed to do. He probably wouldn't become the scientist he'd dreamt to be, but at least he could publish his book with all the things he'd learnt on the island, and he could keep studying botany at his leisure while dealing with the House of Lords.

A scream jolted him. He sat bolt upright. Another muffled sound, like a child whimpering, echoed from the other room.

"Be still!" Quentin said in a raspy voice.

What was going on?

He jumped off the bed and inched the door open. The cold wooden floor chilled his bare feet. More muffled noises came from Quentin's bedroom. It sounded like a struggle. A new feminine scream shocked him. He marched to Quentin's room and pushed the door open without knocking.

Half-undressed, Quentin towered over a shivering, crying girl.

All the air rushed out of Hector's lungs. Hell, she had to be barely fifteen. A child. The front of her gown was ripped, and she clutched the torn fabric with trembling fingers.

"Leave. Now!" Quentin strode to him, muscles tensing under his unbuttoned shirt.

Hector didn't move. Quentin's pupils were so dilated the blue irises were barely visible, and even in the dim light, his face appeared flushed and glistening with sweat.

Hector ignored him. "Do you wish to leave, child?"

She nodded, rouge smearing her cheeks.

Hector didn't need to hear more. He shoved Quentin aside and headed for the scared girl.

"Get out." Quentin's voice sounded cracked and raspy. He lunged, staggering on his feet, but Hector blocked him by grabbing him by the shoulders.

"You are..." He was about to say drunk but wasn't sure his cousin was just drunk. He shoved him again and crouched in front of the girl. "Are you hurt?"

She shook her head, curling up in a corner.

"Do you need a physician?"

"I want to go home," she whispered.

He moved to haul her up and take her out of the room but

paused, not sure how she'd react. "Leave. Wait for me in the hall-way. I'll take care of him. He won't hurt you."

She sprang up like a rabbit and fled the room in a flutter of torn silk and dishevelled hair.

"No!" Quentin went to grab her arm, but Hector pushed him away easily.

Quentin tottered back and fell over, groaning and clutching his stomach.

Hector snatched a few guineas from the dresser and a coat before leaving his cousin muttering nonsense on the floor. One word arrived loud and clear though.

"Bastard," Quentin said.

As if Hector cared. He walked over to the girl who was halfway down the stairs. "Here." He handed her the coat and the money. "Take a hansom cab. There's always one or two passing by. Would you like me to escort you home?"

Her horrified face said it all. He didn't look reassuring, bare-foot, shirtless, and with wild hair.

"No." She rushed down the stairs faster than he could ask her if she wanted a maid's company.

Well, he couldn't blame her. He shuffled back to his bedroom, pausing at Quentin's door. Nausea roiled his stomach. If he needed one more reason to claim the title, Quentin had just given it to him.

nineteen

HECTOR FOCUSED ON Maddie's feet as she showed him the style of the gentlemen's bow that was in fashion. It wasn't his fault if the quick glimpse of her slender ankles and calves distracted him. As part of his becoming a duke, he had to learn, or learn again, manners, and apparently, the way gentlemen bowed had changed in the past years. Verity and Mr. Merriweather were both present. Apparently, an entire entourage of peers was necessary to reacquaint him with the so-called civilisation.

"You move your left foot towards your right one." Maddie did just that, lifting her skirts. The frilly lace of her petticoats made an appearance. "Then shift the right foot half a foot back. No, don't move the left foot." She stretched out a hand when he moved.

"Perhaps I should show him." Mr. Merriweather stepped next to Hector. He made a few quick movements with his feet before bowing from the waist, balancing his weight on the front foot. "Your right hand rests on your belly, and the left is slightly pulled back. I'll do it again slowly."

Hector repeated the steps after him. Right, left, right foot back, weight on the right leg, bow. What a complicated deed.

"Excellent." Mr. Merriweather patted his shoulder. "If you meet a lady in the street, you won't perform this complicated bow but a simpler one and remember to remove your hat but to keep its inner side towards you." He showed Hector the movement by using his tall hat. "We don't want to show the inside of the hat in case it's dirty."

Hector nodded, memorising every detail.

Verity watched them, eating bonbons on the sofa. "It's very decent of you, Lord Wentworth, to fight for your title to take care of those workers."

"After what I saw and what Maddie told me about the prime minister, I couldn't remain indifferent to their pain. I believe their lives are even worse than my years on the island. I had to search for food constantly, and the monkeys attacked me, but I wasn't a slave."

"I would have been terrified to live alone for so long, surrounded by wild animals," Verity said, offering him a bonbon. "You're so brave."

"Desperate." He took one and popped it into his mouth, savouring its sweet, fruity taste. He'd never realised how lucky he was when he'd been a foolish young man, taking food and shelter, title and wealth for granted. Never again. "Some of those monkeys were my friends."

"Friends?" Mr. Merriweather asked, earning a glare of disapproval from Maddie.

"They would bring me fruits sometimes, and I returned the favour." Hector practised the sequence of the steps again. "I believe they could be considered friends since we took care of each other."

Maddie arched a brow at Mr. Merriweather as if challenging him to say anything. But he bowed his head in acknowledgement.

"Heavens, that painting is terrible." Verity pointed at the bucolic landscape on the wall. "Sorry, Lord Wentworth, for my bluntness. I blame Maddie for having taught me what a good painting is. I'm afraid she ruined my enjoyment of mediocre art for good."

He grinned. "I agree with your assessment. Quentin chose it." He practised the bow again in front of Maddie.

She rewarded him with a smile that stopped his heart for a moment.

"Are the shoes too uncomfortable?" she asked.

He twirled his foot. "These larger shoes are better, and I—"

The door swung open, and Quentin came inside with a lady Hector had never met and who clung to his cousin's arm like an extra limb. Her silk dress and velvet cloak were of the finest quality, and her large brown eyes and dark hair made her an attractive woman, but somehow her lopsided, smug smile ruined her beauty a little.

The sudden entrance caused Hector's throat to tighten and his muscles to contract. He stepped in front of Maddie, almost blocking her view. Instead, Verity withdrew to a corner of the sofa and focused on its floral pattern.

"Merriweather. Will I ever get rid of you?" Quentin's mouth formed a displeased line.

The solicitor didn't flinch. "Only time will tell, your grace."

"Cousin. I didn't know you were here," Quentin said. "Jones told me you left the house earlier today."

"I went with Merriweather , here, to see the factory in Clerkenwell."

A deep crease appeared between Quentin's eyebrows. "For what reason?"

"To show Lord Hector in what terrible conditions your employees work," Mr. Merriweather said with too much passion.

Quentin didn't flinch. "I suggest you don't talk about what you don't understand."

Mr. Merriweather opened his mouth, but the lady cut him off.

"Verity!" Her glossy black curls bounced on her rouged cheeks. "What a pleasant surprise."

"Do you know Hector's friends?" Quentin sounded shocked.

The lady smiled. "I know Verity, who always tells the truth, don't you, darling?"

Verity flushed to the roots of her hair. "Annabelle, fancy that."

Mr. Merriweather offered a stiff bow. "May I present Miss Madeline Debenham and Lord Hector Wentworth. I am Earnest Merriweather, Esquire."

Annabelle dropped a half curtsy. "It's a pleasure to meet you, Mr. Merriweather. Verity has told me everything about you. I doubt she told you everything—"

"Everyone, this is Miss Annabelle Fanshaw." Verity sprang up from the sofa and let out a cheerful laugh.

Quentin wrapped an arm around Annabelle's waist. "How do you and Annabelle know each other?"

Verity waved a hand. "We met here and there and at the piano concerts each week."

"Indeed." Annabelle propped her elbow over Quentin's shoulder. "But Verity and I have other interests in common. For example—"

"Does anyone want a bonbon?" Verity rushed towards Quentin and Annabelle but tripped on the carpet and fell forwards. The bonbons flew in the air and landed on Annabelle's head and Quentin's white jacket.

Annabelle raked a hand through her hair, smearing the chocolate on her curls, while a stain of mint cream splattered on Quentin's chest.

Verity clamped her hands over her mouth. "I'm so sorry."

Hector chewed his bottom lip. All that delicious food wasted.

"Miss Verity..." Clenching his teeth, Quentin brushed bits of chocolate from his clothes, making a mess.

"Let me help." Verity went to use her handkerchief on the green stain on Quentin's chest, but he took her wrist, blocking her.

"I believe you've done enough, silly girl."

Mr. Merriweather sucked in a breath. "Don't talk to my bride-to-be in that tone."

Quentin tried to clean his jacket with his own handkerchief. "You and Miss Verity deserve each other. Troublemakers and stupid."

"That's enough!" Mr. Merriweather marched towards the duke who shot forwards, too.

Hector reacted on impulse. He stepped between the solicitor and Quentin but put too much strength in the process, ending up shoving both of them. Mr. Merriweather staggered backwards, and Quentin bumped into Annabelle and together they tumbled onto the floor in a froth of petticoats and silk. The scene would be comical if not for Maddie's horrified face.

Quentin shot a burning stare at Hector. He was surprised he didn't catch fire.

"I didn't mean to push you." Hector offered his hand to Quentin who ignored it and picked himself up, helping Annabelle.

She wiped smeared chocolate from her face. "You were right, Quentin. Your cousin is wild indeed."

Quentin tugged at his jacket and brushed his dishevelled hair back. "There's a reason the newspapers call him the Savage Duke."

"That's unfair," Maddie said. "Hector is a perfect gentleman."

He wasn't sure about that and judging by Quentin's pitched expression, he agreed.

"We should leave, Quentin." Annabelle took Quentin's hand, keeping her wide gaze on Hector.

"I agree." Quentin stomped out of the parlour, followed by Annabelle. She lingered a moment to glance at Verity before shutting the door behind her.

Maddie exhaled when the two left. "Oh, bother."

He turned towards her and frowned at her pale face.

"I'm sorry." Verity picked up the empty box of bonbons. "What a disaster."

"Yes, all those delicious bonbons." He clicked his tongue, searching for a piece that could be salvaged.

"Not the sweets, Hector." Maddie rubbed her forehead. "Your cousin is going to use this incident against you, and Annabelle is his witness."

The bonbons were scattered on the floor, and Mr. Merriweather gathered them, muttering something Hector didn't grasp.

"It's done," Mr. Merriweather said. "It's no one's fault. Lord Hector is a tad stronger than he looks." He massaged his chest. "Definitely stronger. With due respect, you punched the air out of me with that shove."

Maddie exhaled. "Even the duke seemed breathless."

"I disappointed you." He dared to close his fingers around Maddie's hand.

"No, you didn't. Really. Let's think of our goal, which is to help those people."

"And you." He squeezed her hand. "Once I'm the Duke of Blackburn, I'll help you realise your dream and become a painter."

She didn't have the enthusiastic reaction he hoped for. He would love for her to wrap her arms around his neck and kiss him. Not that he'd made the offer only because he wished to be kissed. He firmly believed she was a great artist. But a kiss would be wonderful, wouldn't it? She remained still, her lips flattening.

Damn. "Did I say something wrong?"

"I'll help you no matter what I receive back because I believe you'll be a great duke."

"I want to help you in turn, and before you say I'm doing it only out of my sense of duty, let me tell you that's not true. You're an artist. The entire world must know it."

Tears welled in her eyes, and he wasn't sure if it was a good or a bad thing.

Verity sighed. "That's so romantic, especially since Maddie will paint something a hundred times better than that horrible thing."

"Perhaps we should leave them a moment." Mr. Merriweather kissed Verity's hand again before leaving the room with her.

Verity rested her head on his shoulder. "You're right."

The moment Hector and Maddie were alone, he took a deep breath. "I'm sorry if I offended you."

The rest of his apology was cut off by Maddie throwing herself at him. She hugged him and rose on her tiptoes to kiss him. So, dreams do come true. Laughing, he kissed her tears away, gladly taking her weight and wrapping his arms around her waist.

"I hope you become the Duke of Blackburn and not because of your promise." She cupped his face, making him feel like a king. "But because I can't imagine a better man for the job."

Had he been doubtful about him becoming a duke? Not anymore. If Maddie believed in him, he wouldn't disappoint her.

twenty

AFTER THE INCIDENT in the parlour, Maddie moved Hector's the etiquette lessons to her house to avoid another encounter with the duke. Unsurprisingly, her mother hadn't raised any objections. Maddie had never enjoyed so much freedom. In fact, she was practising dancing with Hector in her sitting room without her mother or a chaperone hovering around. It both delighted and concerned her. But then again, the duke's great wealth was a good reason for her mother to forfeit a need for a chaperone, apparently.

She tried not to think of Hector's big hand sprawled over her waist or his large body looming over her. But what she couldn't ignore was his stare so intensely focused on her face. He stared at her as if he wanted to memorise every detail, as if she were the centre of his universe. Never a man had made her feel so beautiful and adored as he did.

"Now the left foot goes back," she said, mirroring his steps.

He moved with precision and elegance without needing to stop or check his position. Despite being such a tall, broad man, who hadn't danced in years, he danced with a natural fluidity she envied. She bumped against him when she brought forth the wrong foot. So much for teaching him. But he didn't flinch. When she stomped on his foot, she winced.

"Sorry," they said together before bursting out laughing.

"I'm afraid I'm not a great dancer." She wished she'd paid more attention to her dance lessons.

"I beg to differ." He swept her around the sitting room, avoiding the low table, armchairs, and sofa without hesitation.

"I've trampled your feet a few times, bumped into you, and led you the wrong way. You should be the teacher."

"I've been rude to you many times, sitting down before you or not addressing you properly."

She jutted her chin out. "I've sketched you, stealing a piece of your soul."

"I've raised my voice and scared you."

"You gave me hope to be an artist again."

"You made me believe I can be the man my brother would have been proud of."

She brushed his hand with her thumb. "I'm sure he was."

His face brightened. He twirled her around. She couldn't contain a laugh. He was an excellent dancing partner, gentle but protective, careful but not oppressive. He led her through a series of turns that made her head spin. The only problem was his close-ness. He danced too close to her. It would be the reason for a scandal in a ballroom. Oh, she wished she were the lady at the centre of that scandal.

"You're enjoying the dance." He beamed.

"Very much. You're a natural-born dancer."

"Mother insisted I learn, and I loved it. I often danced with her, especially after my father died. My parents met at a ball. Dancing was special to her. She missed my father very much, and I did what I could to cheer her up. Although I now realise, I didn't do enough. My obsession with botany came before everything else. Even her." The smile disappeared as he stopped dancing.

"You're being too harsh on yourself. We all have obsessions

when young." She didn't step away from him, enjoying the comfort of his strong arms.

"I'm ready. I'd like to see her grave." He frowned. "Something I should have done earlier. Would you come with me?"

"I'd be delighted."

"You don't have to if you don't feel comfortable." He stroked her waist with gentle fingers, and she couldn't suppress a delightful shiver.

"I want to be with you when you visit her." Besides, it wasn't going to be easy for him. "Let's go."

During the short trip to Grosvenor Place, Hector remained still. He hadn't fiddled with his cravat or shuffled his feet. She wondered if the fabric of his shirt or the shoes had stopped bothering him, or if he was too upset to fidget.

"Are you nervous?" She slid her hands in her velvet warmer as a chill sneaked inside the carriage.

"I feel that I disappointed my mother." He let out a bitter chuckle. "She's dead, but I can sense her disappointment. It doesn't make any sense, I guess."

"Quite the opposite, but I'm sure she would never be disappointed in you."

"Robert died to rescue me, she's buried in common ground, and on top of that, I haven't made amends to you." He hung his head and twirled the bunch of flowers he'd bought for his mother. "Plenty of reasons to be disappointed."

"Oh, Hector." She pulled her hand out of the muff and closed it around his. "You do worry too much. No one could be disappointed in you."

"Your hand is cold." He took her hand between his, and, good Lord, began to rub it with gentle fingers.

She hitched a breath. His warmth heated her from her fingertips to her toes as he rubbed her knuckles gently and pressed his thumbs against her palm. Oh, she grew warmer. No doubt about it. She felt his touch throughout her body as her temperature rose.

The rough spots on the pads of his fingers added a touch of illicit pleasure going straight between her legs. She wondered how those rough hands would feel on other, more sensitive parts of her body.

He paused. "Am I being rude or inappropriate again?"

"No." The answer came out quickly. But perhaps she had something to learn from his candid sincerity. He deserved to receive the same honesty. "I enjoy it."

His whole face brightened with boyish happiness. "I shall do it more often then." He placed her hand over his chest, right where his heart thumped a steady beat. "You're my angel, Maddie."

No one had ever called her an angel before. Besides, she was no angel. But that wasn't the reason why her face warmed. As usual, he spoke with disarming frankness, something difficult to come by in modern society. His simple compliment struck a chord within her, threatening to reduce her to tears.

When he'd told her she was a great artist with his usual passionate honesty, she'd wanted to weep. She hadn't realised how important his spontaneous support was until he'd offered it to her so freely. Her dream had been buried deep in her soul for years, under layers of cowardice and doubts. But now she wondered if she could realise it with his help. Not economical help, but emotional.

"Why do you say I'm your angel?" Her voice broke with emotion. "I didn't do anything special."

"You did everything. You accepted me even when I was wild." He kissed her hand, and even through her glove, his passion reached her heart. "Not to mention you found me."

"It was luck."

"It was fate." He kissed her fingers, sending her pulse into a frenzy.

The carriage rolled to a stop, breaking the moment between them. The happy light brightening his face dimmed the moment he stared at the gloomy wrought-iron gates of the cemetery. From the outside, the place looked like any other cemetery, but at a closer inspection, it lacked any floral decorations. There were no wooden benches where one could sit in front of the grave of a loved one, or crypts. No flowerbeds, mown grass, or neatly arranged trees. Just plain stones and dirt. Those souls were alone, forgotten and unwanted. The air itself pulsed with despair.

She saw Hector swallow hard before he stepped into the desolate cemetery. He kept holding her hand as they walked along the gravel path weaving across the cemetery. The further they advanced, the more he tensed with shadows darkening his expression. They walked past tombs so old the names had faded into oblivion.

The Duchess of Blackburn's grave marker was a simple grey stone. No statues of angels or crosses adorned it. Her title wasn't even stated. All the graves in the communal cemetery were as anonymous as possible with barely the name of the person buried in that spot.

Hector gently placed the flowers on the grave. "She should rest next to Robert and my father. Not here. Alone. In this sad place."

"Once you're the Duke of Blackburn, you can move her to your family crypt." She regretted her words. He didn't need more pressure about becoming the duke. "I'm sorry. I didn't want to sound commanding."

The ghost of a smile graced his sculpted lips. "Now you worry too much."

She helped him remove the grass and cleavers clinging to the stone. With each layer of weeds removed, Hector tensed further.

His features tightened in anger, or perhaps pain, as he crouched next to the grave. "All these past years, I wanted to leave the island. I cursed it. Cursed my fate. Hated it. But now that I'm here...I miss it. I miss the sky at night, the birds' songs, and the warm sun on my skin, especially now that my mother and brother are dead." He tilted his head up. Hot turmoil swirled in the depths of his sapphire gaze. "Does my wish to be there make me a terrible son and brother? I want to leave this city with its choking air and stupid rules. I wish for silence and the beauty of nature, instead of these dull buildings and the endless, meaningless chatter. People talk too much. Expect too much. And they are cruel to each other." He shook his head. "Why do I feel like that? Why am I not happy to have returned? Am I as mad as Quentin says I am?"

"Good Lord, no." She couldn't stand the distance between them any longer and crouched next to him. A knot of emotion grew in her throat at his pain and confusion. "You aren't a bad person, Hector. Quite the opposite. You're the best gentleman I've ever met, and you aren't mad or savage. Bad things happened to you. That's all."

He lowered his gaze, his eyelashes fanning over his cheek. Was *she* a bad person for wanting to draw him now?

She stroked his sharp cheek. "You need time to adjust to London, but I agree. People do talk too much and are cruel to each other. You've met my mother, after all. I understand your lack of optimism about humans."

He cracked a smile.

"But there are also good people. Ernest has a temper but is a kind soul. My sister is compassionate, and the sailors on the *Empress* risked their lives to rescue you. Even Dr. Landon helped you without asking anything. Not everything is rotten."

"You're right." He pulled at another weed. "But what if it's not a matter of time? I believe the island permanently changed me. I can't be the same man as I was. Everything we do," he gestured around, "the importance we give to propriety, the clothes, politics. Everything seems so meaningless to me. On the island, I had a reason for doing everything. I woke up knowing I had to catch fish or I wouldn't eat. I listened to the wind to understand if a storm was coming. I watched the flowers grow, wilt, and give fruit. What is my purpose now?" He sounded so lost that a phantom pain stung her chest.

"Society is complicated. We have rules, but not all of them are useless. With so many people in one place, we must control what people can or can't do, or we'd be at each other's throats. Some rules are meaningless, but you saw those Irish workers. You felt their pain. You care for them. That's why you wake up. You can make London a better place. This is something worth fighting for." The rest of what she meant to say was cut off by his embrace.

Hector hugged her. He fully enveloped her in his strong arms and pulled her closer to his chest. Goodness, he smelled divine. Citrus and soap. And he was so warm she wanted to rest her head on his shoulder and think about the best way to paint the peculiar blue of his eyes, or how she'd draw his body. She leant against him and didn't care if it was inappropriate or not, or if someone saw them. She needed the contact with him, and he sought comfort too.

"Thank you." His lips brushed against her temple, and she couldn't suppress a moan. "You truly are my angel. You keep saving me."

She caressed his cheek. "I think we keep saving each other."

He kissed her inner wrist. It wasn't a sensual kiss, though, but a reverent one, like a sinner would kiss a saint. "Would you dance with me? I think my mother would like it."

She laughed. "Here?"

"What better place?" He rose and offered her his hand.

The moment she took it, he drew her closer and twirled her around. The hem of her skirt lifted the dry leaves on the path. She stumbled and stomped on his feet, but he threw his head back and laughed, a laugh so filled with life that brightened the whole cemetery.

That was why she knew, without a doubt, she was falling for the Savage Duke.

twenty-one

MADDIE AND HECTOR returned to her house in silence, holding hands and sharing their burdens. As she rested her head on his shoulder and he caressed her hand, she didn't mind the fact he seemed incapable of letting her go. She couldn't let him go, either.

They remained in silence even when they sat in her drawing room, exchanging glances and little touches of their hands. The more she explored his fingers and knuckles, the less harsh his skin felt. Every hard spot and scar told a story she wanted to share with him. The pale sunlight danced on his profile, teasing her with the shadows cast over his features. A natural chiaroscuro—a game of shadows and light—tempting her.

"May I sketch you?" She rummaged through her bag for her sketchbook. "I don't mean to steal a piece of your soul again."

He laughed. "By all means. You stole my heart. You may as well steal my soul."

"Oh, I..." Bother. Did he mean that? Most likely, yes, he did. He only said what he meant. "Then, I'll sketch you now."

He sat still, his chin casually resting on his open hand, and she did her best to capture his god-like beauty. His eyes were the most difficult to draw as usual because her stiff fingers traced lines too harsh for the softness of his eyelids. The shadows in his curly hair forced her fingers to tense in a painful manner.

"It looks better than you think." He angled his head towards the sketch. "You might be disappointed, but you're probably too critical."

"I don't know. I can't control my hand as I'd like to do. But since I started to sketch more often, I can see a difference."

"The academy won't reject your application." He spoke with absolute certainty, and she couldn't ignore the fluttery feeling his words started in her chest.

"It'd be wonderful." She paused when the doorbell rang.

Hurried footsteps sounded from the corridor, and a moment later, the maid knocked on the sitting room door.

"Miss?" Mary inched the door open. "There's a message for you." She handed her a cream-coloured envelope.

"Thank you." She opened the envelope, still watching the shadows changing on Hector's face. "Dr. Landon invited us for an afternoon tea." She put the invitation on a table. "Would you like to go?"

He kept staring at a squirrel in the garden and not in a 'how cute it is' way. He looked like a predator. "Yes. I'd like to see the good doctor again."

"Great. Now please don't talk and don't move."

He flashed a lopsided smile that was going to be her next sketching project. "I'll do my best."

She picked up the pencil and focused on his profile, stubbornly forcing her hand to do what she wanted. And it worked...? Maybe it was her sheer determination, or the kind words Hector had always had for her, but her fingers seemed more obedient that day. A few lines were still too straight for her liking, but lo and behold, her drawing grew softer.

"It's snowing." He straightened up on the chair, staring out of the window.

Maddie drew the shadows under his jaw as the snowflakes floated down in a thick flow. Goodness. Her fingers didn't pain her much. They were a far cry from being painless, but better. "Lovely. Everything will be covered in white soon—where are you going?"

"I have to see it."

"But I haven't finished."

"I'm sorry." He opened the French door overlooking the garden.

A frosty gust swept inside, disturbing the flames in the hearth and shuffling the pages of her sketchbooks. The smell of wet soil thickened the air.

"Snow. I forgot how beautiful it is," he said, inhaling.

"Yes, I love it too—what are you doing?" She was repeating herself, but, good gracious, he was unbuttoning his shirt.

"I know I shouldn't, but I need to feel it on my skin." He removed his jacket and shirt with one yank, revealing his chiselled torso and golden skin, and dropped his clothes on the portico.

It'd take hours to sketch all his muscles, and she'd be glad to do it. Her mouth became dry. "I..."

A part of her was aware she should turn around and give him some privacy. Another part was too mesmerised by his tanned skin, the taut muscles, and even the scars to care. Just because she was an artist. Her curiosity and eagerness were simply an artist's desire for knowledge. The tingle on her skin and the quickening of her breath were all about art.

When he unbuttoned his trousers, she should have stopped him, but aside from Verity, who was in her room, and Mary, they were alone in the house. No, that shouldn't be the reason why she didn't say a word to stop him. If anything, being alone with him made everything worse and—Lord, his thighs! Thick and muscular. A study in anatomy.

And his backside was...she meant glutaeal muscles. Yes. They were a lesson in sculpting. Perfectly rounded and looking firm. And goodness, even his shaft was proportioned to everything else.

Stark naked, he walked into the garden, letting the snow caress his skin. He spread his arms and reclined his head, exposing his strong neck. The flakes started to deposit on his golden hair, the tip of his nose, and eyelashes. She wished she could draw him now in all his male glory with the snowflakes fluttering around him. His body looked like sunlight lay trapped underneath his skin, and the snow flickered like glittering specks around him. The smile stretching his lips was half celestial, half sinful. Completely charming. He put a spell on her because she could easily believe he was the king of the fairies.

He turned towards her and stretched a hand out in an invitation she couldn't refuse. She walked over to him as if in a trance. It was definitely a spell because she didn't like the snow. She liked a snow-covered view. She loved watching the snow from her warm sitting room while sipping hot tea, but not being in the cold and feeling the freezing flakes slipping down her neck or inside her boots. Yet when he took her hand and pulled her closer, it wasn't cold that made her shiver.

"I want to kiss you," he said that with the same devastating honesty he said everything, daring the world to tell him he couldn't speak his mind. He gently brushed a snowflake from her chin. His thumb lingered on the curve of her jaw and caressed her bottom lip. "I wanted to kiss you the first time I saw you, when I spotted you painting in your bedroom. You're so beautiful I can't breathe when you smile. I want to capture your smile with a kiss."

"Then do it," she whispered, her lips already tingling in anticipation.

He dipped his head while cupping her face in his warm, gentle hands. His curly locks of hair fell forwards and stroked her face. His lips brushed against hers in a heated touch warming her whole body. Her nipples tightened, and the urge to press her thighs together couldn't be ignored.

What would she do if they were both naked? Wilt in his arms? He tilted his head to the side and repeated the soft kiss. She no longer felt the snow on her skin or the cold. His presence shielded her from the frosty air and from the entire world. He transported her to a place where they could be whomever they wanted.

The third time he kissed her, he pressed his mouth against hers harder. They were standing so close their hips touched.

She parted her lips in an invitation he didn't decline. The tip of his velvety tongue slipped past her lips in a shy exploration. Oh, the shivers. They danced on her skin, making her feel every little sensation the kiss caused to burst within her. He grew bolder and deepened the kiss, stroking her tongue with his, no longer exploring but claiming. She sagged against him, aware he was fully naked and erect. She was kissing the Savage Duke who was naked in the snow. The contact with his hard length both shocked and excited her. How would it feel in her hand or inside her? He broke the kiss but didn't move away from her. His lips were half an inch from hers, sharing their heat with her.

"I can't stop kissing you." His voice sounded deep and low and started all sorts of illicit tingling in parts of her body that shouldn't tingle.

She took a moment to speak. "Then don't."

"May I kiss you again?"

Her reply was to grip his biceps and pull him closer. His next kiss was all raw passion and dominance. Gone was the shy boy from a moment earlier. He took possession of her mouth with long lashes of his tongue, stroking, teasing, and pleasuring her. Little bites on her bottom lip had her moaning and making sounds she wasn't aware she could produce. He cradled her head gently while sliding a hand around her waist. He held her up, taking all her weight. If he let her go, she'd float away in the snow. Why hadn't they kissed like that before? How much time had she wasted doing menial chores when she could have kissed him?

The more he kissed her, the harder his shaft grew. She grabbed his shoulders as a maddening need flustered her. Now she understood his dislike for clothes because she wanted to remove her constricting dress and feel her naked skin against his, sharing heat and passion in the snow.

A loud scream jolted her.

Hector broke the kiss again but didn't release her. "Your sister."

Verity stood on the threshold of the French doors, her mouth hanging open. There were footsteps and the noise of a door being slammed.

Verity shut the French doors and pulled the curtains, blocking the view. "Nothing, Mother." Her voice came muffled from the other side. "There's a...rat in the garden. Two actually. Two big rats. You don't want to see them. They're, ahem, doing things to each other, naked. I mean, they're rats, for goodness' sake. A scandalous affair but completely natural."

"Mother." Maddie stepped away from Hector. "You must leave, or at the very least get dressed. Hurry." She snatched his clothes from the portico and handed them to him. Her mother might have shown an unprecedented leniency towards Maddie, but a naked man sporting a full erection in her garden was a naked man.

He didn't accept the clothes immediately. Frowning, he took them. "I apologise for having broken another rule."

"That's my mother we're talking about. You'd be surprised by what she considers wrong. A very wide range of deeds."

His eyebrows knitted together as he slid into his trousers and shirt.

"Hector, I'm sorry to hurry you out." Her face flamed with desire, shame, and a million other emotions she couldn't process right now.

He knelt to tie his shoes and gazed up at her. "Don't worry about me." When he straightened, with his dishevelled hair covered in show and his shirt half-buttoned, he looked completely ravishing as if he'd just finished a thorough fumble. Her knees threatened to buckle. He seemed about to say something, but then shrugged. "I'll see you soon, won't I?" He grabbed her hand in desperation.

"You will." She glanced at the French doors still closed.

He kissed her hand before releasing it. And she was hot all over again.

"You may leave through the rear entrance." She pointed at the gate on the other side of the garden.

"I don't need it." He climbed over a tree and jumped to the top of the wall. He blew her a kiss. "Thank you for the kiss, my angel." Before disappearing on the other side, he waved at her, leaving her heart galloping after him.

She waited a few moments before walking around the house and entering through the back door. Her dress was wet, mud drops stained the hem of her skirt, and surely her cheeks were all flushed and scandalous. But she'd never felt better.

From the kitchen, she stepped into the corridor, avoiding the parlour, when Verity almost attacked her. She grabbed Maddie's shoulders and shoved her to the pantry among sausage chains and barrels of spices.

"He was naked," she said, her chest heaving.

"Shush." Maddie glanced around. "I noticed that."

"I want to marry him."

Maddie laughed. "No, you don't, silly. You love Ernest."

"Then you're going to marry Hector. You were kissing him." Her eyes lit with too much enthusiasm.

"Yes, well, it was the spur of the moment. Thank you for covering me. Mother would have had a fit."

"*I* had a fit." She fanned herself. "Good gracious. The kiss was so romantic and scandalous at the same time. The snow, the lack of clothes, the way he kissed you. I want to be kissed like that in the snow with Ernest naked. It's that or there won't be a wedding. And I thought I was the scandalous sister! Amateur. You're the real scandalous one."

"You? The scandalous one? What do you mean?"

"I want a naked kiss in the snow."

Maddie kissed her sister's heated cheek. "Nothing happened aside from the kiss."

Verity stared at her as if she'd been blasphemous. "That wasn't a simple kiss. Promise me you'll kiss him again."

That was an easy promise to make. "Oh, Verity. I will."

"I must talk to Ernest and tell him to get naked in the snow. I have to see him later for a piano concert. That's it! Only piano music would make a naked kiss in the snow perfect."

"Speaking of piano concerts, what did Annabelle mean when we were at the duke's?"

Verity's smile dropped. Her flushed cheeks lost their colour. "Oh, nothing. Don't mind her. I guess she referred to the secret code I told you about. She's such a tease."

"She seemed to imply something more serious."

A high-pitched laugh came out of Verity. "No, no. Anabelle opens her mouth and breathes. Don't pay attention to what she says. I have to go now." She went to leave.

"Verity." Maddie took her sister's trembling hand. "You know you can tell me anything, don't you? Did Annabelle do something to you?"

"Don't be silly. Oh, look at the time. I have to go." She rushed out of the pantry and down the corridor, leaving Maddie concerned for her.

If Annabelle had hurt Verity, Maddie would burn her.

twenty-two

BEING CIVILISED WASN'T difficult. Hector had concluded that piece of wisdom after his second week of taming, as Quentin called his training. All that was required of him was to stay silent as much as possible when in the company of other civilised people. When he was alone with Maddie, he could be himself, but with others, he avoided talking, moving too much, or even frowning when someone said something he disagreed with. Wonderful.

Sitting at the table in Dr. Landon's house, he sipped his tea and bit into a cream cake while the other guests talked about something he didn't care about. Mrs. Debenham and Quentin were present as well, taking small sips of their tea.

"I'm glad to see you healthy and well-rested, Lord Wentworth," Dr. Landon said, straightening his glasses to give him a clinical gaze.

"Being stranded on a deserted island must have been such an ordeal for you." Lord Captain Naylor, captain of the Fifth Northumberland Fusiliers, or maybe it was sixth, paused sipping his tea to focus on Hector with the same interest as a shooter aiming at his target.

Maddie gave Hector an encouraging nod. For a moment, her lips distracted him with the memory of the kiss they'd shared in the snow. Desire clawed its way out of his chest every time their gazes locked. Perhaps he was a savage indeed.

"It was." He found it more difficult to navigate society than to live on an island, but he kept the comment to himself.

A happy squeal broke the moment as Albert, Lord Naylor's son, ran around the room, laughing and putting in his mouth everything he found from a doily on a table to a pencil. Hector was reminded of himself on the island when he'd tried to understand what was edible and what wasn't. He enjoyed watching the child be free and happy, and to hell with rules. At least children could still do that. His smile froze when a young lady walked inside. She was the young lady he'd rescued from Quentin's unwanted attention.

"I apologise for my tardiness. I was busy..." She came to a grinding halt upon seeing him. Her lips parted in mute shock. She paled further when Quentin bowed his head to her.

If she worried he was going to blather about her misadventure, she was mistaken. Hector gave her the slightest shake of his head.

Lady Naylor waved the girl closer. "Don't stand there, darling."

The girl shuffled forwards, her gaze on the carpet. "Good afternoon." She bobbed an unsteady curtsy.

"Everyone." Lady Naylor pulled out a chair. "This is my daughter, Frances."

A round of introductions and greetings followed, to which Hector paid little attention. Albert was a far more interesting subject. He was now looking inside an empty vase with a fascinated expression. Hector guessed Albert might become a scientist one day.

"Albert, darling, stop tasting everything. You're too old for that." Lady Naylor blocked her son from doing another round and putting a saucer in his mouth.

Judging by how Quentin scowled, he didn't share Hector's enthusiasm about children's freedom. Instead, Maddie smiled. Every time she glanced his way and their gazes met, she'd blush. He wanted to kiss her again, feel her soft cheeks in his palms, and see how her skin tasted. He wanted her in his bed, sharing heat and secrets until they fell asleep.

Frances studied him from underneath her thick lashes. Her hand trembled when she picked up her cup of tea. At least Quentin behaved honourably, not mentioning his acquaintance with Frances. Although his behaviour was surely due to a sense of self-preservation rather than chivalry.

"Is it true you fought against savages who tried to kill you?" Mrs. Landon asked.

She resembled her husband in her appearance. They had the same rounded glasses, short nose, and constantly rosy cheeks.

"No." He savoured another oatcake. Delicious with a bit of butter. It was perfect.

Maddie raised her eyebrows, encouraging him to say more.

He cleared his throat. Answers that were too short or direct were frowned upon. "Not savages, but hominids belonging to a species of primates I know nothing about. Some specimens were over four feet tall and broad. Fierce opponents."

"It sounds frightening." Mrs. Landon offered him a pastry with custard and strawberries on top.

His mouth watered as he picked one.

"But Lord Wentworth is strong enough to fend off fierce opponents," Mrs. Debenham said. "Doesn't he look brawny?"

Frances blushed to the roots of her hair. "I believe you're right, ma'am," she said in a low voice.

Mr. Merriweather narrowed his keen gaze on her. Hector wouldn't be surprised if the clever solicitor suspected something.

Oh, strawberries. A perfect balance between sweetness and sharpness. Hector went to snatch another pastry and stuff his mouth but caught himself in time and selected one gently. He'd dreamt of such delicacies for years.

"You should write your story," Verity said.

"And Maddie would illustrate it," Mr. Merriweather added.

Why hadn't he thought about that before? "That's a wonderful idea."

Maddie didn't return his smile this time. "I'm not a professional artist."

"Your sketches are beautiful." When he took her hand under the table, she let out a small noise she covered with a cough. "I can describe to you the plants and animals I saw. It'd be a good way to let your name be known."

"I'm not sure." She sipped her tea.

Mrs. Landon selected a different type of pastry from the china plate. "What are you going to do, your grace, after Lord Hector becomes the duke?"

Silence dropped like a theatre curtain. Even Albert remained silent on his mother's lap. Mrs. Debenham smiled so widely he could see her back teeth.

Quentin seemed about to choke on his lemon pastry. He coughed into his closed fists and sipped before answering. "I'm afraid that day isn't close, ma'am."

"You'd never know." Mrs. Debenham lifted her cup as if in a toast.

Hector half closed his eyes as the velvety taste of the lemon pastry hit his tongue. The cream was perfect. Not too tangy, not too sweet.

"But Lord Wentworth isn't the savage everyone talks about." Mrs. Landon grinned. "I'm a little disappointed, if I may say so. I don't see why he wouldn't find a champion. Any peer would be happy to support him and..." She frowned at the pastry. "This lemon pastry is terrible."

Hector took another. Sweet and creamy, there was nothing wrong with it.

Mrs. Landon waved a hand, summoning the maid. "These aren't good enough. Take all these away. Horrible."

When the maid tried to take Hector's plate, he held it. "My pastry is fine."

Mrs. Landon huffed. "Nonsense. Too much lemon. That silly baker doesn't know his job. Please, Lord Wentworth, put it on the plate. My cook will serve you something else."

"I agree." Mrs. Debenham twitched her mouth. "Rather tangy."

"My pastry is good," he said through gritted teeth.

Mrs. Landon sniffed, her glasses slipping down her short nose. "I assure you, Lord Wentworth, you'll enjoy the other pastries more. These are going to the rubbish."

"What?" he said. "This is the most ridiculous thing I've ever heard!"

Maybe he overreacted, but why did they have to insist on taking the delicious pastry from him? It was like that time he'd fought the monkey over a large fruit. A battle had ensued, and the monkey had won. Except the monkeys had wanted to eat the fruit, not to throw it away.

"Lord Wentworth." Dr. Landon scowled in the same fashion as his wife did. "I beg you."

Albert watched him with childish admiration, or maybe fear. Frances flushed red again. Lord Captain Naylor pretended to find his cup of tea fascinating, and his wife clenched Albert as if worried Hector might hurt him. Everyone at the table fell silent. Even Verity and Mr. Merriweather showed matching, concerned expressions. Maddie was the only one who gave him her support by holding his hand under the table.

Rage cast a shadow over Hector's sight. "Do you know what it means to be starving? Having your stomach so empty it cramps? Fainting because you haven't eaten enough? These pastries are perfectly good, and you want to throw them away?" His voice rose. He wanted to upturn the table and smash that silly pink vase on the mantelpiece. He wanted to yell at the grey sky of London and tear his clothes apart—Maddie squeezed his hand.

"Perhaps you want to take a walk with me?" She stood up.

The gentlemen stood up as well. Mrs. Landon scowled, a hand on her chest. Dr. Landon shook his head. Mrs. Debenham's smug expression turned into one of worry. Quentin smiled, throwing his half-eaten pastry on the plate for the maid to take away.

"Yes." Hector scraped his chair back. "I want to take a walk."

The noise of the wooden legs scratching against the marble floor caused the guests to wince. Without waiting for a servant to escort him, he strode down the corridor and pushed the front door open. As he marched down the pavement, the coal-smelling air didn't improve his mood.

"Hector."

Quick footsteps pounded behind him. He screeched to a stop on the pavement.

Maddie reached him, breathless. "Goodness me. You're fast."

"I'm sorry." He couldn't meet her gaze.

"Don't worry. I caught you." She took his arm.

"I mean, I'm sorry for raising my voice." He stared at her small hand in the crook of his arm, feeling calmer.

"You had a valid point." She resumed walking with him. "I understand your frustration. Throwing food away is shameful, although I agree with Mrs. Landon. The pastries were too tangy." She pursed her lips in a tight 'O', puckering them. "I think my lips will never be normal again."

He laughed, releasing all the suppressed anger. "I didn't mind."

"Where are we going?"

"The park. I need to touch the trees." He shook his head. "Throwing away good food. I can't believe it. I dreamt of eating delicacies, cream, custard, butter, and strawberries. I forgot how they tasted. And people throw them away?"

"You're right to be outraged." She shifted closer to him. Her dark-green velvet dress matched her lovely eyes and exalted her figure. The more time he spent with her, the more her presence calmed him. "Did you spend many days in hunger?"

"Before I became an efficient berry gatherer, hunter, and fisherman, yes. Thanks to my knowledge of plants, I survived by eating fruit, but at first, I didn't trust my judgement, worried I might stumble upon a poisonous plant. There were species I didn't recognise. Only later did I start to eat more. The choice was between dying of starvation or of poison."

She closed her hands around his arm, her delicate eyebrows drawing closer. "I'm so sorry for all the suffering you had to endure."

"Still, I shouldn't have yelled, should I?"

"Alas. The duke will use today's incident to spread the rumour you are a savage, and Lady Naylor is one of the queen's court. She won't be generous towards you. She seemed frightened you might kill us all. Did you see how she clutched her son? And even Frances looked terrified."

He inched closer. "I didn't tell you something that happened a while ago. One night, a helped a young woman getting away from a rather drunk Quentin. She was terrified by him, her dress torn. Frances is the young lady I found in Quentin's bedroom."

"Goodness me." She placed a hand on her chest, coming to a stop.

"I thought about using the incident to convince Quentin to renounce the title, but exposing him means exposing her."

"She'd be ruined forever."

He raked a hand through his hair. "Yes."

His chest rose more easily once they entered Hyde Park. Finally, a piece of nature. The park was too well kept, the bushes too neatly trimmed, and the path too clean to be similar to the wild nature he needed, but it was better than being surrounded by bricks and metal. Even the snow had been set aside and piled up at the border. It was a shame he couldn't crunch it with his feet.

The weight of what he'd done weighed down his shoulders. He hated having disappointed Maddie, and the more beastly he behaved, the less those workers would be paid. Honestly, he should control himself.

"Hector, don't be sad." She rested her head against his shoulder. "You didn't ruin anything."

"I have responsibilities, and responsibilities are the meaning of life."

"What do you mean?"

He paused under a majestic, sweet chestnut tree. The branches were bare but formed an intricate pattern overhead he found soothing. "A father would tell you his children give meaning to his life. A doctor would tell you his patients are the reason he wakes up every morning. When we care about someone else, that responsibility becomes the meaning of our lives."

"That's very noble, but those workers...they aren't the only meaning of your life." She closed her eyes for a moment. "I didn't mean it in a bad way. They do matter, but you have a life. Your responsibility as a duke is a part of it. There are other things in your life you'll enjoy and that aren't responsibilities. You love nature. You enjoy walking in a forest. One day, you might find a wife, too," she said the last words in a whisper.

A wife? He'd already found one. He caressed her cheek. Every time he touched her, even with a small caress, a fire started in his abdomen. He wanted to remove the layers of clothes between them and hold her, just hold her, to feel their naked bodies touch.

She leant against his hand. Should he propose again? The last time he'd done it, it hadn't ended well at all, and he didn't want to hound her. He wanted her to be happy with him first, to know him for the man he was now. A man she might not like. Not as her husband, anyway.

He dipped his head, inhaling her lavender scent. She drew in a breath and parted her plush lips.

He wanted to be gentle, to taste her lips slowly and not scare her with his passion. But as soon as he brushed his lips against hers, the fire that always lurked inside him flared up. He thrust his tongue into her welcoming mouth and explored every corner, licking and sucking at her plush bottom lip. She tasted of tea and cream and something else sweet belonging to her. He pressed her against him, holding her with one hand on her nape and the other on her waist. She moaned, and the soft sound was like a stroke of her hand over his aching shaft. He moved his hand up from her waist to the underside of her breast. How he wished to feel its fullness in his palm, tweak the rosy peak, and hear her moan louder.

"You should thank me for interrupting you." Quentin's voice intruded on Hector's heated thoughts with the same sweetness as a cold blade slipping between his ribs.

He stopped kissing Maddie but didn't let her go.

"Your grace." Maddie brushed a lock of her hair behind her ear.

Crimson blossomed in her cheeks, turning her lips, swollen by his hard kiss, even redder. With effort, he controlled himself and didn't dip his head to take those tempting lips again and beg her to marry him.

Quentin stood stiffly. His tall hat cast a shadow over his serious face. "You behaved in a beastly fashion to Mrs. Landon, Hector." He shook his head as if in disapproval, but the smirk quirking up a corner of his mouth belied his inner triumph. "And now you're causing scandal by kissing a lady in broad daylight in the middle of Hyde Park. It's a miracle no one spotted you. The Savage Duke spoiling a maiden. You'd make the front page."

"You're one to talk," Hector said.

Quentin quirked up his eyebrow. "By all means, go ahead. Tell everyone who Frances is. Her parents, friends, and the entire ton would be thrilled to know her little secret."

It was amazing how quickly anger could spread through Hector. A moment ago, he'd felt only bliss with Maddie in his arms. Now he wanted to punch his cousin.

"You're a disgrace for our family."

"Tosh." Quentin shrugged. "Instead, you should care about Mrs. Landon and Lady Naylor."

"We'll present our apologies to Mrs. Landon." Maddie tilted her chin up. "As for what you saw, there was no spoiling."

Quentin whipped his head in her direction as if realising just then she was there. "I fail to understand why you include yourself in my cousin's predicament. He's the one under scrutiny and has just proved to be the savage everyone fears he is." He raked a slow glance over her. A glance Hector didn't like. "You must have fallen for the charm of having a tryst with a savage, a forbidden fruit, because this dalliance with him will only be your downfall."

She stepped away from Hector's embrace, which he liked even less. "I believe Hector would be an excellent duke, and I beg you to stop talking about him as if he weren't here."

"He never speaks much," Quentin said, "aside from insulting people. Thus, he deserves society's scorn." He touched the rim of his hat. "I'm afraid I'll have to take some unpleasant actions, Hector." He turned to leave but paused. "Unpleasant for you, obviously."

twenty-three

MADDIE FOUGHT THE urge to cry. It was her fault if Hector found himself in this horrible situation. The fact he didn't seem affected by the devastating news Ernest had delivered them made her more anxious. She opened and closed her hands on her lap, wishing to keep them busy with a pencil so as not to think.

"There must be something we can do." Her voice sounded high-pitched to her own ears.

Ernest rubbed his forehead. A few documents were spread in front of him on the low table in her drawing room. "I'm afraid legally Bkackburn has every right to request a medical assessment of Lord Hector's mental abilities. His solicitor rejected my petition to divert the title to Lord Hector and replied with this request."

"But he isn't insane," she said, closing her fists. "Hector is the sanest person I've ever met."

Hector placed his hand over hers and squeezed it gently. "I'm not afraid of this assessment. Any doctor would realise I'm not a danger."

Ernest shifted in his seat with a nervous twitch Maddie didn't like. "Lord Hector—" Ernest paused, which she didn't like. He was a man with a direct manner, never stalling. "I'd like to say the doctors in Harley Street are all well intentioned and professional. Unfortunately, that's not the case. Blackburn has led a..." He glanced at Maddie. "Shall we say a licentious life? He enjoys every illicit pleasure London has to offer. He is discreet, but rumours spread. I don't dabble in gossip. Yet I've heard of Blackburn's habits and licentious company." He paused to take a sip of water. "The duke cannot lead such a hidden, dissolute life without the support of other prominent figures in London's society. To put it bluntly, Blackburn wouldn't have to look far to find a doctor willing to produce a document containing blatant lies on your health."

Hector's hand stiffened on hers. "He wouldn't go that far."

Maddie trapped her quivering bottom lip between her teeth. He was so trusting of others he had no idea what people like the duke were capable of. "The duke needs to keep his money and title," she said. "I believe he'd be desperate enough to do everything in his power to keep his life unchanged." Lord, what would she do if Hector was locked up in a mental institution? He'd never come out. "What can we do?"

"Legally, ask for a second medical opinion in case the duke's physician gives an unfavourable diagnosis." Ernest gathered the documents, the gesture lacking confidence. "Socially, I'd strongly suggest you show yourself at as many social events as you can to quell any rumours about the Savage Duke." He paused to gaze up at Hector. There was no hint of the caring and attentive man he was with Verity. His hard expression held only ruthlessness. "And I strongly advise you to behave flawlessly. As for. Blackburn, it would best if you kept an eye on him and pretended everything is fine."

"Is that all?" Maddie asked.

He cleared his throat. "There might be something else."

"Yes?" Maddie prompted.

Ernest took his time before continuing, straightening the

documents. "Miss Frances Naylor. I guess she's the young woman Hector saw with his cousin."

Maddie froze. "How do you know about Frances?"

Ernest scratched the back of his neck. "You told Verity. She told me. Don't be angry with your sister," he added quickly. "She was concerned about the girl and asked me if there was a legal way to help her."

"I won't use Frances against my cousin." Hector shook his head. "Quentin would destroy her reputation."

"But there is the possibility that if Blackburn fears you might reveal what happened with Miss Frances, he will withdraw his request. We can protect Miss Frances's reputation," Ernest said.

"No, it's too risky."

Maddie's admiration for him only grew. He was ready to face a false accusation rather than let Frances be ruined. But still... "You'd save dozens of families."

"Good point," Ernest said. "As unfortunate as Frances's situation might be, the lives of the workers will be saved."

Hector pressed his lips. "Sacrifice Frances for the workers? I'm not sure I can do that."

Maddie understood his desire to do good. "But, Hector—"

"No." His voice hardened. "We'll find another way."

Ernest cradled his chin. "Then I don't have any other ideas for now." He rose, his shoulders hunched. "I'll do everything in my power to further your cause."

Hector rose as well and shook Ernest's hand with energy. "And I'll do everything in my power to behave properly."

The two men grinned at each other.

"I'll visit Verity shortly, then I'll have to write a counter reply to the duke's solicitor." He bowed his head, and after a brief exchange of nods, Ernest left.

The moment he stepped out of the room, Maddie shot to her feet and paced. What had made her believe she could have helped Hector? She'd made the situation worse.

"This is terrible." She wrung her hands.

Anxiety was tightening a knot in her stomach. Perhaps, if they found a way to protect Frances as Ernest had said, they might convince the duke to leave his title. But again, the duke might not care about exposure. No, Hector was right; using Frances would be vile.

It was horrible enough that Hector was deprived of his right to the dukedom and that those poor labourers were condemned to work in horrible conditions, without the added fear that Hector could be trapped in a mental institution. She'd heard horrible stories of those hospitals. If that happened, then she'd find a way to help him escape. She could hire one of those highwaymen who— Hector taking her hand interrupted her sad train of thought.

"You don't have to worry," he said, rubbing her knuckles with his thumb.

"How can I not? Your cousin is a duke and a well-connected one. He could harm you, have you locked up somewhere, even in prison."

Hector trailed his fingers up her arm, starting the usual tingle in her body his touch triggered. "If he has me locked up, I'll escape. I lived on a deserted island for years. I'm sure I can survive in the English countryside if necessary."

"Surviving doesn't mean living. After all you've been through, you should take back what's rightfully yours." She heaved a sigh, but she wasn't sure if it came from her fear for him or from his wandering fingers caressing her neck.

"I promise I'll be more careful and control my anger. What happened in Mrs. Landon's house wasn't your fault. It was mine. All mine. I learnt my lesson. I won't do it again. I want to help the workers who have served my family for years. And I want you to be proud of me."

"I already am." Shock crept into her voice. How could he think she wasn't proud of who he was?

He tangled his fingers through her hair, toying with a long

tendril. "Then I want to dispel your fear of me. I want you to trust me completely." He ran his fingers over the curve of her cheek and neck, making it difficult for her to think. "And I want to kiss you."

"You can kiss me anytime you want," she said breathlessly. "As long as we're alone, that is." She rose on her tiptoes and pressed a kiss to his lips.

He kissed her back, but not with his usual hunger. When she withdrew, he sucked in a breath.

"What is it?" she asked.

"I want to kiss you here." He inched his hand lower over her collarbone, breast, hip, to stop between her legs. "When we kiss, you always squeeze your legs together, and I want to see what happens if I kiss you here."

The shock of his honesty robbed her of words for a moment. What was she supposed to reply to at a request like that? Her lips parted, but not a sound came out. Although wetness pooled between her legs at the thought of his soft, warm lips on her aching core.

She wasn't an expert, but she knew his lips and tongue would soothe the throb tormenting her every time he touched her. Just feeling the weight of his hand through the layers of her petticoats and skirt caused the illicit pulse to pound harder. Everywhere. Her whole body came alive with sensation.

He removed his hand and stepped away. "I must apologise. It seems my request was too bold and inappropriate."

"No!" she nearly shouted.

She clutched his retreating hand by pure instinct without having made the conscious choice to move. She licked her suddenly dry lips as she pondered once again if she was making the right decision. But good heaven, she wanted to experience all the sinful sensations his lips had to offer, and she couldn't imagine a better man to share such intimacies with. Hector wouldn't judge or scorn her. He wouldn't gossip about her wanton behaviour at a gentlemen's club like too many men. He wouldn't discard her afterwards. So, she did the only sensible thing her body and mind told her to do.

She took his hand. "Not in this room. Anyone could see us." She peeped in the hallway.

The noise of pots and pans came from the kitchen while her mother's voice sounded from the parlour. On her tiptoes, Maddie led Hector up the stairs, her pulse thudding in her ears. Only a few feet from her bedroom. Anticipation itched along her body. She gasped when a door opened.

Verity stepped out of her bedroom and skidded to a halt. She took them in, and a smile curled up her lips. Tilting her head to the opposite side, pretending to haven't seen them, she went down the stairs.

Maddie smiled. She loved her sister. She exhaled when she finally locked the door to her bedroom, Hector at her side.

"Look at your face." He cupped her cheeks. "All flushed. But it's worry, not pleasure."

"It's a little exciting as well." She leant into his touch.

"May I kiss you now?" His voice sounded low and husky.

She placed his hand where it'd been a moment ago, right where she ached the most. His eyes lit up with enough raw desire to knock her off her feet.

"I want it as well," she whispered the words about to seal her fate as a woman and a lady of London's society.

His fingers seemed to burn her skin through the fabric of her skirts as he dipped his head to kiss her lips. He took her mouth without hesitation, conquering it with a few lashes of his tongue. She was losing herself in the ardent kiss when he lifted her by the waist. She grabbed his shoulders for balance and gasped when he laid her on the thick rug next to the four-poster bed.

He loomed over her, stroking her cheek and neck. "I can't believe you let me kiss you."

She couldn't believe how beautiful his hungry gaze on her made her feel. He dragged a hand down her body, pausing over her aching breast to rub her nipple through the fabric of her white shirt.

"Next time, I'll kiss you here," he said before kissing her breast.

She already wheezed, her muscles tensing with anticipation and her drawers getting soaked with desire. He gently spread her legs and nestled between them. He was so broad that he made her feel even more petite than she was. When he bunched up her skirt and petticoats, she held her breath, waiting for his reaction.

He drank in the sight of her, awed. He caressed her leg reverently. Even through her silk stockings, his calloused fingers teased her skin.

He pushed the skirt further up and revealed the silk garters at her thighs. Up again, and her drawers were fully exposed. He paused, crouched between her legs, and admired his work.

Her chest rose and fell quickly as he bent her knees and pushed her thighs wider apart. The fabric of her skirt and petticoats frothed at her waist, leaving her silk drawers fully uncovered. The slit at their opening parted when he spread her legs. Cool air hit her tender flesh currently hot and wet. She should be ashamed of being so exposed to a man, but instead, she ached to feel his lips, fingers, anything on her core.

He took his time though, running his large hands over her calves and thighs, and toying with the garters. He kissed her knee before stroking her thigh again, leaving behind a trail of goosebumps on her skin.

"Your scent is delicious," he whispered against her inner thigh.

She couldn't say anything because, if she opened her mouth, only moans would come out. She gasped when he pulled apart the opening of her drawers and stared at her for a long minute. The more he stared, the wetter she became.

Yet he didn't touch her. He tilted his head and widened his eyes but didn't kiss or touch her. She was one breath away from begging him to do something. Anything. But she didn't need to wait long. He stroked her wet folds, causing her to jolt. Her hips jerked up as he caressed her intimately with gentle fingers.

"You're so beautiful." His thumb brushed against her throbbing nub, and she had to bite into her bottom lip not to scream in pleasure. "Especially now. You're all flushed and pretty. Everywhere." He spread her wetness over her folds and nub, gently touching her entrance. "I could watch you for hours, study every single inch of your skin."

He pinched her nub lightly, but the moan escaping her was nothing but wild. He slid a finger inside her, and no amount of reading scandalous novels, anatomy books, or indecent chats with other women had prepared her for the onslaught of sheer pleasure overwhelming her. The intrusion was both strange and delicious, powerful and not enough. The fact he kept watching her and his finger inside her only drove her mad with need. He stroked her deeply, brushing her little bud of nerves with his thumb. She was all sensation and pleasure. Never could she have imagined how powerful his touch could be.

"I'm going to kiss you now."

"Yes, please." She begged, and she didn't care.

Her body was on fire, her core was wet, and the throb tormented her. Only he could soothe the ache.

She held her breath as he lowered his head. Closer, closer to where she wanted him. She was going to burst like a star out of sheer anticipation.

The first blow of his warm breath on her heated, tender flesh tore another moan from her. Her hips jolted when he finally kissed her. Oh, the heat. She'd never experienced such intense, all-consuming heat.

His tongue was gentle on her, stroking and lapping at her, but the result was a devastating wave of ecstasy she quickly became addicted to. She now understood why people sought carnal pleasure with obsession. The feeling was intoxicating. Although she couldn't imagine receiving the same pleasure from anyone else but Hector.

He used his fingers, tongue, and lips, tasting her deeply. She moaned and clawed the rug with her fingernails as he slipped a second finger inside her while using his tongue on her nub. The strokes of his tongue were both slow and delicate, but now and then, he'd make her feel the pull of his lips by sucking at her. It was so wrong, but it felt so right. He slid his fingers deeper, touching places inside her she had no idea existed.

As he licked and suckled at her, a restless feeling grew within her, starting from the spot he tormented with his tongue. It spread from her core to her chest and head, making her moan and writhe until delicious spasms took hold of her.

She couldn't stay quiet any longer and released a liberating scream she muffled with her hand. He didn't stop. His merciless tongue and lips kept lapping at her, and his deft fingers slipped deeper, stroking secret spots she wasn't aware could produce so much pleasure. Even his teeth grazed her most sensitive skin, scattering shivers throughout her body. Too much pleasure, yet she wanted more. She pushed her hips towards him, arching her back.

He licked her and moved his fingers until a new wave of energy built up and another release burst out of her. The second one was more devastating than the first, leaving her boneless and exhausted. She had to muffle another liberating scream. Never would she have believed that such pleasure was physically possible. She was surprised her body didn't float away with the pleasure.

She lay on the rug, her eyelids so heavy as he lifted his head from her core. He pulled down her skirt and arranged it around her legs, but if he did a poor job, she wouldn't know or care. How could she return to her normal life after this moment? How could she be a functional human being after being torn apart?

He stretched next to her and brushed her flaming cheek. "I gather you enjoyed it."

Only a muffled, undefined noise came out of her. She didn't even know what she meant to say with it. Was it a laugh or a snort?

"Will you let me touch and kiss you again?" His eyebrows pulled together as if he were worried she might say no. Ha! He had no idea.

She swallowed and struggled to emerge from her state of bliss. "Any time you want."

He smiled so widely a dimple appeared on his cheek.

"But on one condition," she added, touching his chin.

"Anything."

"You'll let me do the same to you." After today, she was curious to watch him becoming undone by her kisses. Everywhere.

She wanted to explore his body as well, touch his taut muscles, and hear him shout in pleasure. To her surprise, he flushed to the roots of his hair. He'd undressed in front of her and stood in the snow stark naked while being aroused, yet he blushed now.

"Are you embarrassed by my proposition?" she asked, worried she might offend him.

"I'm not sure you will like it." He licked his lips, capturing a few drops of her wetness.

The tingle started all over again, threatening to consume her.

"That's not possible." She caressed his golden hair. "I want to make you feel what I feel."

"My skin isn't as soft or pleasant to the touch as yours."

"Let me decide that." Now she couldn't wait to taste him.

She touched his chest and slipped her hand under his waistcoat —he finally wore one. His skin gave off enough heat to warm her hand. He stilled, and his lips parted in what seemed to be shock. She paused.

"Does my touch bother you?" She wasn't an experienced lover, so the possibility she already did something wrong was real.

"No. Quite the opposite. It's very intense."

"I want to touch your skin." She barely finished saying it

before he unbuttoned his waistcoat and shirt, revealing his golden torso.

She disagreed. His skin felt soft and silky under her fingers. She touched his hard pectorals, the defined ridges of his abdominal muscles, and the tendons in his neck.

Each inch of him revealed a little secret about his life on the island, the hardship he'd endured, the long hours in the sun, and the fight for his survival. He closed his eyes and groaned deep in his throat as she explored him both with a lover's fascination and an artist's interest. The hard ridge straining beneath the flap of his breeches caught her eyes, and curiosity won. She unfastened the opening, pouting when she realised it wasn't a quick task. Lord, so many buttons. She'd never paid attention to a man's breeches. Her breath hitched when his hard, thick shaft came out. Goodness. She'd already seen it, but the sight triggered a new flush through her. He was thick with a glistening drop on the blunt head. How could it fit inside her? Just the thought shot another wave of pleasure to her core.

"Maddie." He propped himself up on his elbows, reddening furiously. "I apologise."

"For what?" It was with effort that she averted her gaze from his inviting length to his face.

"I know it's...I can't stop it. When you're close, I feel my body tensing." He spoke faster. "If it offends you—"

"Offend me?"

"I might have forgotten much, but I do remember Robert commenting on the fact a gentleman should hide his physical reaction to a lady. He said it was the most vulgar thing a gentleman could do."

"Poppycock." Right. She should have chosen another word. "He was partially right. When in the company of other ladies and gentlemen, you should follow Robert's advice, but it's only you and me now, and I want to see you."

He reddened further. Gosh, he looked adorable. She closed her hand around him in reply.

He jolted and closed his eyes again as a guttural noise came out of his throat. A curse escaped him, but she wasn't shocked. Quite the opposite. She stroked him and caressed his smooth tip with her thumb. The effect on him shocked her. He clenched his fists tightly at his sides as if in pain, his whole body tensing. She worked his length gently, memorising the feel of him in her hand, the hard muscles, and the silky skin. A pearly drop appeared on the tip, and she spread it around, noticing how his shaft twitched and swelled under her hand.

He panted now, utterly beautiful with his flushed cheeks, parted lips. He was at her mercy, and she shouldn't find it so heady. She moved her hand faster, and the rhythm of his breathing matched that of her hand. Spasms caught him as his muscles tightened and he spilled in her palm. She watched fascinated as his release came out in thick ribbons and wondered how it'd feel inside her or in her mouth. How she wished to capture his moment in a painting, his expression of ecstasy.

"I'm sorry." He sat bolt upright, producing a handkerchief from his pocket. "I'm sorry." He wiped her hand clean while avoiding her gaze.

"Don't apologise."

He shook his head.

"Hector, please look at me."

He did as he was told while wiping her fingers.

"You don't have to apologise. It was wonderful. I loved every moment of it." She caressed his cheek with her free hand. "I liked it. Why are you so bold when it's you who touches me and so shy when it's my turn?"

He drew in a shaky breath. "Because I can't believe you like me as much as I like you."

His usual honesty caused her heart to clench.

"Let's dispel any doubts then, once and for all. I like you. I like touching you, and I want more. So much more. I want you, Hector. You. No one else. I want to feel you inside me and give you as much pleasure as possible. Will you share this journey with me? Will you let me be with you?"

He hugged her so quickly and with such strength she was shoved back. His strong arms wrapped around her and held her tightly. She hugged him back and rested her head on his chest.

Yes, she wanted so much more.

twenty-four

HECTOR COULDN'T THINK, breathe, or move without thinking of Maddie.

He'd tasted her only once, but her scent and the feeling of her soft skin would forever be imprinted in his memory. Too many emotions overwhelmed him from his desire to be alone with her again to his sense of duty and worry about his family's legacy. It was out of sheer determination he attended an afternoon tea at the Serpentine that day just because he'd promised Ernest he'd do his best to fight Quentin's allegations.

As he sat at a table surrounded—thank goodness—by trees, his cock twitched when the vision of Maddie touching him flashed unbidden across his mind. Yes, Robert had been right about gentlemen's reactions being the worst affair possible. Hector couldn't find a comfortable position and was terrified that one of the other attendees might see what happened in his breeches. If it weren't for his intimate discomfort, he would appreciate the sunny corner of Hyde Park where they had luncheon. Tall sycamores and Scottish pine trees waved their branches in the breeze, carrying the fresh scent of moss. Ladies promenaded along the path, twirling their parasols. The view was lovely but for Mrs. Landon, who hadn't yet forgiven him for his outburst, judging by the way she ignored him.

Maddie sat next to him, laughing about something Verity had said, but he'd be damned if he followed the conversation. Maddie's laughter was too distracting on top of everything else. Quentin and Annabelle chatted at the other side of the table, but he didn't pay attention to them either. Ernest had insisted that keeping a civil relationship with Quentin and his peers would make things easier for him. He wasn't sure. Mrs. Landon looked like she wanted to stab him with her parasol.

The winter frost had left room for an unseasonable warmth. Saint Martin's summer, they called it. The ice had melted on the Serpentine, and the gentle breeze caused the water to quiver. He fiddled with his teaspoon but perked up when Ernest mentioned the unrest in the streets due to new protest marches. Even Maddie stopped chatting with Verity and turned towards Ernest.

"The reasons for the protests are always the same. The labourers demand better wages, better work conditions, and more hours of rest," Ernest said. "If we don't do something, we're going to face a revolution, mark my words."

"If we yield to their absurd requests, they'll demand more privileges until they want to be paid without doing any work," Quentin said. "Then we'd face a more disturbing revolution."

Annabelle nodded seriously as if Quentin had said something wise.

"The parliament repeatedly failed to keep its promise to the Irish," Ernest said in a hard tone. "The majority of workers in our factories are Irish. Conceding to their demands wouldn't be a sign of weakness, but of wisdom and human compassion. A massive riot is brewing, and the whole kingdom will plunge into a financial depression if we don't intervene."

"A riot is always brewing when the Irish are involved." Quentin sounded harsh. "Lazy and whiny. That's what they are."

"Honest people who know the meaning of hard work and an empty stomach," Ernest said, baring his teeth.

The others fell silent, turning their heads right and left between Quentin and Ernest like at a tennis match.

"The empire will go to the dogs with your compassionate philosophy." Quentin shook his head. "We should preserve the establishment of the British Empire because it guarantees order."

Ernest thumped a fist against the table. "This isn't order, but slavery."

Quentin propped his elbow on the table. "You're just like the other Irish."

Ernest opened his mouth but was cut off by Annabelle. "Enough talking about politics." She waved a hand. "This beautiful weather will not last. Soon the cold will return, and I have no intention of wasting time discussing boring subjects with you. I want to take a boat across the Serpentine. What do you think, Verity?"

"Yes." Verity shoved up to her feet so quickly her napkin dropped to the ground, avoiding Annabelle's gaze. "It's a wonderful idea. Shall we go?"

"A boat trip?" Ernest wrinkled his nose.

"Why not, darling?" Verity took his hand.

"Not for me." Mrs. Landon opened her parasol. "I'm prefer to stay here on firm ground."

The gentlemen rose as well. Hector was a moment late. Sailing? He wasn't sure he wanted to. He'd had his share of sailing, thank you.

It took a matter of minutes for Ernest to organise the tour, urged by Verity's impatience. Too quickly for Hector's liking, but the ladies were excited about the idea of sailing across the Serpentine.

Maddie beamed, her cheeks glowing, and watched the sunlight glinting off the calm water. "What a wonderful idea."

He hated being a spoilsport. He scrubbed the back of his neck as an itch started there. Perhaps he should stay with Mrs. Landon. No, she'd probably murder him.

"I've never been on a boat on the Serpentine." Maddie clung to his arm. "It should be fun."

Not really. He conjured up a smile for her sake only because he didn't share her enthusiasm.

Amidst laughter and squeals of delight from the others, he sat on the boat with Maddie, Ernest, and Verity while Quentin and Annabelle took another boat. He suppressed a groan as the boat rocked right and left after Ernest dropped himself onto the bench. Maddie and Verity laughed, and Ernest made the boat roll again on purpose. Hector's chest tightened. He almost lost his grip on the oars.

"The duke's boat is going faster than ours." Maddie pointed at the other boat cutting smoothly along the Serpentine.

"His boat is lighter." Verity shrugged. "But I don't care. I want to enjoy the view. Isn't it lovely, Lord Wentworth?"

Hector gave a curt nod, too focused on the water's movements to speak. The rhythmic sound of the oars dipping in and out of the water triggered a buzz in his ears. There had been a time when he'd found the patter or slosh of the water soothing. Not anymore. Snow was great, but anything water related sent goosebumps down his back.

For a moment, the dark water of the Serpentine turned into the blue sea around the island. The vision disappeared as soon as he blinked.

"Is something the matter?" Maddie touched his arm. Not even her touch could calm the odd pricking on the back of his neck.

"I'm all right." But he wasn't. Something, a sharp sensation he couldn't define, burned at the back of his throat.

He and Ernest rowed the boat deeper into the lake where a few slabs of ice floated. If he weren't so anxious, he'd appreciate the weeping willows, oak trees, and evergreen bushes around the lake. Even without leaves, the trees formed a thick wall around the shores. One could almost believe to be somewhere else wilder than London. It was ironic that he'd searched for such a spot for weeks, only to find it now when he didn't need it.

"I want to go faster than Blachburn," Ernest said, clenching his teeth. "So, the Irish are whiny and lazy? I'll show him."

"Oh, please, don't." Verity huffed. "I don't want a competition. Can't we simply enjoy the warm day and forget about the duke?"

"No. The way he treated Hector was despicable." Ernest rowed harder, and Hector had to match his strength. "And he insulted my people."

"He's despicable to everyone," Maddie said. "Don't take it personally."

"It is personal." Ernest nodded. "One more reason to row faster."

The boat rolled. Maddie and Verity laughed, but Hector's stomach clenched with a cold feeling. Rising anxiety caused him to breathe harder and his sight to become blurred. He was on a boat, not on the raft. He was in London, not on the island...he blinked. The view changed. Tall waves threatened to devour him.

No, he wasn't in London. It'd all been a lie, a cruel dream. He'd never been rescued. He was still on the raft at the mercy of the sea. Or lack thereof. The waves would swallow him. The wind hissed in his ears. Salty water stung his lips. The scent of the sea choked him. He'd sink into the bottom of the ocean. He'd drown. He'd never see England again. He couldn't fight the waves. They were too big for him. All he could do was grab the raft and hope the sea wouldn't kill him. His supply of fresh water and food ran low. If the sea didn't kill him, he'd die of starvation. He was tired of holding on and hoping to be found. He was exhausted. The sea would eat him alive.

"I don't want to die," he whispered or maybe shouted.

Something touched him, but he swatted the thing away. He needed to leave the raft. He shouldn't be here. He stood up. The raft rocked with the strength of the waves. Someone screamed. Hands touched him. Then a face swept into view and became sharp as he focused. Maddie. What was she doing on the raft?

"Hector?" Her voice sounded distant and muffled. "Stop moving."

Another dream? No, he couldn't stop. He had to move. The sea was going to get him and—icy cold water shocked him. Splashes and the sound of bodies diving resounded around him. He blinked as the wave of panic receded, leaving him shaking. The raft disappeared, and his memory returned. He was in London, taking a trip across the Serpentine. He'd been rescued. It was real. Maddie had found him.

The boat had capsized, likely his fault, and Maddie, Verity, and Ernest struggled to keep their heads above the water.

"Help them! They can't swim. Their skirts drag them down!" Ernest held Verity up while trying to undress her. "Maddie. Help her! Go, Hector!"

Ernest's words shocked him into action. Maddie tried to grip the upturned hull, but between the freezing cold and her heavy clothes, she slipped down, swallowing water. He swam towards her and coiled an arm around her waist. She gurgled and sputtered as she grabbed him for dear life. Her fingers dug into his shoulders and pushed him down. Even though he was a strong swimmer, between the icy water freezing his lungs and her hands shoving him down, he could barely keep himself and her afloat.

"Maddie, loosen your grip, or we'll both go down," he said, controlling his voice.

She stopped struggling, paling. Hell. He'd hurt her and put her in danger again.

"That's it. Stay still. Trust me." *Trust me.* He was such a hypocrite. He didn't deserve her trust.

His heart broke when she obeyed him and snuggled closer to him. She shivered but remained still when he unfastened her petticoats, yanking at the strings hard enough to rip them. Holding her, he swam towards the shore where Quentin, his friends, and other people had gathered. He reached the shore before Ernest did and laid Maddie on the grass. She trembled so hard her teeth chattered. She was so pale.

"Maddie." He cupped her cold cheek and checked her eyes that showed too much white. "Take deep breaths."

"You idiot." Quentin shoved him, pulling him away from Maddie. "What was all that about? The shouting, the madness? You caused the boat to capsize, you cur."

He couldn't say anything. Maddie was everything that mattered to him.

Mrs. Landon shook her head. Annabelle was as pale as Maddie, and the people gathered on the shore muttered, shooting sideways glances at him.

"To the receiving house. Quick." Dripping water, Ernest gathered a shivering Verity in his arms and headed to the house at the end of the path.

Quentin moved to haul Maddie up, but Hector would have none of that. Maddie was his responsibility.

"Don't touch her," he gritted out.

Quentin held up his hands. "I'm sure she's perfectly safe with you."

Curse him to hell. Hector picked her up and marched towards the house. Maybe it was the cold, but an odd numbness descended upon him. A numbness that aimed at his emotions. Had he really risked killing his friends by behaving like a man possessed? He'd almost killed his angel. Maddie clenched his drenched jacket with stiff fingers. Her wet hair was plastered to her pale face. Too pale. A blue tint coloured her quivering lips. The sound of her raspy breath was like a stab to his chest.

"Help!" Ernest shouted, stomping inside the house. "We need help. Two women fell in the lake."

A flurry of activities started. Nurses and doctors gathered

around them, providing blankets and comforting words, but Hector had eyes only for Maddie.

"To the examination room." A nurse opened the door to a white room smelling of carbolic acid.

Staggering, Hector laid Maddie on a narrow bed and brushed a wet strand of hair from her face. "I'm so sorry."

Her lips trembled. If she tried to say something, he wouldn't know.

"Please wait outside, sir." The nurse waved him out as Ernest placed Verity down on the bed next to Maddie.

Hector didn't move.

"Let's go." Ernest grabbed his arm and dragged him out of the room.

On trembling legs, Hector sat in the waiting room, his stare on the door behind which lay Maddie.

Another nurse handed him a blanket and a hot mug of tea he took on reflex. He was so focused on the door he didn't even thank the woman. A nurse walked in and out of the room a few times, but aside from that, nothing else happened.

As if the warmth from the tea thawed not only his fingers but his feelings as well, his emotions returned with a vengeance, and they weren't pleasant. Shame and anger at himself soured his mouth. Worry churned his stomach. Tears welled in his eyes. He'd behaved like an idiot, believing he was on the raft again.

"I'm so sorry," he said to Ernest. "I don't know what possessed me. The water...it upset me."

Shivering in his blanket, Ernest stretched out a trembling hand to take his arm. His thick brown eyebrows were pulled together in a fierce expression. "I don't know what happened to you on the boat, but I don't want to see it ever again. You must promise you'll do everything in your power to avoid a repeat of today and control yourself." His fingers tightened around Hector's arm. "I can't lose Verity. She's the love of my life. I like you, Hector, but if you put

my bride in danger again, I swear I'm going to see you at dawn."
He was serious. His voice didn't waver.

Hector couldn't blame him. He felt the same way towards
Maddie. He ran a hand through his wet hair. "I didn't mean for
any of this to happen. I had no idea that being on a boat would
make me behave that way, but I assure you I won't endanger
Maddie's or Verity's life ever again."

"Tell me what you thought on the boat." Ernest's tone didn't
lack kindness, but there was a tightness Hector couldn't ignore or
blame.

"I believed I hadn't been rescued. I thought I'd had a nightmare and that I was still alone. I didn't see the Serpentine or you,
Maddie, and Verity, but only waves. I was so scared..." His hands
shook so hard the mug fell from his fingers and shattered on the
floor.

He crouched and collected the fragments despite his quivering
fingers. Ernest helped him. They worked in silence, cleaning the
floor from the spilt tea. He wiped the tears from his face, not sure
if he cried for his fears or for having almost lost Maddie.

Ernest put a hand on his shoulder, jolting him. "I'm not a
physician, but the problem is here." He put a finger on Hector's
temple. "Not here." He touched Hector's chest. "That's why I'm
worried."

So was Hector.

"I know you wouldn't hurt Verity and Maddie." Ernest's
expression softened only for a moment. "But you must collect
yourself and master your fears, or someone will get hurt."

Hector could only nod. He'd promised to make amends. He
had to keep that promise.

twenty-five

T HE FIRST THING Maddie was going to do once she recovered completely from her ordeal would be to learn how to swim.

She'd become a swimming champion. She'd learn to swim forwards, backwards, and whatever else people who swam did. Never again did she want to experience the absolutely frightening sensation of being dragged down and suffocating while freezing water flooded her nostrils and mouth. And next time she went to Hyde Park, she'd wear only one layer of petticoats. Sod fashion. Her clothes had been so heavy she'd barely kept her nose above the water.

In her bed, she shivered despite the fact a log fire blazed in the stove, two thick quilts covered her, and she'd drank enough hot tea to have significantly lowered the tea supply of her country. Earlier in the receiving house, she hadn't had the energy to reassure Hector and tell him she didn't blame him, too stunned by fear and cold. Although the way he'd shouted and moved on the boat had terrified her. His eyes had been too wide, and his breathing had been so shallow she'd worried he might have fainted. He'd swatted her hands away when she'd tried to calm him. He'd kept shouting he didn't want to die. Then the boat had gone upside down and the cold...Lord, the cold. The shock from the icy water had been her worst enemy at that moment. Saint Martin's summer her foot. The Serpentine had been freezing. Her lungs had turned into icebergs. Breathing had been difficult, and panic had nearly killed her.

She shivered again at the memory of her lungs hurting and cold water filling her mouth.

The house was finally quiet after her mother had suffered from a fit of hysteria upon seeing her two daughters soaked and shivering. Mother had behaved as if she'd been the one about to die.

Anyway, Maddie preferred to be alone in her silent room than surrounded by her shrieking mother, and even Verity needed rest. Gosh. Ernest had looked like he'd wanted to murder somebody. That somebody being poor Hector.

She reclined on her pillow and closed her eyes. Peace and quiet, finally. No, there was a tapping noise from the window. Then a soft thud. She propped herself up and peered in the semidarkness, having left her oil lamp burning. Was the exhaustion playing tricks on her mind?

Another tapping noise came. She craned her neck to look at the window, the very window Hector had broken years ago.

"Maddie?" Hector's deep voice came muffled through the glass.

She sagged in relief. "Hector." She pushed aside the covers and padded to the window. "My goodness." She hurried to open it since Hector held himself up by gripping the ledge. A swift gust of wind swept through the room. "What are you doing?"

"May I come in?"

"Please." She stepped aside, clutching her nightgown.

He leapt through the window and hurried to close it, muttering something about her having frozen enough for one day. The golden light from the lamp shone upon him.

He shoved his hands into his pockets. "I...I climbed your wall."

"Yes, I gathered that much."

He removed his flat hat. "I'm sorry for the intrusion, but I needed to know how you were faring." He swallowed hard. "Your mother didn't allow me to see you, and I didn't want to argue with her. She seemed rather upset. Understandably so."

She wasn't surprised. "I'm doing well. Just tired."

He bowed his head in a formal manner. "I won't disturb you any further. I hope you might forgive me one day." He turned around to open the window, but she stopped him.

"Hector, wait. I'd like to say something, but first, please be a dear and lock the door, just in case."

He did as told and faced her again, his head hanging over his chest. "You can tell me whatever you wish. Don't hold back your words on my account. I deserve your anger. It's the second time you nearly died because of my actions. Unforgivable. If you don't want to see me again, just say the word and I'll disappear."

"Good gracious, I don't want you to disappear." A warm, fluttering feeling lit her chest. "I'm not angry, and there's nothing to forgive." She shivered again. Would she ever be warm again? "Why don't you sit with me for a moment?" She sat on the bed and patted the spot next to her.

He shuffled forwards and sat on the edge of the bed, but his eyes shone with unshed tears. "I'm so sorry, Maddie." His voice cracked with sobs. "I don't know what happened to me. I panicked. I wasn't on the boat with you anymore but on the raft, scared and alone. I didn't mean to hurt you."

"Oh, Hector." She hugged him. He rested his head on her shoulder and shook, stifling his sobs. "I've never thought, not for one second, that you meant to hurt me. I understand what happened to you, darling. You couldn't know that being on a boat would trigger your fear. After what you've been through the boat was a stupid idea. Don't blame yourself."

He wrapped his arms around her waist and held her closer. She caught a whiff of his scent—citrus with a hint of mint. So refreshing. His warm body fended off the chill. She caressed his hair and hugged him until he stopped shaking.

"Your skin is cold," he said, raising his head. "Why are you so cold?"

"I'm having trouble keeping myself warm."

"Let me help. It's the least I can do."

She was about to ask him what he wanted to do, but as he started to undress, her silly question was forgotten. Who cared about his intentions? He removed his shoes, socks, trousers, and shirt until he stood naked in front of her. The light from the lamp kissed his skin. If getting naked was his strategy to keep her warm, it worked because her face already grew hot. He tucked her under the covers and slid into the bed beside her.

"You aren't shy now," she said, shivering but not from the cold.

"No, because we aren't going to make love. Come here." He opened his arms, and she willingly went into them.

Immediate warmth seeped into her as she rested her head on his chest. His arms and legs held her, and he caressed her back in slow circles. His body enveloped her in a warm cocoon.

"I nearly killed you all. I'm so sorry," he whispered, brushing his lips against her temple.

"Shush. You've apologised enough. Besides, we're fine. You took me to the shore. You saved me."

"You're too kind. I was the one who put you in danger to start with." He rubbed her neck and back.

"I'm not kind." Her eyelids became heavy as even her toes began to warm. It felt so good to be held and warmed by his strong body.

He kept caressing her, rubbing warmth into her stiff muscles. One by one, her limbs thawed, releasing a delicious exhaustion. She couldn't keep her eyes...

She woke up in his arms. The oil lamp didn't burn anymore, and even the stove had exhausted the wood and coal. But she was nice and warm, snuggled against him. She stirred, and he moved as well.

"Do you need anything?" he whispered, kissing her cheek. "Tea? Another cover?"

She blinked. "Is it morning?"

"Not yet. Not even dawn."

"Then I want to stay here in your arms."

"I'm more than happy to hold you." He pulled her closer.

Her thin nightgown let her feel his warm skin against hers. And more than that. His hard shaft pressed against her belly, sending a shot of liquid desire between her thighs. It wasn't her fault if her hips rolled and rubbed against him of their own accord.

"Maddie." He stiffened, which was a good thing. "What are you doing?"

"Getting warm." She slid a hand between them and reached down, heading for his glorious—he took her wrist, stopping the happy trip of her hand.

He swallowed hard. "If you touch me now, I won't consider myself responsible for my actions."

She rocked her hips again. "Will your actions involve your lips on my body?"

"You need to rest." He scowled at her, the scoundrel.

"Interesting answer." She freed her wrist and resumed travelling down all his delicious muscles. His thighs were as hard as steel, and his buttocks as firm as leather.

"Maddie." His plea didn't hold any confidence.

When she closed her hand around him, they both groaned. She ran her hand up and down his length, feeling his whole body grow tense. His breath fanned over her cheek as he panted.

"You're killing me," he whispered.

"I want you, Hector." She twined her leg with his and guided his shaft towards her wet entrance.

He let out a low growl that would have scared her in other circumstances. "Maddie, you need rest."

"I need you. Please."

He grabbed her hips with rough hands and pulled her closer. She spread her legs more widely to accommodate his build as her core pulsed in anticipation, but he didn't move. His muscles were taut and ready, and his chest heaved with heavy breaths, but he didn't thrust forward.

"I've hurt you twice." He gripped her hips more gently. "Are you sure you want me?"

"Yes." She pushed herself towards him to show him how much she needed him.

She bunched her nightgown up until her bare skin touched his. He growled again. The tip of his shaft touched her throbbing spot, and she couldn't repress a moan.

"Hector, please."

"It's going to sting," he whispered, kissing her lips with a light brush of his mouth.

"I don't care."

"You might not like it."

"I need you. Don't make me beg again."

"You must tell me if it hurts though." He inched inside her, and yes, he was right.

The foreign sensation of being stretched burned her tender flesh, but the need of him overcame the pain, and she got wetter.

"How do you feel?" He remained still.

"I'm fine. You may go deeper."

He did as he was told and paused again to give her time to adjust. She moaned as her inner muscles contracted against his length. The sensation was both painful and extremely pleasurable. He caressed her cheek before thrusting further. She inhaled. The combination of pleasure and pain spread warmth throughout her body. He slid a hand between them and rubbed her with gentle fingers. Instant relief. The sting vanished and only pleasure remained. Now she wished he'd pound inside her.

She shifted her hips forwards, meeting him. "Please."

"We must go slowly."

"No." She took his shoulders. "Do it. With one push. I want to feel it."

His features tightened with concern. "Are you sure?"

"Do it." She was going mad with need, lust, desire, and whatever else brewed within her.

The bedsheet fell off his body as he laid her on her back and he stretched himself out on her top. Having him over her, in all his broad masculinity, sent shivers down her back. He was so heavy and strong he could easily overpower her. Yet only kindness and sweetness radiated from him and his touch.

He nestled between her legs, propping himself up on his elbows. She lifted her hips, desperate for more friction, more contact, more everything.

"Ready?" he asked before kissing her.

"Yes, yes."

Her pulse went faster the closer he came. He shoved his hips onwards. The moment of sharp pain tore a gasp out of her, but Lord, it was worth it. He was buried in her to the hilt, his thick shaft stretching and filling her completely. Feeling him inside her was the strangest yet most wonderful sensation she'd ever experienced. He remained still, giving her body time to welcome him.

"How are you?" His tone held too much worry.

She smiled, savouring the feeling of him inside her. "Wonderful."

He started moving slowly, thrusting in and out of her. Each delicious friction brought a tiny sting of pain and a hot wave of pleasure.

She needed more of his strength, deep thrusts, and raw power. Seemingly reading her mind, he sped up. He rubbed her sensitive spot between her thigh again until she couldn't keep her eyes open. His chest brushed her taut nipples as he moved back and forth, adding a new layer of bliss. Between his thrusts, the rubbing of her nub, and brushing of her nipples, pleasure burst within her suddenly. There was no build up. No warning. The release shattered her and caused her inner muscles to clench around him.

The more her muscles contracted, the more pleasure shuddered through her. She moaned, writhed, and arched her back, seeking more contact, more friction, more pleasure. He groaned deep in his throat, all his muscles pulling taut. He withdrew abruptly to spill over her belly. She watched, mesmerised, as he squeezed his eyes shut and his entire body tightened, each muscle becoming more defined underneath his silky skin. The tendons in his neck stood out in sharp relief as he gritted his teeth. If she didn't know better, she'd think he was in pain.

She caressed his sharp cheek as he stopped trembling and finally opened his eyes. The way he stared at her was both frightening and awe-inspiring. A promise—no, a vow lingered in the depths of his sapphire gaze as if he took an oath right then and there.

Without them exchanging words, she knew he would do anything for her, be anything she needed, and cherish her. Utter adoration was etched on his handsome features. It almost brought her to tears.

He bent his head to take her mouth in a hard, possessive kiss that sealed their silent pact. His tongue thrust inside her mouth and took possession of it unapologetically. She was breathless as he bruised her lips with the raw kiss. But he hadn't finished. He kissed his way down her breasts and thighs until he dipped his head between her legs and lapped at her.

"What—" She couldn't finish. A moan erupted from her.

She clenched the bedsheet as he kissed her deeply. She wasn't ready for this. Too much pleasure. Every inch of her skin burst with it. And watching his golden head dipped between her shouldn't be so erotic. His expert tongue circled her nub and stroked it until it triggered another powerful release. She had to press her mouth against the pillow not to scream.

He twirled his tongue over her wet entrance and nub until she writhed again, helpless against the fierce need shaking in her body. The third release was fiercer than the first two, shocking even. It went straight to her head, leaving behind a path of fire. How could her body produce so much ecstasy? When he raised his head, she lay in the bed, unable to move or speak.

"I'll be back in a moment." He placed a reverent kiss on her thigh.

He slid off the bed to take the towel and the basin of water from a corner. He wiped her belly and washed her between her legs, which should have made her feel self-conscious, but instead, it only sparked warmth and affection towards him. When he was satisfied she was clean, he lay next to her and covered her with the quilt, careful not to leave any inch of her body uncovered.

"The sun is rising. I must go now." He brushed her hair from her face.

"No." She caught his hand in hers.

Although the noises coming from downstairs meant the cook was already up to light the fire. Soon Verity and her parents would be up and about, and someone might enter her bedroom to ask how she was faring.

He kissed her knuckles, fingers, and wrists. "I'll see you later. I promise. It kills me to leave you now, but I don't want to cause you more trouble. This was the best night of my life. I feel so honoured that you let me be with you."

"Oh. I enjoyed it too." More than enjoyed it. What a stupid thing to say to such a lovely speech. But she couldn't say more. She was too stunned by the experience and his adoration.

He glanced at the bed. "There's a little bloodstain on the bed."

"Don't worry about it. I'll manage. I'll say I'm bleeding."

"Hope you are all right." His brow furrowed with concern.

"More than all right." She was about to say more, but footsteps padded from the corridor.

They both froze but then slackened when the person walked past her door.

He kissed her hand again. "Sleep for another few hours if you can. I've disrupted your sleep too much."

He dressed quickly, his gaze never leaving her face. Before jumping out of the window, he smiled like a dashing pirate and blew her a kiss. Then he was gone, but his warmth lingered in her heart.

twenty-six

FROM THE MOMENT Hector had left the warmth of Maddie's bed, his heart had pounded fast. A part of him wanted to enjoy the memory of being inside her, kissing her, and the lovely expression on her face when she'd found her release. Another part wanted to marry her now. Immediately. Without delay. Eloping if necessary. Gretna Green.

He had no idea why the urge to make her his wife sent him into a frenzy, but he wanted to be sure she didn't think, not for one moment, that he would leave her after a fumble with her. He wasn't one of those rakes who seduced a lady and then left her. He scoffed as he tried to tie his cravat for the third time. Stupid thing.

His restless fingers didn't seem able to button his shirt as well. Yet he ought to be quick. Ernest had sent him an urgent message, requiring his presence in Maddie's house. An emergency meeting. He had an idea of what Ernest wanted to talk about. The cravat fell loose on his chest. To hell with the cravat. He simply knotted it around his neck like a scarf and hurried out of his bedroom, only to skid to an abrupt halt.

Quentin stood in the corridor with an arm around the waist of a woman. Not again. He clenched his fists, ready to defend himself or the lady if his cousin got aggressive again.

Quentin rubbed his chin, giving Hector a long once over. "You know, I'm sorry to have called you an idiot."

Hector ignored him and angled towards the woman. "Are you here on your own free will, ma'am?"

She rolled her red-painted lips together. "Very much."

He bowed his head. "Then enjoy your company."

Quentin pulled her closer and stepped in front of Hector, blocking his path. "Please commit other atrocities as the one you performed in Hyde Park. It makes my solicitor's work easier."

"Go to hell, Quentin." He sidestepped the couple.

"Your mother will never rest in the family crypt." Quentin's angry words echoed in the hallway.

Hector skidded to an abrupt halt. Red spots blotched his vision. He turned around, fighting the urge to punch the smile off his cousin's face.

"Well?" Quentin darted his tongue over his bottom lip. "Do you want a fight?"

"What is this all about?" the woman asked.

Quentin released her and waved Hector closer. "Come here, Cousin. Show me what you can do."

Oh, Hector was tempted to pummel some sense into His Disgrace. But he'd taken an oath to behave like a gentleman, and a gentleman didn't go around punching people, not even those who deserved it. Besides, likely Quentin hoped for just that. He wanted Hector to lose control before crying bloody murder. He'd caused enough trouble to fall into Quentin's little trap. If he weren't worried about the Irish workers, he'd slam his fist against his cousin's jaw. He was finally learning a duke's job.

"Give me the Savage Duke," Quentin said.

Hector clenched his jaw and started down the stairs. "At least today your lover isn't a child. It was about time you decided to pursue a woman."

As he pulled the front door open, the high-pitched voice of the lady came from upstairs. "A child? What did he mean by that?"

Hands shoved in his pockets, he strode down the pavement towards Maddie's house. He needed a walk and, to be honest, wasn't fond of the carriages. Too much rocking and jolting. Thank goodness there weren't many people around. The freezing air had returned, bringing rain and icy gusts, discouraging the Londoners from promenading.

His mind was crowded enough with thoughts to deal with people. Should he propose to Maddie right now? What if she felt oppressed by him? Maybe he should wait. No, he didn't want to. But it'd be better if he became a duke first and solved the chaos with Quentin. God, it might take months. His head was about to explode.

He slowed his pace as he arrived at the spot where he'd discussed his passion for botany with Robert. It'd been right before the incident with Maddie. No, he hadn't forgotten his promise to make amends. Once he was the Duke of Blackburn, he'd help her become the artist she wanted and deserved to be. Then he'd propose, and if she rejected him, he'd provide for her anyway. He'd always be ready to help her, no matter what she decided to do.

His heart beat more slowly when he entered Maddie's house. Just smelling her scent had a therapeutic effect on his nerves. The maid showed him to the drawing room where Ernest and Maddie were having tea. Hector hurried to her as his pulse quickened again. His heart was confused. Lord, he wanted to sweep her off her feet, kiss her, and beg her to marry him.

"How are you?" He took her hand and was pleased to find it warm and steady. Even her cheeks had returned to their usual healthy colour.

"I'm well." She blushed fiercely, which brightened her beautiful eyes. "I slept soundly. It was a very restful night." She flashed a coquettish smile that stirred his blood.

Not that it took much to stir it. He'd want her even if she'd made a comment on the weather.

Ernest cleared his throat. "Shall we start?"

Reluctantly, Hector turned towards the solicitor. "I'd like to apologise for what happened in the park."

Ernest put down his cup of tea. "It was unfortunate and tragic for Maddie and Verity, and a complete disaster for our plan to make everyone believe you aren't a savage. Blackburn sent me a letter from his chosen physician." He showed the document. "The physician, Dr. Trevor Smith, declared you with mental and emotional issues thus unsuitable to hold the title."

Hector took the letter and read it. "But no one visited me."

Ernest spread his hands in a 'what did I tell you' gesture.

"What can we do?" Hector asked.

If he was going to be honest, he hadn't the foggiest idea of how he could restore his reputation. He could build a shelter in a matter of hours, catch fish in minutes, and fend off rabid monkeys with only a stick. But convincing society he was a civilised person? Not a clue.

"You must make an appearance at another party to quench the rumours." Ernest shook his fist as if he gave a speech to a demoralised cricket team. "The boat trip was a disaster from every point of view. Pardon my bluntness. The ladies are shocked, Blackburn spreads the rumour the Savage Duke is deranged, and even the prime minister expressed his concern."

Hector slouched his posture. The last few days had been filled with strong emotions—the fear of facing the water again, his first, and hopefully not last, night with Maddie, and now the disappointment of having ruined all the hard work Maddie, Verity, and Ernest had done.

"And it can't be just a dinner party," Ernest continued. "But an event organised by a well-respected member of the ton. Someone whose word means something to the peers. Thankfully, we finally have a bit of luck." He turned his attention to Maddie.

"Lord Naylor is hosting a charity lunch in his house this week," Maddie said. "His daughter Frances convinced him to invite you."

"Frances?" Hector rubbed his forehead. "She couldn't even glance at me when we had tea at Dr. Landon's."

"Yes," Ernest said, "but I think she appreciated your silence and by asking her father to invite you, she's returning the favour. I guess not having involved her turned out to be the right thing to do." He gave a quick smile.

The idea of another party didn't thrill Hector, but after all the damage he'd caused, he could only nod and do his best. "I'll do exactly what you ask me to do."

Ernest didn't seem pleased. Since the incident, he regarded him with coldness, and Hector understood his concern.

Maddie smoothed a wrinkle on her skirt. "Ernest, would you mind if I have a word with Hector?"

"Of course not." Ernest stood up and bowed. "I have to see how Verity is faring. Good day."

The moment he was out of the room, Maddie sprang up and wrapped her arms around Hector's neck. He closed his eyes for a moment, welcoming her soft body and scented skin.

"I'm so sorry." She tilted her head up, her emerald eyes shining with tears. "Your cousin isn't only a terrible duke, but an awful person."

He caressed her dark curls. "That's why he's going to lose his title."

She hugged him tightly and rested her head on his chest. "I've missed you today. I kept thinking about you."

"So did I. Are you sore?"

"A little." She giggled, and the sound was like that of the angels singing for him. "But I feel wonderful."

"I'm not going to leave you. You know that, don't you?"

"I do."

"I mean it." He stroked her cheek with his knuckles. He

opened his mouth to tell her again he wanted to be with her no matter what, but she gazed up at him and placed her chin on his chest.

"I want to sketch some of those plants and animals you saw on the island."

"Do you want to illustrate the book?" That was his opportunity to make amends.

She beamed, and her whole face became radiant with happiness. "I want to try. Since you're here, I keep sketching more." She wiggled her fingers. "And my fingers are less stiff. I can control them a little better."

He kissed her fingers. "Let's sketch then."

HECTOR COULD WATCH Maddie draw all day. Her face tightened and relaxed, depending on what she sketched. When she drew the chiaroscuro, her brow furrowed, but when she drew the lines of a silhouette, her expression softened and she smiled. After the conversation with Ernest, they didn't have much to do but wait for the lunch. In fact, it was better if Hector didn't show himself around, lest the rumours grow. So he was with Maddie, working on his book.

"Was the flower like this?" She showed him the sketchbook with flowers, plants, and animals he'd described to her.

He tilted his head, forcing himself to focus on the sketch and not on her delicate hands which he wanted to kiss and feel on his body. "Yes. The petals were more pointed though. Aside from that, it's wonderful. You're an amazing artist."

"Not really." She focused on the petals and reshaped them with quick strokes of her pencil.

"How can you say that?" He gestured at the dozens of sketches she'd already completed.

There were the trees from the island, insects, birds, and flowers, all sketched with great details and realism. He could almost smell the scent of the orchids and hear the flamboyant birds sing.

"I'm not a professional. My knowledge is limited." She added a few shadows on the petals. "No one would buy my paintings. But book illustrations might be good enough to help me earn something."

Yes, earning. That was the crux of her problem.

He propped his chin on his closed fist. "What if I help you pay the academy's fee?"

She raised her right hand and wiggled her fingers. "It's not a matter of money. My hand still hurts sometimes. My fingers don't always do as they're told."

"But you said they got better since you started sketching more. You need to practise." He opened and closed his thick fingers. "I did exercises to strengthen my fingers to climb trees. You can do the same. Have you ever tried?"

She paused and stared at her scar. "Actually, yes. I mean, I worked hard to draw again, and my fingers got a little better. But I've never done specific exercises to strengthen my fingers. Do you think it might work?"

"I'm sure it will."

She lowered the sketchbook. "Great, but let's focus on getting your title back first."

"After that, may I help you?" He raised his eyebrows. "May I have the privilege to pay for your studies? Provide for you while you concentrate on your art?" *Please say yes.*

She'd refused his money years ago. But surely, things between them were different now.

She laughed. "You don't have to."

He took her hand, lacing his fingers through hers. "There's nothing I want more than to help you become the great artist you can be." He kissed her knuckles and the scar. "I want everyone to know how talented you are. I want you to be happy."

Her lips parted, but whatever she wanted to say was cut off by her mother who barged inside the drawing room in a flutter of blue skirts.

"I've been quite tolerant with you." Mrs. Debenham pointed a finger at Hector. "I gave Madeline more freedom, turned a blind eye to her sudden disappearances, and for what? To have her almost drowned in the Serpentine of all places and find you kissing her hand? And you still haven't reclaimed your title." She stretched out an arm towards the door. "I kindly request that you leave."

Maddie lowered her sketchbook. "But Mother—"

"Besides." Her mother folded her arms over her arms across her chest. "Rumour has it that a physician produced a certificate stating you, Lord Wentworth, aren't mentally stable." She huffed. "Your chances of finding a champion are quite slim."

Maddie exhaled, but Hector didn't see the point in lying.

He rose and bowed his head. "Dr. Trevor Smith didn't even visit me."

Mrs. Debenham spiked her brow. "Dr. Smith you say." She narrowed her gaze. "Tell me, Lord Wentworth, do you want to be the Duke of Blackburn, or are you looking for a past-time, or worse, a way to ensnare my daughter?"

Past-time? "The dukedom is my legacy. My brother believed I would be a great Duke of Blackburn. Yes, I want to be the duke. I want to honour my family's legacy, and I want to do the right thing for Maddie." Ensnare Maddie. Ridiculous. If anything, it was the other way around.

"Smith." Mrs. Debenham paced, a hand on her hip. "I might be able to do something and help you with Dr. Smith's certificate."

"How?" Maddie asked. Scepticism dripped from her tone.

"Leave it to me. Maddie, you go to your bedroom and rest." She pointed upstairs. "Now. And you, Lord Wentworth, leave."

Hector bowed to the ladies. Mrs. Debenham had a point. Maddie needed to rest. "I will see you tomorrow, Maddie."

From behind her mother, she scribbled something on the

sketchbook and showed him the page where the word 'window' was written. "See you tomorrow. Lord Wentworth."

Hector walked around the house and waited in the same spot he'd stopped before climbing her window years ago. The chilly wind blew from the park, and thunder boomed from a grey sky. He kept to the shadows, watching commuters hurrying home and constables huddling their cloaks more tightly.

When the street became less crowded and the constables had turned around the corner, he hauled himself up. He didn't even need to pause. His muscles were so trained he didn't hesitate. The window was half open, so he slipped inside and landed on the balls of his feet. He had barely time to straighten before Maddie hugged him.

Laughing, he hugged her back and inhaled her sweet lavender scent. "You didn't answer my question. Will you accept my money?" He pulled back enough to see her face, needing to stare at her eyes.

Her cheeks reddened. "I can't pay you back unless I become famous."

"You'll become famous, and I don't want to be paid back."

"Not even in kisses?" She unbuttoned his waistcoat and tugged at his pathetic excuse for a cravat.

Just watching her slender fingers working on the buttons of his shirt caused his pulse to spike. "That's another matter. When do we start this payment in kisses?"

"Now. Because it's my turn."

"Your turn?"

She removed his jacket, waistcoat, and shirt with one yank. She drew in a breath, admiring him. "You must promise me that one day you'll pose for me." She ran her hands over his chest, exploring and studying him.

"Yes. Anything you want." Oh, his cock ached, but he let her explore his body without interrupting her.

Her fingertips caressing his nipples were sheer torture, but he pushed down the urge to rip her clothes off her beautiful body. He sucked in a breath as she traced his abdominal muscles and biceps. Blazes. He had to focus to remain still. Her delicate touch fed a fierce dark hunger inside him. It nearly frightened him.

When she opened his trousers and knelt in front of him, he couldn't repress a groan. She wouldn't do that, would she? No, he was wrong. She parted her plush lips and smiled before dipping her head. He hissed a breath between his teeth when she took him in her hot, velvety mouth. Fire of hell. His body was aflame with need, pleasure, and the deep desire to marry her. No, not because she obliterated his reason with her tongue and lips. He wanted to marry her because he couldn't imagine his life without her.

Another tortured groan tore out of him as she sucked him deep in her throat. He sank his fingers into her silky hair and fought a shout crawling up his chest. She swirled her tongue over his tip before taking him deeper. It was good that his thigh muscles were taut and strong, or he would collapse. Desire welled so fast in his abdomen that he shuddered with it. He jolted when she stroked his balls with curious hands. He felt her touch everywhere. She changed rhythm but took him even deeper in her mouth. Hell. He was dying from pleasure.

He couldn't resist. The release built up quickly, burning him from the inside out. He gently took her face and moved her away before he spilt into her mouth.

She pouted, her pillow-like lips red and glistening. "Why did you stop me? I wanted—"

He cut her protest with a kiss. Even to his standards, it was a savage one. Raw and furious. He poured all his burning desire into that kiss. But she replied by wrapping her arms and legs around him. They kissed with their mouths open, biting, tonguing, and grazing at each other. He lifted her and walked blindly towards the bed. When his legs touched the covers, he laid her down. He took a moment to admire her kiss-swollen lips and her rising chest before unbuttoning her dress. It was curious how earlier that day his fingers had struggled to tie the knot of his cravat, but now they managed to unbutton her shirt, untie her skirt and petticoats, and remove her boots in a matter of seconds. In her chemise and drawers, she was simply irresistible.

She spread her legs, showing him her glistening core without hesitation. He started kissing her from her neck, smiling against her skin when she moaned. He bunched up her chemise and closed his mouth around her inviting nipple. Her hips bucked up as he sucked hard before tonguing her breasts. She was perfection in everything. All creamy skin, sweet scent, and delicious moans. He fondled her breasts and tongued her hardened nipples until she writhed underneath him.

"Please," she whispered. "Make me feel it."

He buried himself in her with one thrust and paused, worried to have hurt her. But she arched her back and lifted her hips, so he started to move back and forth until he found a rhythm she matched. God, she was so beautiful it hurt.

"Harder," she said in a commanding tone.

He obliged. When her inner muscles squeezed around him, he stroked her engorged nub. She clamped her hands over her mouth to muffle her scream of pleasure, which he didn't like. He wanted to hear her scream. He wanted her fully unbridled with passion, free to express her ecstasy.

All in good time. If she'd ever agree to marry him. He pulled away before finding his release. Its power rocked him deeply. It bordered on pain, so shockingly strong it was. Swallowing his shout of pleasure, he waited for his brain to become functional again and his heart to slow down.

"Come here." She spread her arms, and he went to her willingly, scattering kisses on her face.

The words 'would you be my wife' burned on the tip of his

tongue, but he reined himself in. If Quentin's doctor managed to declare him insane, he'd be locked up in an institution, and he didn't want Maddie to suffer because of him, being tied to a man proclaimed insane. So he held her, feeling her soft breath on his chest, and promised—no, swore that he'd ask her to marry him when he could offer her the whole world.

twenty-seven

MADDIE COULDN'T BELIEVE what her eyes saw.

She stared at the document her mother had given her in disbelief. In an official letter, signed by two solicitors and even a judge, Dr. Smith declared he'd been mistaken about Hector's mental state and after a second assessment—which she doubted had ever happened—he was ready to testify that Hector was perfectly sane and fit for his ducal duty.

She lowered the letter, speechless. She wanted to ask her mother how the devil she'd managed to convince Dr. Smith to change his diagnosis, and above all, why.

"See? I'm not completely useless." Mother smiled, and for once, it wasn't her smug smile but a genuine one.

Finally, Maddie appreciated the similarity between herself and Mother. "How did you get this?"

Mother blushed, and blazes, she looked ten years younger and beautiful. "I always listen to your father when he talks about his work. So, I happen to know about some financial problems Dr. Smith is going through due to his passion for gambling. The man squandered his daughters' dowries. How irresponsible. His poor wife doesn't know. His dire financial situation is actually confidential information, but I didn't publicly divulge it. I simply reminded him that everyone can make mistakes and his wife should be informed. It's only sensible. He didn't seem to agree with me, though."

"You blackmailed him." Maddie didn't know if she should be proud or horrified.

"Good gracious, no." Mother put a hand on her throat. "It was a perfectly civil conversation."

Maddie would like to argue that blackmailing was never civil, no matter how polite the exchange was. Anyway. "Why did you help Hector?"

"Why? A vast and wealthy dukedom with five estates. Well, four now that Blackburn sold one of them. I bet he and Dr. Smith attend the same gaming den. I don't want to mingle with such scoundrels," said the woman who blackmailed a doctor. Mother gave her a kiss on the cheek. "Only the best for my daughters."

As her mother sauntered away, a shock of stillness went through Maddie. She held the letter and read it again. Hector wouldn't be locked up in an institution and, if their luncheon with Lord Naylor went well, he could find a champion. They had to thank Mother for the opportunity.

Blimey. Her mother had done the right thing for the wrong reason.

But did it matter?

~

LORD NAYLOR KEPT LOOKING at Hector as if expecting Hector to attack him at any moment, which was a pity because Hector liked the man.

Lord Naylor's house on the outskirts of London was surrounded by old oak trees, birches, and tall Scottish pines. Just inhaling the fragrant scent of pine resin and wet soil gave Hector hope.

The glasshouse, where they were strolling, held species from all over the world. Some of them looked remarkably similar to those he'd seen on the island.

He walked along the wide aisle, watching the beautiful flowers and ignoring Lord Naylor's worried glares. Maddie chatted with Lady Naylor, and he loved hearing the sound of her laughter. Albert, Lord Naylor's son, touched every flower and leaf he could get his hands on while Frances flashed at him a shy smile he returned.

Lord Naylor cleared his throat. "May I inquire about a matter that worries me, Wentworth?"

Ah, there it came. "Ask away, sir." He stepped aside to let Albert rush past him, holding a bright red hibiscus.

"Would you tell me what happened in Hyde Park?" He surveyed the conservatory, following his son's meandering. "I heard the most outlandish accounts of your adventure on the Serpentine. Some are too outrageous to be true."

"Like what?"

"Like you tried to kill Miss Debenham and her sister."

Hector sighed. At least Lord Naylor didn't fully trust the rumours. "The truth is quite simple and, I'm afraid, less exciting than the stories you heard. Being on the boat and surrounded by water took me back to when I was floating on the raft in the ocean before I was rescued. It was a harrowing experience. And there I was reliving it in that boat. I panicked." He paused as a choking sensation gripped his throat. Just thinking about that moment of panic caused sweat to break on his skin. The darn cravat was too tight all of a sudden. "The fear was so real...I absolutely, without a doubt, believed I was on the raft. I understand it might sound absurd, ridiculous even, and I was shocked to realise my mind tricked me into believing I was in the middle of the sea. But that's what happened, and I don't have an explanation for it. But yes, Maddie and her sister's lives were at risk because of my reaction."

Lord Naylor's expression softened, and his eyebrows lowered

over his suddenly sympathetic brown eyes. "I understand what you went through. After I returned from Afghanistan, my mind tricked me into thinking I was in the middle of the battlefield many a time. The sensations were very realistic. The illusions went away after a while, but my strength had little to do with them. Even now, sometimes I fall prey to nightmares." He gripped Hector's shoulder and gave it a squeeze. "I don't believe you're as deranged as the rumours say. I admire you for having survived in conditions that would have discouraged the bravest of men, and I know how a man's mind can take time to heal."

Hector wasn't sure he deserved the praise but bowed his head. "I feel for you. Living the nightmare of a battlefield must be even more horrifying than being on a raft."

"I don't believe that. The fear is the same. But above all, I hate the feeling of not being able to control myself." He rubbed his arm stiff at his side. "I ruined quite a few parties as well. The sound of a bottle of champagne being uncorked would bring me straight to the battlefield. A shattered glass would have me search for my rifle. Even loud voices would make me sweat. Lord Hector, you have my sympathy. I'm grateful that my wife has always been patient with me and helped me through those awful years. Believe me, the illusions will go away, or rather, you'll learn to live with them."

A scream rent the quiet of the conservatory before Hector could say anything.

Lady Naylor rushed towards them, her skirt flapping around her legs. "Keith, come!"

Her panicked voice caused both Lord Naylor and Hector to run towards her. They followed her to the fountain where Albert made retching noises, crouched on the floor. His skin had a blue tint that hinted to suffocation, and his dilated pupils could be both fear and poison. Maddie stood petrified next to the child. Frances clamped her hands over her mouth.

Lord Naylor knelt next to his son, panic widening his eyes. "What happened?"

His wife sobbed. "He swallowed one of those orange berries."

Hector studied them quickly. The rounded berries and shiny dark-green leaves pointed to a willow leaf plant. "They're poisonous. Keep his mouth open and make sure his tongue stays out, lest he choke on it."

He ran down the aisle, searching for the leaves of the *Phillotaria elongata* he'd spotted earlier. Behind him, Albert kept choking and gasping for air. Come on. Where was that damn plant? Hector snatched a few tender leaves and dashed back to the child.

"Keep his mouth open." He stuffed the boy's mouth with the crushed leaves none-too-gently, being careful to break them so as to release their juice.

The boy swallowed hard, tears welling in his eyes. Lord Naylor rubbed his son's back, his features etched with fear. "Swallow it, son."

Albert pulled a face, but he stopped convulsing and breathed normally again. His skin lost its blue colour but didn't return a healthy shade of pink.

"Papa," the boy said in a weak voice.

Lord and Lady Naylor hugged him. Frances joined them. Happy tears fell down Lady Naylor's cheeks as she whispered how much she loved her son. Hector's legs shook. He needed to sit down, or he'd collapse. He stretched out an arm, searching for something to grasp, and found Maddie.

"I'm here, Hector." She took his hand and steadied him.

As always. She was always there for him.

"He's fine. He's fine," Lord Naylor kept saying, caressing his son's face.

Hector leant against her, not too heavily, though. "He needs the physician. It takes a few days for the body to get rid of the poisonous juice of those berries. He'll likely have problems with his stomach for a few days, but if he drinks a lot of water and avoids spicy food—" The rest of his list of recommendations was cut off by Lord Naylor crushing him in a bear hug.

Hell, Hector could barely breathe, trapped in the captain's thick arms.

Lady Naylor copied her husband and, still holding her child, wrapped an arm around Hector. He waited for the rising tide of anxiety that being squashed and crowded might bring him, but nothing came. If anything, he enjoyed the comfort of the embrace. Maddie never left him, her arms wrapped around his waist.

"We could never thank you enough." Lady Naylor wiped her tears. "Without you, Albert would be dead."

"Thank you, Lord Wentworth," Frances said, taking his hand. "For everything."

The boy flashed a weak smile and waved as if agreeing with his mama. "Thank you, sir."

Lord Naylor stared at Hector with the determination of someone who'd made a firm decision. "Wentworth, I'll vouch for you with the queen. I'll present your case myself. You are neither deranged nor dangerous. I owe you my son's life."

Hector shook his head. "You owe me nothing."

Maddie poked him with her elbow.

Lord Naylor's determined expression didn't change. "I do, and I'll show you what gratitude means."

"Yes, yes!" Ernest shook a fist in the air, his enthusiasm contagious. "We have our letter from Dr. Smith, and we have our champion, and a fine one at that." He kept waving the document signed by Lord Naylor after Maddie and Hector had returned from the lord captain's house.

Maddie couldn't believe it. Thanks to Lord Naylor's intervention, Hector was about to become the Duke of Blackburn. Sitting next to her, Hector grinned as if he couldn't believe it either.

"Your brother and your mother would be so proud of you." She squeezed his hand. A sob remained lodged in her throat as his eyes misted.

"Will I be a good duke though?" he whispered. "Will I really make them proud?"

"You'll be the best," Ernest said before Maddie could reply. He grabbed Hector's shoulders and shook him. "Now we have to talk to your cousin, Your Grace. Let's go."

"Now?" Maddie and Hector asked together.

Ernest snatched his hat and leather bag. "No time like the present."

The trip on the carriage was a frantic affair. Ernest couldn't remain still and kept tapping his feet or shaking his fists. Hector jolted at every noise, and she wondered if panic would seize him again.

When they arrived, Ernest was the first to jump out of the carriage, singing *The Bonny Bunch of Roses*. Maddie couldn't help but smile at his great voice.

Ernest knocked on the door, still humming.

The door swung inwards, revealing Jones, the butler. "May I help you?"

"We must see Quentin Wentworth immediately," he said before the butler could even say good afternoon.

Their enthusiasm doused after they'd waited twenty minutes in the parlour. Apparently, his grace had to finish getting dressed and shaven, even though it was almost noon. In the parlour with Ernest's nervous company, Hector's silence, and the ugly painting, time slowed down to a crawl.

Finally, his cousin came into the sitting room with measured steps. The smile he flashed was strained and did nothing to ease the tension tightening his features.

"Hector, Miss Debenham, and Merriweather. What a charming trio." He barely finished the sentence before Ernest slammed the documents on the low table with an air of triumph.

"Ha! It's done. Lord Hector Wentworth is now the Duke of Blackburn," Ernest said. "You may leave the premises immediately, thank you. Shut the door behind you."

Maddie wasn't an expert, but she didn't believe that was the right procedure. Besides, Quentin Wentworth's air of superiority didn't falter. He cast a glance at the documents and skimmed them, nodding.

"I see. Lord Naylor. How generous of him to be Hector's champion. Oh, and dear Dr. Smith had a change of heart. I'm not surprised. He's such a coward." He gestured at the armchairs and sofa. "Please take a seat."

Ernest's enthusiasm faded a little. Likely, he'd expected a more dramatic response from the ex-duke. He sat on the armchair while Maddie took the sofa and Hector remained standing.

"It's official." Ernest tapped the documents. "His Grace wishes you should leave the house immediately, resign your position at the House of Lords, and even return all the family's belongings you have used in the past years."

Hector tensed.

Quentin slouched back in his armchair. "I admire your enthusiasm, Merriweather, but I'm afraid I'm not going anywhere."

"It is done." Ernest gritted his teeth. "Soon, even the queen."

Blackburn sighed. "This conversation won't be an easy one."

"What conversation?" Hector said. "Everything is done. I will finally restore my family's factory to its former glory and take care of the labourers."

"Bloody labourers." Quentin tugged at the cuffs of his shirt. "The problem is that I have no intention of being cast aside so that a simpleton can play the good Samaritan with those workers. You scared Dr. Smith. See, I know Smith. I play cards with him regularly. I was afraid he might get scared. But I have, shall we call it, taken precautions."

She pressed her lips and bit down a comment about them not caring about his precautions.

Ernest chuckled. "We can involve the police. You can leave quietly or noisily. Your choice."

"But see..." Quentin rummaged through his pockets and produced a brown envelope. He exhaled as if he were about to do something he didn't want to. "I happen to know something that will change everything. Hector must forget about his title and leave me alone."

"No." Maddie's voice rose. "Hector will be a better duke than you are because he knows how to be compassionate. Becoming the Duke of Blackburn is his birth right."

"Indeed. I'm glad you mentioned his compassion because it'll play a role in what I'm going to show you." He handed her the envelope. "This is for your eyes only, Miss Debenham. I'm being a gentleman and let you see the content of this envelope first."

Maddie hesitated before taking the envelope. When she opened it, she couldn't understand what the matter was. The envelope contained a few pictures. Ernest craned his neck, trying to catch a glimpse of the picture, but Quentin chided him.

"Now, now, Mr. Merriweather. Give the lady a moment of privacy, will you? I'm talking in *your* interest as well."

Maddie skimmed the pictures. Why would she care about the pictures of a scantily dressed lady? A lady who was in the company of two equally scantily dressed gentlemen and who pleasured her in different manners? Why would she—her throat clenched, and her pulse drummed in her ears when she studied the woman's face, going past the wig and makeup. Good Lord. It was Verity with two men Maddie didn't recognise. Not that it mattered. Verity lay on a plush bed surrounded by cushions, half-naked and a coquettish smile on her painted lips. In the pictures, her face was easily recognisable, even though she was in, er, different poses.

Maddie swallowed past the lump crawling in her throat. "How did you get these?"

"What are *these*?" Ernest asked, impatience radiating from him in waves.

Hector didn't say anything.

Quentin leant closer. "The right question is, what will happen when *he* sees these pictures?"

"He who? What is going on?" Ernest stomped a fist on the armrest.

Maddie released a shaky breath, hiding the pictures from view. "The pictures are personal and involve me." She wasn't going to offer any further explanations, especially since she needed to talk to Verity first. "They're compromising pictures." She cast a glance at Hector who squeezed her shoulder. Not a trace of reproach tightened his features. Only love came out of him. One of the many reasons she loved him.

Tarnation. Maddie's hands shook. Verity's life would be ruined. She loved Ernest dearly, and if he broke the engagement because of those pictures and the rumour spread, no one would want to be near her. The scandal would affect the whole family. Even Maddie would become an outcast. Her father's business would suffer. But Verity's life worried her more. She'd never recover from something so scandalous.

Ernest paled. "Maddie, surely you understand the importance of Lord Hector regaining his title. The future of many families is at risk. Your reputation—"

"Ernest." Hector's nostrils flared. "Perhaps I should decide with Maddie."

Ernest shot to his feet. "No, dammit! I've waited years to take Quentin Wentworth down and see him punished for the miserable way he treats his employees." He pointed a finger at Hector's cousin. "Maddie, I love you like a sister, but I can't let him continue hurting people, my people." He beat a fist against his chest. "Because of a scandal that will be forgotten in a matter of weeks. I can help you get past the scandal. I promise."

Maddie's bottom lip quivered as a sob threatened to break free. Ernest was insensitive but had a good point. It was the dilemma they'd dealt with about Frances, only worse. She'd seen the labourers. So many families lived in poverty, and Hector would help them. He would keep the children safe. But Verity was her sister. She didn't deserve to be ruined for life. If it were only Maddie, then maybe she would have agreed with Ernest, but Verity was another matter.

"Maddie loves her family deeply, and a scandal would affect them." Hector touched Maddie's trembling shoulder. "We need to discuss this."

"There's nothing to discuss." Ernest clenched his fists. "It's your duty to become a duke. You cannot leave those people in the hands of a heartless man."

"Ah, the Irish. Such passionate people." Quentin shrugged. "You can keep the pictures, Miss Debenham. I have the originals." He rose from the chair, a smug smile on his face. "I expect Hector to officially renounce his title by tomorrow. Have a nice day, all of you."

twenty-eight

MADDIE DIDN'T REMEMBER having left Hector's house or the trip home. She remembered Ernest voicing his disappointment and sense of injustice and her chest tightening with worry about Verity. The atmosphere in the carriage parked in front of her house was so thick that she felt its weight against her stomach. After his outburst, Ernest was silent, lips pinched in a flat line, and Hector had the same expression he'd worn after he'd been rescued from the sea—tired and defeated.

She swallowed past the lump in her throat. "Please let me talk to my family. Perhaps there's something I can do to avoid a scandal."

Ernest stared stubbornly out of the window. "Even if the scandal damages your family, I'll marry Verity all the same. I want you to know that."

But that was the point. Would he insist on letting the scandal burst if he knew Verity would be at its centre? It was Verity's decision whether to tell him the truth or not. For now, Maddie was more than happy to take the blame. "I will tell her, thank you."

Hector took her hand. "I understand you need to talk to your family. Would you like me to be with you?"

Oh, dear. No. "I'd like to talk to them in private, please."

He nodded and opened the door for her. "Let me know if you need me. If you need anything. I'll be here in a moment." He jumped out of the carriage and offered her his hand to help her out. "And Maddie?"

"Yes?"

"I don't care. Whatever is in those pictures, I don't give a damn. You have my unconditional, full support."

"Thank you."

On trembling legs, she walked the few steps to her front door and turned around to wave at Hector. His eyebrows were drawn in concern. He was more worried about her than about his future. But those workers needed his help. His mother deserved to rest in the family's crypt, and Hector had to take what was rightfully his. He shouldn't renounce his title because she'd been blackmailed. She went upstairs without removing her hat or coat and knocked on Verity's door.

"Verity?" Her voice came out strangled.

"Come in."

Maddie inched the door open, pondering how to break the news.

Verity stood next to her bed where a few frocks of different colours were sprawled. "I can't decide which one is the best for tomorrow. Ernest wants me to go to his aunt's birthday and I want —why that face?" She hurried to Maddie. "What is the matter? Hector? Did he hurt you?"

"No." She should make a short speech and explain to Verity what had happened, but she didn't have the energy to recount the whole story. So, she showed the pictures to her sister. "Are they real? Did you do these things?"

Smiling, Verity took the envelope. "What is it, dear? What are these...oh." Her bottom lip quivered as she went through the pictures. The more she watched them, the paler she grew. "How did you get these?"

"Duke Quentin. He threatened to make these pictures public unless Hector renounced his title."

She exhaled, shaking her head. "It was a long time ago, before I even met Ernest. Annabelle introduced me to a group of poets, musicians, and artists. They believe people should be free to enjoy all sorts of pleasure and to experiment with different things. I joined them only twice. Annabelle scared me. In these pictures, I...we were enjoying ourselves. That was all. These pictures were meant to be a game, nothing more. I guess Annabelle gave them to the duke."

Maddie plonked down onto the bed. "What a disaster."

"I'm sorry, Maddie." Verity let out a sob. "I know my behaviour was horrible, and you have every right to judge me, but I didn't mean for this to happen."

Perhaps before making love with Hector, Maddie wouldn't have understood what had urged her sister to dally in such illicit activities. But now, after having experienced the pleasure Hector gave her, she couldn't so easily dismiss her sister's behaviour. "I don't judge you, my dear. You weren't betrothed to anyone. I think about Hector, and—" She glanced at her sister. "You said you've never seen a naked man when you spotted Hector in the snow."

"I told the truth. See?" She showed her a picture. "It's not as terrible as it is. I mean, if people knew about these pictures, it'd still be a disaster, but we aren't fully naked. It's a trick. The gentlemen aren't naked. I'm not naked as well. We are in our undergarments, and...oh, Maddie. I'm so sorry." She dropped herself next to Maddie, crumpling her dresses. "We simply touched each other a bit, but not engaging in actual intimate activities."

Maddie rubbed the spot between her eyebrows. "What will Ernest say if he sees these?"

Verity bit her bottom lip. "I don't know, but if we want to help Hector...I guess I have to tell him the truth. But even if he doesn't care, the scandal would be too great. He wouldn't..." She sobbed and covered her face. "He's a solicitor. His career would be ruined, and he worked so hard to get it."

Maddie wrapped an arm around her shoulders. "Let me talk to Hector again. Perhaps we can find a solution."

THE IDEA of becoming a duke and improving the lives of others had grown within Hector's heart to the point where he'd become eager to start a new life. But after seeing Maddie's sad and defeated face, he wasn't sure about what to do. He couldn't give her any further pain, but at the same time, the lives of many people depended on his decision. Yet how could he hurt the woman he loved? Hell. These questions tore him apart, and Ernest's frustrated attitude didn't help.

Sitting next to Hector in his parlour, Maddie fiddled with her gloves and stared at her lap. "It's true. My family's future would be compromised if those pictures are made public."

"What about the lives of those families?" Ernest asked, steepling his fingers. He exhaled. "I'm sorry Maddie, but what do you consider more important? The lives of two hundred people working in miserable conditions or a society's scandal that will be forgotten in a matter of months?" His voice rose, causing Maddie to shiver. "I told you that I'd marry Verity all the same. I don't care what scandal hits you or your family. My feelings for her won't change."

Maddie shuddered, and Hector wondered why Ernest's honest reassurance didn't please her.

Hector glared at the solicitor. "Ernest. There's no need to push Maddie."

"Dammit, Hector!" He slammed a fist on the law table, causing the cups to tremble. "Weren't you the one who hated society's rules? Who believed manners were overrated? Well, scandals are part of those rules you so blatantly broke many times in the past months."

Maddie inhaled deeply. "I don't know what to do. That's why I'm here. I realise helping the workers is a more pressing matter, but see, the scandal might last for a few months. The damage would last forever. My family and I will become outcasts. We can't survive here without help. And most importantly, even my sister will be ruined. I..." She shook her head.

Ernest huffed. "Nothing can keep me away from Verity.".

A muscle in Maddie's face twitched. "I know it's not my decision to make, and despite what I just said, I want Hector to do what he thinks is best for him and his family. The fact Blackburn plays with Hector's affection for me is too cruel. But Hector should decide independently from my personal tragedy." She lifted her teary gaze to him. "Hector, my love, whatever you choose, I will accept and I won't think ill of you if you decide to carry on with your title. Nothing will change between us."

Ernest threw a hand up. "Finally, some sense."

My love. Did she realise what she'd said? Because Hector's brain was stuck on that word. He took her hand, feeling her pain. She loved him. "I cannot cause you and your family more harm than I've already done."

"Hector." Ernest regained his tense posture. "You saw those people, how they live. You saw how the duke treats them."

Hector forced himself to turn his attention to the solicitor because if he kept staring at Maddie, he'd kiss her right there and then. "Can't we find a way to help them even though I won't be the duke?"

"Another way?" Ernest scowled. "Since your disappearance and your brother's death, I've been working relentlessly on finding a solution. Years. I tried petitioning the politicians, raising concerns among the citizens, and protesting. And what did I get? Nothing. Children get sick in that factory. Young mothers faint from exhaustion. Getting rid of Blackburn is the only solution."

Maddie discreetly wiped away a tear. "I'm distraught over what happened to them. Hector, you should do something. We can't let the duke continue to abuse those people."

"Can't you leave London before the scandal erupts?" Ernest exhaled. "What we're trying to accomplish with Hector's work is more important."

Maddie bit her bottom lip. "You're right. I can leave London and see what happens."

A pang, so sharp and deep to be like a stab, hit Hector's heart. He was sure Maddie would support him. Her selflessness was one of the reasons he loved her. But there had to be something he could do to help her. "I'll renounce my title."

"Hector—" Maddie and Ernest said together in two different tones. Maddie's was concerned, Ernest's was furious.

"We'll find another way to help the workers. I have Lord Naylor's support. He's close to the queen. Surely, this can help our cause."

"Don't you bloody understand?" Ernest thumped a fist against the table again. "It's not only the workers. It's your family's legacy, the money your cousin is squandering to pay for his darkest pleasures. Is this what your family worked for? Your parents and your brother are rolling in their graves. And your mother, one of the finest ladies I've ever met, isn't even buried in holy ground."

Hell. Ernest was right, but what was Hector supposed to do? Not care about Verity and Maddie? Yes, if he was the duke, he would help them, but the scandal wouldn't help his cause, and if he wanted to change the law, he needed the support of the House of the Lords, which meant no association with scandals. If he helped Verity and Maddie, the lords wouldn't support him. And without his title, how could he propose to Maddie? It was a problem without a solution.

"Give me a bit of time," Hector said. "I'll tell Quentin he can keep his title while I think about a solution."

"That's madness!" Ernest shoved himself up, hitting the table in the process. Tall stacks of papers fell to the floor.

"At least we need to give Maddie the chance to find another solution." Hector owed Maddie's family that much. "I'm not giving up, Ernest. I just need more time to think."

"Do what the hell you want. I hope you'll sleep well at night when one of those workers dies in the factory."

Hector rubbed his aching chest. Ernest was right. As much as it hurt him, he had to do something. "Maddie, I—"

Verity entered the room. Her face cream couldn't hide her puffy red eyes and the shadows underneath them. "Ernest." She swallowed hard. "I couldn't help but hear."

"Verity." Maddie stood up, shaking her head.

"It's time." Verity lifted her trembling chin. "I can't let you take the blame and the responsibility for something you didn't do."

Hector frowned. What was she talking about?

Ernest held up his hands. His expression softened when he faced Verity. "I know what you're about to say, but Hector's work is more important than your sister's reputation. I'll marry you anyway. Maddie could leave London, and together we'll face this crisis."

Verity took a step forwards. "I hope you mean it because—"

"Verity, don't," Maddie said.

"You've done enough. It's my turn now." Verity shook her head. "Ernest, the pictures are of me."

"I don't think..." Ernest stilled. He was so motionless Hector wondered if he breathed at all. "I beg your pardon?"

"The compromising pictures the duke gave to Maddie are me. I used to spend a lot of time with Annabelle. She likes to play some silly games, taking pictures posing with her friends as if in intimate situations." Verity thrust her chest out. "It was before I met you, I swear it. It was only a stupid game, but the pictures make it look like something different. Yes, I'm quite undressed in those pictures in the company of other men, but I swear there was no fumble involved, if this might help you feel better."

Hector's skin tingled with the thick tension in the room. Despite the revelation, the only thing he could think about was Maddie. She'd been ready to take the blame, maybe being ruined forever, to protect her sister. If he didn't already love her, he'd fall in love with her now.

Ernest didn't even blink. For a few long moments no one talked. Everyone was staring at Ernest, waiting for his reaction.

He put a hand on the wall. "The compromising pictures are of you?"

Verity nodded, wiping a tear from her cheek. "As I said, it was a silly game."

Ernest raked a shaky hand through his hair. "I...I..." He put his coat back on the back of a chair, only to take it again. He paced and stopped, muttering something.

"Please say something." Verity sobbed.

Maddie rushed to hug her, but Ernest seemed oblivious to them.

"Ernest." Hector grabbed his shoulder. "You love Verity. You said so yourself many times. Do the right thing."

Ernest raised a lost gaze towards him. It was the first time Hector had seen the passionate solicitor so frail and pale. "If you claim your title, everyone will see Verity's pictures."

Hector wanted to tell him that, until a moment ago, Ernest had dismissed the scandal as something fleeting, but he didn't want to add salt to the wound. "Your lady waits for an answer."

"May I have some time?" Ernest turned towards Verity, begging her. "Please, I just need a moment to..." He waved his hands. "To process this. To think."

Maddie's face hardened. "You're such a hypocrite. If you love Verity, the fact the pictures show Verity—"

"I said please!" Ernest roared.

Verity nodded. "Yes, go, take your time."

He patted her cheek quickly before striding out of the room. Hector exhaled.

Verity burst into tears. "What have I done?"

"If he really loves you," Hector said, "he won't care."

"He looked shocked." She wiped her tears with a handkerchief.

"Because he was surprised. Once he ponders the situation and realises how much he loves you, everything will be all right." Otherwise, Ernest didn't deserve Verity's affection.

"Let's go home." Maddie went to lead Verity out, but her sister swatted her hands away.

"It's a disaster." Verity sagged against her sister.

"Do you want me to come?" Hector asked.

Maddie shook her head. "Thank you. We'll go home and wait for Ernest to finish thinking." Sarcasm tinted her voice.

"Be patient with him." Hector held the door open for them. "He'll see reason."

"Or I'll force him to." Maddie held her sister, leaving the parlour.

twenty-nine

MADDIE PACED WHILE Verity and Ernest sat together and talked on a bench in the garden. It was their *big* discussion. She was dying to hear it because if Ernest hurt Verity, if he shamed her or broke the engagement, she'd intervene and kick him out of the house herself. But it was difficult to understand how the conversation went. Both were flustered and agitated and waved a lot. Only Ernest sometimes looked petrified, and Verity shook his arm with some strength as if to spill some good sense into him.

"What's happening?" Mother stopped next to Maddie, jolting her. "Why are you spying on them? What are they talking about?"

Maddie lifted a shoulder. "Oh, nothing really. The duke is blackmailing Hector, using his affection for me and some nude pictures he has of Verity to force him to renounce his title."

Mother's gaze shot up. "You and your silly novels. If you don't want to tell me, just say so." She hurried away, her back straight. "I'll ask Verity once she's done."

Maddie held her breath as Verity and Ernest walked towards the French doors. They didn't hold hands. Bad sign. She held the door open for her and studied her sister's face to understand if Verity's heart had been broken.

"How are you?" Maddie took Verity's hand, ready to punch Ernest.

"Tired." She turned towards Ernest and hooked her arm through his. "But I think we've understood each other."

Ernest raked a hand through his already dishevelled hair, his face turning the colour of raspberry jam. "If there's a good thing about the incident in the Serpentine is that it made me realise how much I love Verity." He paused. "I'm not going to lie. Those pictures made my blood boil and I want to chase those men down and punch them senseless and beat them into a pulp and then—"

"I think Maddie got the point, darling." Verity stroked his cheek.

He took her face and gave her a passionate kiss that caused Maddie to blush. He poured more than love into that kiss. There was a healthy dose of possessiveness and carnal desire, too. She wouldn't be surprised if Verity got pregnant after that kiss. Gosh, Maddie could see their tongues. And could they breathe? No one could survive that long without air.

She cleared her throat, shifting her weight. "So I suppose everything is all right between you two."

They broke the kiss, taking deep breaths as if emerging from a deep dive.

"I love Verity more than anything," Ernest said, having eyes only for Verity. "I'll face the world for her."

Verity giggled and brushed a lock of hair from her red cheek.

Maddie hugged him. "Thank you, Ernest. You're wonderful." Not as wonderful as Hector though. "What are we going to do now?"

Ernest draped an arm on each sister's shoulder. "We face the world."

~

ONCE AGAIN, a sense of impotence and uselessness pressed against Hector's chest. Maddie had told him Ernest was ready to face the scandal and marry Verity, which was great, but nothing could hide the fact Hector didn't know how to force Quentin to leave.

At least Maddie was happy for Verity.

He held her hand in his parlour. "Listen, a man like Quentin must have secrets we can use against him. It's a matter of time. We'll find something to force him to forget about Verity and leave this house. We might talk to Dr. Smith. Perhaps he'll share some of Quentin's secrets. Or what if he really stole *The Lady of the Lake*?"

"He seems too clever to be exposed easily. But I guess you're right. We can dig into his life and find some secrets we can use...oh, look at us. Plotting to blackmail someone." She rubbed her forehead. "Good heaven. I'm like Mother."

"Quentin pushed us to a corner to start with, and I'll take full responsibility for whatever action we're going to take." He kissed her cheek. "Let me fetch you a glass of water."

He had to do something to keep his hands busy because, despite his brave words, he didn't know how to help Verity. His hand trembled so much that when he lifted the pitcher, it slipped out of his finger. The noise of the glass shattering shocked him out of his stupor.

Water soaked the carpet and the dark wooden floor. For a split second, he glanced at the door, worrying about what his mother would say. Sadness crushed his chest again as he crouched to collect the pieces of glass.

"Let me help." Maddie knelt next to him.

He blocked her wandering hand. "No. I'll do it. We already had an incident involving sharp glass shards, and it didn't end well."

She flashed a tired smile and straightened. "Will you ever forgive yourself? Because I forgave you a long time ago." She leant next to the ugly painting.

"I will, when you've realised your dream and become an artist."

She shrugged. "Certainly, I won't paint anything as ugly as—" She fell silent, staring at the painting as if seeing it for the first time.

"What is it?" He set the shard aside and mopped the water with his handkerchief and the napkins.

She pointed a finger at a corner of the painting. "Look. The artist, and I use the term loosely, added the date and the title of the painting."

"As if anyone would want to remember the day that atrocity was produced." He gave up soaking the water.

"No, it's that there's a blotch on number one." She inched closer to the painting and narrowed her gaze.

"And?"

"It might be a code, like the one in Verity's letters."

He frowned. "What code? What letters?"

"If I read only the first word...no, that's not correct. Too few words. But if I read only the first letter of the words, I get...un...der. That's it. The solution to the riddle is '*under*,'" Maddie scratched at a corner of the painting.

She looked adorable, all focused and flushed, but he had absolutely no idea what she was talking about.

"I know the painting is revolting," he said, "but if you want to ruin it, I can think of a few better and faster options."

She beamed so widely that her green eyes shone from within after she lifted an inch of the canvas. "Your Grace, we must summon your cousin. We have something to tell him."

MADDIE'S HEART thumped heavily when his cousin entered the parlour. Hector had been ready to renounce his family's legacy to help her family. Buying time was a good idea, but she didn't believe it'd help. Ernest was right. Hector had to be the duke to help the workers. There wasn't any other solution. But she could save Verity too because underneath the ugly painting was *The Lady of the Lake*. Or at least she hoped so. If the blotch on the number one was the key to solve the riddle, then if she took only the first letter of the place, name of the artist, and title of the painting formed the word under, which might be a coincidence or not. Why would the duke leave a clue about where *The Lady of the Lake was*? Well, that was a question she'd have to ask him.

The problem was that she couldn't simply rip the ugly painting off to see what was underneath. She might ruin *The Lady of the Lake* if she'd guessed right. The procedure to reveal Mrs. Blanchet's work would be a delicate one, and she didn't want to rush it. She'd lifted a corner of the canvas, revealing something else underneath, but it could be anything. Many artists, who struggled to make ends meet, recycled used canvas by painting something else on them or adding a cheap layer on top of an old painting. And judging by how poorly talented the painter of the ugly painting was, she could easily believe the artist had financial troubles. Besides, if she damaged the painting beyond recognition, she couldn't prove Quentin had stolen it. But she could provoke him into confessing.

"Have you decided what to do?" Blackburn gestured at the chairs in front of him. He slouched on the sofa and spread his arms over the backrest, looking like a king about to pardon a criminal.

Hector didn't sit down. "We have. Despite your despicable behaviour."

His cousin chuckled. "This is only a business transaction. Nothing personal. I don't care about what Miss Verity Debenham does with her time. But, alas, society has other standards." He caressed his chin. "In fact, I'd be interested in knowing Verity more intimately. Those pictures—" He never ended the sentence.

"You bastard." Hector lunged, jumping across the room with one swift move.

Maddie shot up to her feet as well. "Hector. Leave him."

Breathing heavily, Hector removed himself from Quentin, his muscles bulging. Goodness, it was the wrong moment, but he looked so handsome, all bothered and angry. Her lady's parts tingled.

She waited for Hector to release his cousin before placing a hand on the painting. "We agree to your terms if you agree to give me this painting."

The duke laughed and patted his hair into place. "Ridiculous. What does that horrible painting have to do with anything?"

Maddie shrugged. "If you don't like it, why do you care?"

He showed his teeth, not smiling anymore. "That worthless painting stays here."

"If it's worthless..." She snatched a poker from the hearth and pointed it at the painting. "I guess that if I scratch it, you wouldn't care." She hoped he did something to stop her because she'd have a fit if she ruined Mrs. Blanchet's masterpiece.

"You silly bitch!" He lunged, but Hector was ready and tackled him with one smooth move.

She winced as a thud resounded when Hector slammed his cousin on the floor. "I'm going to take this painting, because *The Lady of the Lake* is underneath it. Don't deny it. I have proof." She didn't, and her voice shook when she said it, but hey, she had to play the part.

Under Hector's weight, the duke paled. "You are bluffing." He lacked his usual smugness.

"I'm not." She trailed the tip of the poker over the painting. "You made me desperate, and I'm ready to ruin *The Lady of the Lake* unless you do as we say." Not that she knew what that was. What were the terms she should propose?

Hector grabbed him by the collar and raised him, saving her from having to find a solution. "Destroy Verity's pictures and leave my title to me, and we won't involve the police."

Maddie shifted her weight. Hector's proposal was good, and yet she wanted to involve the police and see Quentin Wentworth behind bars. But dragging him to court would likely mean having to show those pictures for the inquest. Oh, bother.

The duke closed his eyes and sagged against Hector. "Why couldn't you stay on that damn island?"

Still holding the poker, Maddie loomed over him. "Why the code?" She had to ask just in case she was wrong.

He shrugged himself free from Hector's grip, his hair dishevelled. "It wasn't my idea." His upper lip went up in a snarl. "There are five more paintings identical to that one."

"Good gracious." She put a hand on her chest. More ugly paintings around? It was like a disease.

"Annabelle—"

"Annabelle?" she and Hector said together.

"She wants a share but doesn't trust me. That's why she marked the painting to make sure I didn't sell it and replace with a copy. It's a special paint, the one with the title. It can't be deleted."

"Mrs. Blanchet will be happy to have her painting back." Maddie dropped the poker and allowed herself to smile at the ugly painting. She felt vindicated because no artist would have ever produced something so horrible. The painting was only a disguise, clever but still as ugly as starvation.

Hector swept her off her feet. "Marry me," he said with his usual honesty.

She laughed, bursting with love. "Yes, with all my heart."

Quentin rolled his eyes. "I might vomit."

"Cousin, don't look so sad," Hector said. "It's only a business transaction."

epilogue

T HE LADY OF the Lake.

Finally, the stunning painting was fully exposed in all its beauty after days of careful work to remove the ugly canvas on top of it. Maddie's breath hitched as she admired the masterpiece. Those strokes of blue and silver were exquisitely done. The lady in the centre of the painting had a tragic yet determined expression that pierced her heart. How could Mrs. Blanchet capture such a heartbreaking moment with the right light and just a few strokes?

She couldn't believe that Mrs. Blanchet had gifted her with the precious painting. *The Lady of the Lake* now hung in Hector's office, surrounded by the soft light of the gas lamps. She admired it while she contracted her fingers around a ball made of sponge. It was harder than it looked and sometimes the exercise pained her, but her fingers grew stronger with each passing day. Her strokes on her drawings were more precise, she felt more confident, and her work got better. That was why the academy had accepted her request to become a student. Speaking of which. She had a pile of books to read.

She propped her hips on Hector's desk as he was busy reading his own pile of books and documents. Among them lay a draft of the island book, as it was called for now. Her sketches and his words had produced a rich story that a few publishers had already expressed interest in publishing.

"I have to read five books by the end of this month. Can you believe it?" she asked.

"You don't fool me." He raised his sapphire gaze to her. "You complain now, but once you start reading them, you won't stop, neglecting your fiancé as well."

Fiancé. She still had to get used to the fact she was engaged to be married to Hector. He'd proposed right in front of the lovely painting. What could be more perfect?

"I would never neglect you. You're extremely busy, too." She sat on the edge of the desk, enjoying the predatory look he gave her. "How are the works at the factory going?"

He pulled her over onto his lap and wrapped his arms around her. "Finally, we have proper windows, the children have been sent to school, the mothers who have small babes are sent home with paid leaves, and the place has been scrubbed to a polish." He kissed her neck and inhaled deeply. "Sick people have been given a salary. I've reduced all the workers' working hours, and Ernest can't stop telling me how wonderful I am."

She giggled when he kissed her again. "What about their wages?"

"All fixed." He darted out his tongue to caress a sensitive spot under her ear. "The problem is the House of Lords. Getting something done with them is a struggle."

"At least your factory has some happy workers now."

"Yes." He nuzzled her neck again. "It's my body that's a little sad now. I've missed you."

"We've seen each other every day." She moaned when he caressed her breasts.

"Briefly, and you were busy with your sketches." He nibbled her earlobe. "I want some time with you. Alone. Naked." He spun her around and lifted her legs so that she straddled him. "You wear too many layers. I've always thought the fewer clothes, the better. Something I discovered on the island. I haven't changed my mind about that."

She chuckled as he pulled her skirt and petticoats up. "I can't go to the academy half naked."

He frowned. "I agree. I don't want all those men looking at you." He opened her shirt and pulled down her chemise.

She reclined her head when he latched his mouth around her nipple and sucked hard. Her hips moved of their own accord. She widened her thighs and rubbed herself against his erection. She unbuttoned his trousers until his length was free and she slid over it. Bliss. Heaven. Holding her by the hips, he helped her move up and down. He paused only to suck her nipple into his mouth and whisper how beautiful she was.

He buried his face in her neck as she dug her fingers into his shoulders. The pleasure left her breathless. He found his release with her and held her tightly as they both savoured the bliss that came after a powerful release. They shared one of their silent, quiet moments when only the beating of their hearts mattered.

He kissed her lips softly. "Do you want to come with me to the crypt?"

"Let me get dressed."

It was a chore. She buttoned up her shirt, he unbuttoned it. She lowered her skirts, he pulled them up again. After a few minutes of laughter, swatting hands, and shuffling clothes, they were ready.

Holding hands, they went downstairs. Maddie took in the beautiful pale-blue wallpaper, the oak wood furniture, and the beige curtains. After they'd renovated the house to its former splendour, the corridor seemed larger and a certain lightness lingered.

After a short carriage ride, they walked hand in hand along the gravel path in the cemetery. The family crypt rose among tall cypress trees and rose bushes. She rested her head on his shoulder as they placed the flowers on his mother the late Duchess of Blackburn's tomb. She finally rested next to her husband and son in a beautiful white marble tomb with an angel on top of it.

"She belongs here." He caressed the stone. Every time he talked about his mother, his voice quivered.

"She'd be so proud of you." She wrapped her arms around him and rested her head on his chest.

"I love you madly, Maddie."

She rose on her tiptoes and kissed his chin. "Please stay savage, my duke."

THE END

about the author

Love stories have always captured my imagination. What's better than two people falling in love with each other? I write steamy romance, usually with a paranormal twist in an historical setting. Add a touch of suspense and mystery and a pinch of darkness. I love stories with  strong, sexy heroes and mischievous heroines who pull no punches.

I live in the City of Sails, New Zealand, drinking tea (coffee gives me anxiety) and devouring books.

Join my newsletter for exclusive content and the chance to receive an ARC copy of my books. Just copy and paste this link into your browser:

Barbara's Newsletter

also by barbara russell

If you love steamy paranormal romance set in Victorian London, my
Royal Occult Bureau series is for you:

The Royal Occult Bureau Series

Are you into shape-shifter romance? Check out my da Vinci's Beasts
series, set in WW2:

da Vinci's Beasts Series

For more Victorian paranormal romance with witches and sexy warriors,
see the Knights of the White Blade series:

The White Order Series

Love steampunk? Check out my Auckland Steampunk series:

Auckland Steampunk Series